THRESHOLD

A NOVEL

To Amëme –
Hope you enjoy!

[signature]

Oct 2019

× EL

THRESHOLD

A NOVEL

DANIEL J. WATERS

Cover Design by Jim Zach,
ZGraphix, Mason City, Iowa
Author Photo © Jean Poland Photography

For Pam, Jessica, Michael & John-
The best Chapters of my Life

Chapter 1

AMJAD AL-SHAHANI FINGERED THE lump under his collarbone. The scab was still fresh and the crude metal staples that were used to close the wound pricked when he touched them. The skin around where they'd cut him had developed a shiny redness and a drop or two of what looked to him like snot extruded whenever he pushed on it. Amjad had asked the elders if he should be given the antibiotic pills but none of them seemed very concerned.

The holy book was under his shirt. In his lap was a tattered paperback by the infidel writer Nelson DeMille. The story's villain was a superhuman terrorist that Amjad heard the old men refer to laughingly as the *jihadi's* John Wayne. The book's last twenty pages and back cover were missing. Amjad did not read English well, his formal education having ended seven years prior, shortly after he turned twelve. He knew more about machine guns, RPG launchers and explosive timers than he did anything else but the sacred scriptures, which were read to him daily by his Uncle Tamal.

The placing of the silver disc under his skin five days ago had hurt terribly. It had been done without any anesthetic and he had not been allowed even a sip of the forbidden alcohol the elders drank freely in front of him. The device, they had told him, would confuse the sensors and the metal detectors at airports and would allow one to carry other, more important objects on to the airplanes. Amjad had expected a plane ticket and a car ride to Lahore, but his cousin Rahim told him they wanted to test the device's signal range in an enclosed space like the cabin of a great jetliner. So here he sat, sweating and aching in the small desert hut, surrounded by cases of green bottles and packing material. He looked at the plastic watch and then at the blue metal circle Rahim had given him. It looked like a round piece o roti, the delicious flatbread his mother often made. It had a hole in the center and it was heavier than he would have guessed. There was English lettering on it but Amjad did not recognize any words he knew. When the watch read four o'clock, his cousin had instructed, he was to put the metal disc on top of the lump under his collarbone and count off five seconds. Then he was to quickly remove it and keep it at least a half- meter away from his body. They would be outside, Rahim said, measuring the signal strength at various distances from the hut. Then Rahim had closed the rickety door. It sounded, by his footsteps, as if he had been running – probably, Amjad thought, to get to one of the signal receivers placed outside.

Amjad laid the paperback on the arm of the wooden chair. He checked the watch again and took the blue object from the table with his left hand. He brought his arm across his chest and up to his opposite shoulder. He tucked his chin so he could see that the disc was centered over the staples and the angry-looking cut. More snot was leaking from it, he noticed. Then he counted out loud.

"One, blessings be upon Him, two blessings be up- "

Outside the hut, Rahim counted his steps. Tamal had assured him that twenty paces would be adequate if he ran hard. He pitied his younger cousin Amjad but at the same time envied him. The fruits of Paradise would soon be his. This thought caused Rahim to briefly shorten his stride and he decided to turn his head at exactly the wrong moment. The massive explosion pushed him to the ground, but not before a lump of molten glass took out his left eye. His screams were lost in the blast of superheated air that rushed over him and he writhed on the ground for several minutes until the roaring sound stopped. The searing pain lasted only a few seconds longer and then suddenly abated as the sensory nerve endings melted and died beneath his charred skin.

Rahim looked up with his concussed but functioning right eye. One of the elders was talking to Tamal but, he realized, now he couldn't hear anything at all. He saw the bearded elder point to something that was behind Rahim. As he tried to turn his head to see what it was he felt the muzzle of a gun hard against the back of his skull. His vision was getting watery but he could make out Tamal rubbing at his prodigious mustache and nodding. Then a burning white light – Rahim thought perhaps it was the inside of the sun – seemed to shine all around him. An instant later, the blackness came.

Chapter 2

"SUCK, SWEETIE. BLOW IS just a figure of speech, you know."

"Sorry, Dr. Roberson," the younger woman said, trying to adjust the gurgling catheter in her right hand. "In twelve days I'll be a Urology resident. I've never even been in an open-heart operating room before."

Johanna Roberson, M.D. was neatly engraved in block letters on the right temple of the black eyeglasses that held the taller woman's surgical telescopes. "You should get a pair of loupes," Johanna said. "It's always best to see exactly what your opponent is seeing." She turned to the circulating nurse. "Any chance we could get the room temperature turned down? I'm sweating like a pig under this gown."

"Pigs don't sweat," her assistant chirped. "Did you know that?"

"Excuse me?" Johanna said, pausing in the placement of the last of the paired valve stitches.

"Pigs, actually all swine, to be more accurate," the younger doctor said. "They don't sweat."

Johanna turned her head slightly to her right. "Valve ready?" she asked.

"Fifteen seconds," said a female voice from the back table.

Johanna tuned back to her assistant. "And you know this... how?" she asked.

"I grew up on a hog farm in Iowa," the younger woman replied.

"Swine can't really sweat. That's why they wallow in the mud – it helps dissipate their body heat. It's the porcine version of sweating."

"Valve's up," the scrub nurse said, proffering the long metal holder.

"Well, fuck me dead," Johanna said. "I did not know that. Hold the valve please." She loaded one of the needles in the jaws of a long, ratcheted instrument. The young doctor assisting her, a PG-1 named Annalisa, grasped the holder with the attached aortic valve prosthesis awkwardly. Johanna reached to put the first stitch in the white Dacron sewing ring that encircled the valve like a tiny skirt, and then stopped. She put down the needle holder and reached across the table.

"Jesus, it's not fucking rocket science, you know." She took her assistant's hand which, she noticed, was now shaking noticably. "Gently but firmly," she said adjusting the girl's fingers. "Hold it like you hold your boyfriend's d-" She stopped herself.

"Just hold it like this."

Johanna picked up the needle holder and began to place the alternating green and white stitches as the scrub nurse handed them to her. "Where in Iowa?" she said.

"I'm sorry. What?"

"Iowa," Johanna said. "Where in Iowa are you from?" The girl's tremor had lessened just a little

"Lansing," she answered. "Lansing, Iowa. It's right on the Mississippi river."

Johanna paused to check her spacing and then drove more needles in succession through the cloth ring. "Anywhere near Waukon?" she asked.

"Yeah," the girl laughed, "about fifteen, twenty miles east of Waukon. How do you know about-"

Johanna cut her off. "I went to medical school in Des Moines. One of the surgeons I spent time with with was from Waukon. In fact, he was actually the Walk-On from Waukon for the University of Iowa baseball team. Ever heard of him?" The girl's shake, she noticed, had dissipated.

"No," she replied. "But I didn't go the U. I went to St. Olaf, a small college in Minnesota. I'm pretty sure everybody there was a walk-on."

Johanna laughed. She slid the now circumferentially-impaled

valve down the sutures and into the root of the patient's open aorta.

"See those two little holes there?" She pointed with the tip of her forceps. "Those are the openings to the two main coronary arteries. If we don't get this valve down below them, no blood gets to the heart muscle; if that happens, this guy never gets out of the operating room and, if that happens, The Cutter Clinic- Pacific Rim gets sued for a shitload of money." She pushed on the valve to seat it firmly. "Look OK to you, Dr. Kildare?"

"Looks OK to me, Dr. Roberson," the young woman answered.

Johanna turned again to her right to locate the circulating nurse at the far end of the operating table. "Would you let Dr. Taylor know the valve is in," she said as she began deftly tying the sutures. "Dr. Taylor is the staff surgeon," Johanna said in a quieter voice. "Technically he was supposed to be in here for all this, but the hospital's not going to do twenty-eight hundred hearts a year that way, sooo…"

"Dr. Taylor says he's tied up in Room 44 for at least another hour," the nurse replied. "He says if something comes up you can't handle-"

Johanna interrupted her. "I know," she said. "Handle it."

As she tied down the last of the stitches the operating room door opened and a head with a bouffant scrub cap and dangling mask poked through.

"Y'OK, J-Row?" a chipper male voice said. Johanna looked up.

"We're good, Dr. Constantine," Johanna replied. "How are things on the Pacemaker and Implantable Cardiac Devices service?"

"The PICD schedule has been done since noon," Michael Constantine replied. "Dr. el-Hamini is a wizard. They don't call him the Afghan Flash for nothing."

Johanna looked at the clock. It was inching toward four o'clock "Fuck you, Constantine," she said with a laugh. "Just because you're done in twelve days doesn't mean you can –"

"Eleven days, eight hours and six minutes. And that's exactly what it means," Constantine replied with a grin. "Come the stroke of midnight on the first of July, you, Johanna Roberson, MD, will be the Chief Resident in Cardiothoracic Surgery here at the WFCC. I'm taking two weeks off to enjoy my new sailboat."

"What's the WFCC?" Annalisa asked.

"World Famous Cutter Clinic," Johanna replied. "Irrigation."

She took what looked like a squat turkey baster and squirted saline solution on the valve. "Prolene for the aorta, please. Then we'll de-air and give the hot shot." She looked over the top of the little telescopes embedded in her lenses. Across the room Constantine was still leaning in through the door. "Eleven days is still eleven days, Dr. Constantine," she said. "Remember Rule Number One."

"I will, Johanna," he replied. 'You're coming to my farewell party on Monday, aren't you?"

"Unless one of the FNG's has a bleeder, I'll be there," she replied. The door clicked shut as she took the loaded needle driver in her right hand. "Big ugly forceps, please."

Annalisa reached for the suction catheter. "What's an FNG?" she asked.

"You are an FNG," Johanna replied. "A Fucking New Guy; or, in your case, Girl."

"Oh," Annalisa said. "And what's Rule Number One?" she asked.

Johanna's mouth torqued under her mask and she paused before answering,

"They can always hurt you more," she said quietly.

Chapter 3

TRIPLETT L. COLLIER, III, *ESQ*. WAS an unhappy man.

This was not totally because Triplett. L. Collier, II, *Esq.* had called earlier in the day with another "offer" to join the family law firm in Redmond, although that certainly hadn't helped. His small cubicle was in the southwest corner of the Department of Homeland Security's office suite on Second Avenue and he had a window. Only three blocks from the Seattle Ferry Terminal, he could see Bainbridge Island across the Puget Sound on most days. But not today. The dark clouds and fog to the west suited his mood but it was the looming glass and steel monstrosity six blocks to the east that was the author of his misery. The Seattle Field Office for DHS Region X included ports of entry not only in Washington, but North Dakota, Montana, Idaho and Minnesota as well. All of the other states put together had not given him as much trouble over the last five years as the new hometown medical Mecca had given him in the last five months.

Collier looked at the stack of folders on his desk. It was easily ten inches high. And none of the folders were very thick. It wasn't The Cutter Clinic's methods that bothered him. It was the goddamned sense of entitlement that wafted from every communication DHS received from them. Those letters and cables were in a separate stack about four inches high. Collier considered on a daily basis just shoving them all in his "Burn" basket and blaming the housekeepers. He was considering it again when the phone rang.

"Collier, DHS," he answered.

"Hey, Trip," a sugary voice said. "It's Amanda over at The Cutter's International Referral desk."

"Yes, Amanda," Collier replied with as little enthusiasm as possible.

"Trip, honey," she said, "Y'all have just got to help us with this backlog. Baby, my doctors are screaming at me asking where these international patients are. We're not talkin' Bedouins, here, Trip. These patients are people of importance in their own countries. And until we can establish a Cutter presence in the Arab world, they just have to come here to get the treatment they need."

"I thought you had an outpost in Abu Dhabi," Collier asked, deciding to pull Amanda's chain just a little. There was a slight delay in her response.

"Now, darlin', we both know that Abu Dhabi did not work out they way anyone planned, Trip. I mean, who are you going to believe? The nurses who said they were drafted as sex slaves or the gracious hosts who said they willingly joined their harems?"

"It's a great porn movie either way, Mandy," Collier said. "Think of the publicity."

Amanda laughed insincerely. "All kidding aside, Trip, I've got several Cardiology patients who've been waiting weeks for clearance. They're here for a new experimental device protocol that's not available anywhere else. They all have very bad hearts and we're worried about their short-term survival if they're not treated soon."

Collier remained silent.

"Did I mention, Trip, that Dr. Lloyd Poole is scheduled to visit The Cutter Clinic-Pacific Rim campus in just a day or two? I've seen his itinerary and I can tell you, off the record of course, that he does have meetings scheduled with the Governor, both U.S. Senators and the mayor. I don't think you want any DHS items to be on his agenda, now do you, Trip honey?"

Collier had been doodling on a pad of Post-It notes and snapped the tip of the pencil simultaneously with Amanda's terminal "honey". Lloyd Poole, MD, Collier knew, was the current Surgeon General of the United States. He'd operated on the sitting President as well as one former Vice- President when he'd been a heart surgeon. He had also been CEO of The Cutter Clinic when it was based solely in Indianapolis. The four overseas Cutter "partner hospitals" and the stateside expansions into Phoenix, Tampa and

Seattle, were widely ascribed to Poole's overarching vision of a healthcare empire on the order of Christendom. Collier decided he could pull Amanda's chain just a little more.

"Come on, Mandy," he said. "The Surgeon General is like, I don't know, like Colonel Sanders. Funny uniform. Bad tie. A lot of public appearances maybe, but no real political juice. Maybe he's just here for a restaurant opening." He paused. "Now, you tell me Ichiro Suzuki wants this done, throw in a couple Mariner's tickets and a baseball autographed by Ken Griffey, Jr., and I'll personally walk the folders to your desk this afternoon. And it's all uphill from here, you know."

"Just like a man," Amanda replied. "When you need him to give you what you want, he thinks about baseball."

Collier had to laugh at that one. "OK," he said, "You keep me and Homeland Security off the Surgeon General's dollar menu and I'll work on clearing some of your patients. Not all of them but enough to keep the wheels turning. Fax me a list and use the words Urgent Medical Necessity somewhere. That will help things on my end."

"Thanks. Trip," Amanda said. "You're a sweetheart." Then she hung up.

Collier grabbed the pile of folders and shuffled through them. Mostly males, he noticed. Many of them surprisingly young. His own father had suffered his first heart attack at fifty-one, so he knew it wasn't an old man's disease any more. Different countries of origin but not all that geographically diverse, really. Several educated or living in the U.K. He looked at the unsmiling but earnest faces on the photos and wondered if they knew the thread that linked them together.

He tapped the folders back into a neater pile.

"They just want to live, I guess," he said quietly.

"So, all looks, as you say here in this country, A-OK?"

Michael Constantine lifted the echocardiogram probe and wiped off the conductive jelly with a stiff and scratchy washcloth. "Looks really good, Mr. Bahan. One might even say better than expected."

"Then that is good, yes? The 'woosh-woosh', 'woosh-woosh' says all is the way it is supposed to be." The question was delivered in a clipped British accent though the man in the bed had skin the color of coffee with a splash of milk.

"Yes, that is good," Constantine answered. "We'll interrogate the device tomorrow before you go home."

"What do you mean, interrogate?" Bahan asked warily. He lifted his head from the pillow.

Constantine smiled. "We'll check its programming, that's all. To make sure it's set the way we want." Bahan laid his head back down. Constantine tugged on Bahan's hospital gown exposing his upper chest and right shoulder. "Your incision looks good," Constantine said. "Just remember to keep it clean and dry. You don't want it to get infected."

"How will I know if it's infected?"

"It will get red and shiny and nasty-looking stuff will probably drain out of it."

"Yes," Bahan said, nodding. "Pus and corruption, Satan's calling cards."

Constantine laughed. "That's right. And well put. Pus and corruption, indeed."

"Then I will keep it very clean. I am good at following instructions," Bahan replied. "Will I see Dr. el-Hamini in the morning?"

"Perhaps," Constantine replied. "It depends on how busy his schedule is in the device lab."

"Excellent, then. I will share with him the good news about this test."

Constantine stood next to the bulky echo machine and tucked the probe in the little compartment on its side. "You don't need to tell Dr. el-Hamini about it," he said. "I'll put a note in your chart." Then he trundled the machine out the door and into the hallway.

"Doing your own echo's now, Mike?" an Asian male nurse asked.

"I was a little worried he had a perforation," Constantine replied. "Wanted to make sure he wasn't going to accumulate a bunch of blood around his heart and tamponade in the middle of the night. Better to know at eight-thirty than be guessing at midnight." He started rolling the heavy machine toward the elevators.

"Whatever you say, gaijin sensei," the nurse said. "So it looked OK, right?"

"Great," Constantine replied. "Maybe too great. And, FYI, I've been here for two years. I know what that means."

♦ ♦ ♦

Johanna had just sat down when the phone rang. She exhaled heavily then got up from her chair and looked for the cordless receiver. She hadn't bothered to change when she'd left the hospital and her scrub top hung loosely outside the waist of her drawstring pants. Her legs ached and she thought about starting to wear the compression socks she kept rolled up in her dresser drawer.
She found the phone on the eighth ring.

"This is Johanna Roberson," she said in an exhausted voice.

"Wake you up?" Mike Constantine asked.

"Nah," she said. "I was just getting ready to have a kale smoothie, run ten miles and review the world surgical literature on something obscure. You?"

"Having my third beer. We definitely picked the wrong specialty, Johanna."

"Really?" she replied. "Think you might like the Defibrillating for Dollars racket as a career?"

"Actually," Constantine said, "That's why I'm calling."

Twenty minutes later Johanna wedged the phone between her ear and her shoulder, reached under her scrub top and unclasped her bra. The handset shifted back and forth as she did so.

"What are you doing?" Mike Constantine asked.

"Getting my tits out of this wringer," she answered. "Sorry."

"Getting your what?"

Johanna took the phone in her hand. "Undoing my bra, OK? You try wearing one of these things under a scrub shirt and gown for sixteen hours."

"I'll take your word for it," Constantine said. "Anyway, what do you think?"

Johanna propped her feet up on the small rolling ottoman. "I think you took a real chance doing an unordered, undocumented but witnessed echocardiogram on a staff cardiologist's private patient. Don't ask the question if you don't really want to know the answer."

"I do want to know the answer," Constantine replied.

"No, you don't. A month from now you'll be a junior attending at Harborview and this will all be ancient history," Johanna replied.

"I think this is a scam," Constantine said. "Nobody's left ventricle goes from a fifteen percent ejection fraction to sixty-percent in forty eight hours. I don't care what kind of magical device you implant. A really sick heart just doesn't get better that fast. Which leaves only one conclusion."

Johanna rubbed at her eyes. "That the ventricle was normal to begin with and the device implantation is a sham."

"Not just a sham. Like I said, I think it's a scam. And a highly lucrative scam at that," Constantine added. "Doesn't it seem odd that these are only international patients on this protocol? Odd that they come with their own echoes and interpretations which we never corroborate with an in-house study. Odd that the devices all come from a single vendor with special lot numbers. And I'm telling you Johanna, these guys don't look like chronic heart failure patients. Something really is rotten in Denmark."

Johanna let out a sigh. "OK, but really all you've got is one surprisingly normal post-implant echo. Not much to make a sweeping allegation with – especially when you're a trainee and a short-timer, at that. You really think you're going to dent the armor of The Cutter Clinic with this even if it is true? You of all people know they'd never let that happen."

"I went back and looked at the echocardiogram that came with this guy. It was supposedly done in Karachi last month. And it did show a fifteen percent E.F."

"See? There you have it - a fifteen percent Ejection Fraction. Exhibit A for the defense, not to mention the Hospital Ethics Committee as they have you and your little cardboard box of belongings escorted out the front door."

"You didn't let me finish. That echocardiogram also showed a one centimeter Atrial Septal Defect," Constantine said. "Of which there was absolutely no sign on the echo I did tonight. A thumb-sized hole inside the heart of an adult does not spontaneously close in the space of a few weeks."

"So, what are you saying? You think these patients are being referred with echoes that actually belong to other patients?" Johanna said.

"Bingo," Constantine replied. "And check this out – they're all private pay. Every last one of them. My guess is el-Hamini is in cahoots with one if not more cardiologists back in the Middle East. I'd bet they're getting a kickback on every device he implants."

Johanna switched the receiver to her other ear. "I don't know,

Mike. The Cutter supposedly has the most sophisticated electronic medical record and billing software in the world. I can't believe they'd miss something like this."

"Who says they're missing it? Maybe they're just ignoring it. Not asking and certainly not telling. We are talking about millions of dollars here, Johanna. They haven't had a foothold in the Arab world since that debacle in Abu Dhabi. El-Hamini's patients are like oil – I think they'd do a lot to reopen the pipeline."

Johanna pursed her lips and thought carefully about what she wanted to say next. "OK, I agree it sounds fishy. But why not wait six months and then make a quiet call to Dr. McCarthy outlining your concerns? He's the chair of The Cutter's Cardiac Institute – hand him the grenade and let him decide if he wants to pull the pin or not. You'll have discharged your ethical duty and acquitted your conscience. And you'll have a lot more credibility as an established staff surgeon at Seattle's venerable Harborview Medical Center than as the lame duck Chief CT Surgery Resident you are right now. Not to mention protection. This isn't the time to be a crusader."

There was silence on the line. Then Constantine spoke. "Yeah, you're probably right. I won't say anything now. But I'm going to quietly review the echocardiograms on patients he's done in the last couple months. Maybe try to get some documentation to back me up when it comes time to make that call. I'm pretty sure I can do that while staying safely under the radar. Eleven days, right?"

Johanna looked at the clock.

"If we don't hang up right now," she said. "It'll only be ten days."

"Thanks, Johanna," Constantine said. "Sorry to unload this on you. I'm thinking of taking the boat out this weekend. Wanna come?"

"Thanks, but I can't. I have Grand Rounds tomorrow and I'm going to need Sunday just to recuperate so I can go back on call Monday. Have fun but-" She paused and yawned loudly. "Just be careful. Rule Number One, right?"

"Got it, J-Row," he replied. "Rule Number One."

Chapter 4

THERE WAS VERY LITTLE foot traffic in the North Satellite Terminal of the Seattle-Tacoma International Airport at one-thirty in the morning and this pleased Charlie Urban to no end. Charlie's TSA uniform had not expanded at the same rate as his midsection but he had found relief by unbuttoning the top of his pants and loosening his belt. This maneuver only worked, he discovered, if he stayed seated. And seated was exactly what he intended to remain.

The latest RapidScan full body scanner had only been installed three days earlier and Charlie really liked it. The nearly naked three-dimensional images it produced of female passengers and stewardesses made the shit pay almost bearable. A government-mandated peep-show, he thought. The technical rep from OSI Systems, the company that built the scanners, was propped up against a baggage cart, snoozing. There was a SkyWest puddle-jumper to San Francisco leaving at three-twenty-six a.m. but those passengers generally didn't arrive until shortly before departure. Charlie figured he had time to catch twenty winks. He grabbed a neck pillow that had been confiscated for just this purpose from a passenger's carry-on and slipped it behind his head. He felt the first level of drowsiness washing over him when the unmistakable echoing sound of leather heels on tile stirred him from his reverie.

Charlie hoped whoever it was was lost and would either turn around or head for another terminal, but such was not the case. As the echo grew louder he straightened his back and saw a well dressed man striding purposefully toward the deserted security line. The man, Charlie noticed, had darker skin but was not black. As he got closer Charlie pegged him for Indian or maybe Iranian. The man was sharply but casually dressed, with a loose-fitting shirt that hung outside his crisply pressed pants. He wasn't carrying a briefcase or any other luggage, which was a little unusual for short commuter flights where many bags were "gate-checked" at the Jetway. He didn't hesitate or look at his ticket, like most fliers did, as he approached the belts and poles that marked the circuitous route to the checkpoint. Charlie gathered his drooping pants and belt in his left hand as he stood.

"Sure you got the right gate?" he asked. "No flights scheduled out of here for almost two hours."

The man reached into his pocket and withdrew his passport and boarding pass.

"Can I just walk around these poles since I am the only one here?" the man asked in a mellifluous sing-song manner. Indian, Charlie decided.

"Sorry," Charlie answered, "You have to follow the path." This was not technically true, he knew, but he was trying to buy time in the hopes of not losing his pants. He fumbled with the top button but the zipper had opened. Pulling everything back together, he decided, was not going to be a one-handed job. He regretted having told Alexus, the other TSA officer on duty with him, to extend her break by thirty minutes. The scanner rep had woken up and was rubbing at his forehead.

Charlie arrived at the little podium at the same time the man did. By pressing his prodigious middle against the back of it, he found, he could keep his pants up temporarily and free his left hand. His belt buckle was pressing painfully into the doughy and dimpled flesh of his belly but he ignored it. Charlie took the passport and scanned it with the ultraviolet flashlight. He picked up the chewed-on Bic pen, scrawled on the boarding pass then handed it and the passport back. "Going to San Francisco on SkyWest?" Charlie asked.

"I believe it is United Airlines," the man replied pleasantly but without smiling.

"Yup," Charlie replied. "United owns the route but the plane will say SkyWest on it, OK?"

The man nodded and put the passport and boarding pass back in his pocket. The scanner rep, Charlie thought his name was Jeff or maybe Jack, was busy booting up the big machine. Charlie had managed to rebutton his pants and he began to walk with the man towards the scanner. "Would you object to trying the new whole-body scanner, sir?" Charlie asked.

"I would welcome the chance," the man replied. "It is important to be a student of new technology. Do you really think it is more sensitive?"

"We're really not allowed to discuss it," Charlie replied. "Right here, please. Turn sideways and extend your arms above your head." As he said this, the large blue button at his waist popped its fraying threads and his trousers and belt began migrating slowly southward. What was worse, they were pulling his overstretched boxers along for the ride. Charlie knew he was in full view of the video recorder now. If he lost his drawers, he thought, he would probably end up going viral on YouTube. He grabbed the waistband with his left hand and pushed the "Scan" button with his right. There was a soft whirring sound and then a click. "You can step through now, sir, and wait on the other side."

The scanner rep was staring at the image on the screen with a quizzical look. He nodded his head toward the picture. Charlie stared at it – this was not anything he had seen before. Just below the man's right shoulder there was a round, bright spot on the screen. This usually indicated metal. The arms, legs, head torso and pelvis were easily distinguishable in a black outline. The guy had quite a crank on him, Charlie noticed, but that wasn't the problem.

Keeping his hand at his waist Charlie walked around to where the man stood smoothing his shirt. "Something wrong?" the man asked.

"Sir, are you carrying any metal objects on your person?"

"Carrying? No, I don't believe so."

Charlie was now a little irritated, mostly by his drooping pants but a little by the guy's attitude.

"Sir, are you carrying something under your shirt?" Charlie asked.

"I am not carrying anything," the man said. He looked almost amused.

"Could I ask you to lift your shirt up please," Charlie asked. Jack or Jeff, the scanner rep, had now come around to stand beside him.

"Certainly," the man answered. He grasped the hem of the cream colored shirt and lifted it clear over his head. Charlie looked at the large lump under the man's collarbone. A thin pink line bisected it. A surgical incision – Charlie knew that much.

"You can put your shirt down, sir," Charlie said. The man dropped the shirt and smoothed it flat. Charlie looked at him. "Sir, the scanner shows a metal object under your left shoulder. Could you tell me what that is, please?"

He thought he saw the hint of a smile play at the man's lips. The guy was jerking him off, Charlie was sure of that. The man rubbed at the lump through the shirt.

"You must be seeing my defibrillator," he said. "I had it put in a few weeks ago. I am prone to irregular heart rhythms and this device can actually sense them and deliver a shock if necessary. Almost magical, no?"

"You look pretty young for heart problems," replied Charlie, who was only sixty one already on his third stent.

"Alas, age does not protect me," the man replied. "They say it is genetic, handed down like wisdom from father to son. May I go to my gate now?"

Charlie knew that he should at least wand the guy. He also knew he should be calling a supervisor. The problem with the first option was that he still only had one hand to work with. The second, well, that would involve explaining why his pants were falling off and, more worrisome, where Alexus was. Giving blow-jobs to baggage handlers was not exactly TSA protocol, but Charlie knew that Alexus was a single mom and the unreported income was keeping her and her kids afloat.

"Have a nice flight to San Francisco, sir," Charlie said pleasantly and pointed toward the empty row of gates and lounges. "Take your time – you have plenty of it."

The man nodded.

"I wish it were as you say."

The morning light was already starting to fill the room. Michael Constantine looked at the clock. It was nearly six a.m. In forty minutes or so the day shift of nurses, aides, unit clerks and bleary-eyed interns and residents would start trickling in, he knew. The light was making the monitor screen harder to read, but Constantine decided he'd seen enough already. He clicked the mouse a few times and logged himself out of the digital viewing system. Since he was still a resident, his "surfing" of the patient records in the electronic chart system wouldn't draw undue notice. Technically he was a Cutter trainee for ten more days and because he was assigned to the device service, he could always claim he was reviewing the echocardiograms for educational purposes. If they asked him why he'd started doing it at four in the morning, he realized, he would need a better answer.

Constantine massaged his stubbly beard and opened the handle-operated Venetian mini-blinds. He squinted until his eyes were able to adjust then peered cautiously through the door of the little reading room. He knew the Echo Lab was closed on Saturdays but he didn't want to take any more chances. Seeing no one, he grabbed his rumpled lab coat and walked out into the ninth-floor hallway. He paused by one of the large banks of windows in the foyer. To the west he could clearly see the Sound with its rapidly vanishing patina of morning fog. The water was sparkling in the early slanting rays of sunlight. To the east, much closer, the near shore of Lake Washington was lit golden while the far side still lay in shadow. He could make out several eight-oared rowing shells angling away from a large dock, their oars making tiny circles with each stroke. He thought about Johanna and wondered if telling her had been a mistake for both of them. He'd drunk a fourth beer the previous night and neglected to eat anything before his early morning sojourn back to the hospital. Now he was famished. Meals were still complimentary for on-call housestaff and he certainly looked the part. He pushed the "down" button on the wall and waited for the elevator.

When the doors opened he shuffled on, head down and hands stuffed in the large pockets of his lab coat. The elevator was crowded with early-exiting night shifters.

"Two please," he said. He kept his chin tucked and did not look up when the doors opened on Six. Constantine shuffled a half step back to make room for the new passengers. Then he heard a familiar voice. He looked up and saw, at the front of the car, a tall, auburn-haired woman in a crisp white coat nodding emphatically to a shorter blonde doctor.

Once the doors closed he lifted his head and spoke:

"Hey, Johanna," he said softly.

The entourage whisked down the sunlit hallway in a blur of white. Two floor nurses, two interns, a beleaguered Physician's Assistant and three scurrying medical students struggled to keep pace. Leading the procession was a man of moderate height, impeccably dressed in pleated khaki slacks, a blue two-button blazer and an azure silk mock-turtleneck. Immaculately coiffed silver hair and a neat silver mustache accented his caramel skin. A large but somehow not ostentatious platinum chain encircled his neck, matched, in both metallurgic content and cost, by the Breitling sport chronometer on his left wrist.

"Quickly, my children, quickly!" he said with a smile. His sockless feet padded the tile floor in a worn pair of Top-Siders. He turned sharply into one of the rooms and strode to the bedside, right hand proffered in greeting.

"Bahan, my friend!" he said. "You look wonderful."

"Thanks to you only," Bahan replied.

Seljuk el-Hamini made a sweeping gesture with his arm. "Not just me, dear friend. All these people you see work hard to make you well." He turned to the group. "And what day are we today?" he asked.

"Saturday," one of the medical students piped, pleased to finally have a question she could answer.

El-Hamini stifled a smile. "Yes," he said, "And quite a beautiful Saturday it is. But what post-operative day is Mr. Bahan today, Student Doctor Joyce?"

The medical student immediately understood her error and turned a shade of crimson that put her strawberry hair to shame.

"Day four," the Physician's Assistant standing next to her answered. "Should be OK for discharge. Chest X-ray looked good."

El-Hamini turned back to the bed. "You wish to leave the hospital today, Bahan?"

"If the great Dr. el-Hamini says I am ready then I must be ready," Bahan answered.

"Ah, Bahan," el-Hamini said, "You are younger but you are wise. We would like you to stay in our fair city until your follow-up appointment in two weeks. You have arrangements?"

Bahan nodded. "All is arranged," he answered.

"Very well," el-Hamini answered. "Pad please."

A light green prescription pad materialized from somewhere in the huddled group and Hamini took it. He withdrew from the inside pocket of his blazer a thick, pearl-colored Mont Blanc pen and scribbled on the top sheet.

"This is for pain," he said, tearing it off. "Use them only if you have to – we want your mind clear at all times."

Bahan took the slip and regarded it. "The ink of the scholar," he said.

"The blood of the martyr," El-Hamini replied. He touched his fingers to his chest and turned to leave. Bahan's voice stopped him.

"The whoosh-whoosh," Bahan said. "The echo. Dr. Constantine said it looked quite good." El-Hamini shot a look at his group. The intern shrugged.

"Then I'm sure that it did," el-Hamini replied with a tighter smile. "When did he tell you this?"

"Last night," Bahan replied, "When he was in here with the big machine. The whoosh-whoosh machine."

El-Hamini slid the pen back into his blazer. "That is good to know," he said as he gently shepherded the group to the door. "That is very good to know."

The Cutter Clinic had spent more than two-hundred million dollars on the Pacific-Rim campus and the staff dining room reflected the expenditure. Only Chief Residents and Fellows were allowed to mingle with staff physicians in its carpeted splendor. Constantine sat across from Johanna in one of the little banquettes and wolfed down the last of his three bagels with cream cheese.

"I'm sure he's just saving it for D and D," Johanna said, setting down the steaming cup of coffee. She had breezed through Surgical Grand Rounds – what the housestaff referred to as "smack-a-rounds" – in a little over an hour. Their chief, Dr. McCarthy, had been the only attending cardiac surgeon present and he hadn't seemed interested in pummeling Johanna for any of the deaths and complications that were discussed aloud in the great amphitheatre. He would save that, she knew only too well, for the more private departmental Mortality and Morbidity conference the next weekend. It was always held in the morning and accompanied by a continental breakfast. The housestaff nicknamed it "Death and Doughnuts."

Constantine chewed and swallowed, then took a large slug from his glass of chocolate milk. He waited for Johanna to continue.

"Anyway," she said, "so he had an ASD. Stuff gets missed. How many times have you –"

Constantine cut her off. "No, Johanna. Not he. They. All of them. They all have atrial septal defects."

Johanna shook her head. "That's impossible," she said. "ASD's don't occur that frequently in adults."

Constantine leaned in and lowered his voice. "They do if they're all the same person."

It took Johanna a few seconds to comprehend what she was being told. Several expressions passed over her face and she started to speak only to stop herself each time. "So you're saying–"

"I'm saying, Johanna, they're all the same echocardiogram. It's one patient back in sand-land somewhere with a bad pump and an ASD." His voice was a stage whisper. "They're not duplicate studies. They're all separate studies done on the same patient."

"You're sure about this," Johanna said.

"You have to look closely," Constantine replied. "They did each one a little different trying to hide it. But when you see them all together, watch them back to back like I did, it's plain as day."

"And there are no in-house echo's on any of them?"

"Except for the stealth one I did last night, no. Not one."

"Holy shit, Mike," Johanna said. "This is really bad."

"I've thought about it a lot since I talked to you. It's not Medicare or insurance fraud since they're privately paying foreign nationals. But it's still wrong. I think I have to tell McCarthy. At least a private heads-up. You know, nothing written or e-mailed."

Johanna considered it. "McCarthy's a player here but he's not the CEO or even the Chief Medical Officer. You need to make sure you leave him one thing."

What's that?" Constantine asked.

"Plausible deniability." She raised her eyebrows. "This is happening on his watch. It could be him with the cardboard box. See what I mean?"

A thoughtful look came over Constantine's face. He nodded his head. Johanna took another sip of her coffee.

"Look, go sailing," she said. "Clear your head. It's going to be gorgeous this weekend. I may even go rowing tomorrow. It's not just Rule Number One, Mike. It's The Cutter ABC's. What do we tell the junior residents to do when the shit goes down?

Constantine half-smiled. "Assign Blame and Cover your Ass."

Chapter 5

"BROTHER, WHY DO YOU call me now and on this phone?"

"I have concerns about the integrity of our vessel," el-Hamini replied

"Do you fear for its safety or the successful completion of its journey?"

"Both. And for the same reason."

"Not from the government or the FBI. On this, I assure you, they are silent."

"I think it is too early for that," el-Hamini said. "That would be like a great wave crashing down. This is a tiny crack and a trickle of water."

"Then the crack must be sealed."

"As you say," el-Hamini replied

"Tell me, brother, how did this tiny crack come to be? An errant sailor or, perhaps, an enemy sailor?"

"No, the sailors remain loyal, I believe," el-Hamini replied. "And the enemy slumbers in his camp. It is the one thing we always fear and cannot control. Chance."

"You mean luck."

"Yes, if you wish. Luck." el-Hamini dabbed at his brow.

"Which one is it?" the voice on the phone inquired.

"The one who assists me this month. His name is on the schedule I sent you."

There was a pause and a shuffling of paper. "How ironic," the man on the phone said. "You know the Arab proverb about the lucky man, brother?"

"Yes. Throw a lucky man into the sea, and he will come up with a fish in his mouth."

"Then we will take the fish and then we will cast the lucky man back into the sea. Call me no more, brother. Use the usual means to proceed. Do not alter the plan. The tiny crack will be sealed. How many so far?" the voice on the phone asked.

"Eight," the el-Hamini answered. "All defibrillators. Six more are awaiting clearance. We don't want them too close together."

"Agreed. Although there is absolutely nothing to link them to one another. That has been assured."

"You forget," el-Hamini said. "I link them to one another. So you must humor me in my cautiousness."

"As always," the voice on the phone replied. "Blessings and protection be upon those who do the work of the Prophet."

"And all blessings be upon Him," el-Hamini said. It was a familiar ritual

"When do you think the rest will be in place?"

"Soon," el-Hamini replied. "One is being discharged tomorrow. I have listed myself as gone on vacation soon so I will want to get the rest of them done before I leave. No one will question that. It is quite a commonplace practice, actually."

"You have planned well."

"I have followed the plan well," el-Hamini retorted, "But I have had much help."

"Brother, that is why we remain here with you in this cursed land. To make sure all goes as it is supposed to."

"Blessings upon you," el-Hamini intoned.

"Upon all who do His work. Stay strong. Be vigilant. We will all be home soon."

"Home?" el Hamini asked

"Paradise, brother. Is there another?"

Closing the cheap but untraceable TracFone, the man gently stroked his mustache. He always inferred that he was half a world away when, in fact, he was less than thirty miles south in a small café in Auburn. It was nearly empty in the quiet of a Sunday morning. He worried about the doctor but felt sure he would remain compliant. The doctor still believed in home as a place. For Tamal Hajiik, home had long since vanished as a point on a map and existed now only as a concept. And Paradise? Well, that was more than a concept – it was something real, something obtainable merely by purchase. And soon he would have the funds to locate it anywhere he pleased. In the shadows at the rear of the café, he sipped strong Syrian coffee from a small cup and pondered the absurdity. Born into poverty, he had raised himself up to professional respectability and then to a level of some refinement. But refinement, he rued, had not been enough. Craving opulence, he'd sold his services to a madman. He had escaped with his life, but little else. Now, he mused, he was in league with another madman, albeit a shrewder and much more powerful one. One, he was sure, who would not have his head snapped off by an ill-fitting noose.

Slurping the last bit of the thick coffee, Hajiik wiped the dregs from his lips and fingered the wrinkled dollar bills in his hand. If he did his part they would someday become worthless collector's items. Yes, he was trading with kafir, but his religious fire had burned itself down to barely a glowing ember long ago. He used it now only to convince others that his murderous motives were pure and unquestionable. He had never seen the Black Sea, but with the rubles he was promised, he was sure it would look just like Paradise.

Trip Collier stopped furling the jib the moment he saw her.

A film of sweat glistened on her skin. Tautly muscled arms and legs strained with each stroke she took. The sunlight turned her hair varying shades of red and auburn as she glided past, her ponytail flipping each time she leaned back and lifted the oars out of the water.

Collier stood with his hand on the forestay, transfixed. The sun reflecting off Lake Union was dazzling. The high pressure system now parked over Seattle had turned the water to glass and the docks and slips were crowded, even for a Sunday. Collier stepped gingerly around the forestay but did not let go of it. He stood on the starboard bow of the O'Day cruiser and watched as she moved toward its stern. She tilted her head up as she passed directly abeam and Collier thought she might have smiled at him. But in that moment the sun glared off her mirrored Oakleys forcing him to squint. He couldn't be sure. Inching along the starboard rail he kept one hand on the lifeline until he reached the cockpit at the sailboat's stern. She was like a machine, he thought - a tall and, from what he had seen, gorgeous machine. Collier knew just enough about rowing to recognize perfect form when he saw it. She was in a racing shell, one of the most unstable things a human could choose tp be in on the water. Collier's freshman roommate at Gonzaga had been a sculler. On a late fall weekend he had tried rowing one of the narrow little boats at his roomie's behest. Three choppy strokes and twenty feet were all he'd managed before "dumping" unceremoniously in the chilly water. That had ended his interest in crew – until now.

Collier flipped down his sunglasses and watched her until she slipped out of sight behind a larger sailboat. He tied off the main sheet, sat down in the cockpit and put his feet up. Rummaging in a beat-up cooler he found a Curveball Summer Brew and twisted the cap off. He knew there were a couple of rowing boathouses along the lakeshore. He put the bottle to his lips and slugged down a third of it. He wondered if she was going out or heading back. There were five more beers in the cooler. Five good reasons, he thought, for him to stay right where he was and find out.

"Have you ever sailed it on the Sound before," the old man asked. His skin was more sun-baked than sun-tanned. You could hide a dime in one of the lines on it, Michael Constantine thought. Puget Sound sparkled in the sunlight behind him. "It's a might different than day-sailing on the lake. Currents are trickier and there's an ocean swell due in from the 'leutians any time now. And they've spotted killers in the North Sound."

"Killers?" Constantine asked

"Orcas," the old man replied. "Punch a hole in yer hull if ya come between a mama and her calf."

The hand-lettered sign read "Launching/Landing Assistance $25", but Constantine decided that the old man didn't really want to leave the comfort of his shack and was digging for a reason to stay parked right where he was.

"I grew up sailing off Amagansett, New York," Constantine replied. "It's near the Hamptons."

The old man's eyes narrowed and the creases on his face increased to nickel depth.

"It's the ocean," Constantine said, "I think I can handle it."

"Suit yerself," the old man replied. "Here's a chart and a tide table. What size motor you got in case you need it?"

"Twelve-horse Yamaha," Constantine replied.

"Twelve whole horses, huh?" the man replied, shaking his head. "Horses are a lot more useful on land, you know." He rubbed at his dimpled chin. "But, if you keep so that you can always see the bottom half of the Space Needle, twelve horses will probably get you back. I wouldn't venture fu'ther out than that. Nope, I wouldn't."

Constantine took the charts and the tide table. He hadn't, he thought, gone to all the trouble of trailering his boat over from Lake Washington to head back now.

"What was wrong over at the pond?" the old man asked.

"Not enough wind," Constantine replied. "I was hoping it would be fresher over here."

The old man nodded and smiled. "Yeah, Yeah. It'll be fresher for sure," he said. "I'll back it in and park the trailer fer ya." He got up from his stool and started walking toward the idling truck and boat trailer. Constantine saw that he was holding a well-thumbed paperback book.

"What are you reading?" Constantine asked.

The old man turned the book so he could see the cover.

The Lion's Game.

"It's an older book but it's a good book," Constantine said. "I read it last year."

With the book back at his side, the old man nodded. "Makes ya' glad we live here and not in New York, don't it?" he said.

Collier nearly missed her.

The second beer and the hot sun had conspired to dull his senses and he had managed to nod off while seated on the cockpit's faded and irregularly padded seat cushion. An air horn blast several slips down had snapped him awake just in time to see her approaching from the stern, her back toward him.

Collier reached for the two lettered signs he'd hastily made on the back of an old grunge band poster he found rolled up in the chart box. Just as she passed he waved at her and held the first one up.

T. COLLIER
555-2492
He figured his cell phone was a safe place to start.

She slowed her stroke and leaned forward. Collier quickly pulled the second sign from behind the first.

"I HAVE BEER(S)!"

He held the sign out in front of him with both hands and gave her his best megawatt smile.

She stopped rowing but was still moving away from him. It looked to him like she was laughing. Then she shook her head from side to side. He held the first sign up again with one hand and waved vigorously with the other. Collier stopped waving when he saw her dig the oars in and start pulling away. He sat back down on the lumpy cushion and checked his watch. There were still four beers in the cooler – two apiece, he figured.

He slouched down and rested his feet on the gimbaled compass. He'd give her an hour.

Chapter 6

THE BREEZE HAD INDEED freshened and Michael Constantine trimmed the main sheet just a little. The twenty-two foot Catalina sailboat was thirty years old but had been lovingly cared for by its previous owner, a retired heart surgeon from Cleveland, Ohio. The brightwork fairly sparkled in the sun and the teak accents had been oiled obsessively. Constantine had replaced the jib and the main with new Melges composite sails but that was all he'd needed to invest after the purchase. The old surgeon had thrown in the trailer for nothing. In deference, Constantine had kept the boat's original name: Sea V Surge.

Heading north up the Sound the boat was nicely making way. Constantine smiled at the old man's concern as he felt the first faint rise and fall of the ocean swells. He'd been caught in nor'easters and had his share of close calls in Block Island Sound but he'd never been in a situation he couldn't sail his way out of – at least not yet.

Passing Mutiny Bay on the starboard side he began to feel the roll a little more. Boat traffic had thinned out appreciably as he meandered north. He planned to come about when he caught sight of Port Townsend, which would be soon. He'd only had to lower the little outboard twice, both times to negotiate the currents. The old man had been right about those. Constantine checked his watch. The days were so long at the end of June he didn't think he'd have any trouble getting back and trailering out before sunset. Breakfast hadn't set well and his sigmoid colon was making its ongoing displeasure known. He really needed to use the head but there was a small boat off to starboard whose course seemed somewhat undecided. He elected to wait until he was abeam of it before leaving the helm. As he glided past it he waved to the two people on board. He could faintly and intermittently hear the staccato whine of its outboard motor.

Constantine locked the wheel in place and went down the companionway to the little chemical head which was tucked forward in the bow. The hull was starting to pitch a little and he had to brace himself at the entrance to the tiny chemical toilet. He managed to get himself turned around and depantsed just in the nick of time. He waited a few minutes to make sure the fireworks were over and then carefully cleaned up. He reached for the header above the little doorway and started to pull himself up when he heard a loud thud. In the next instant Constantine was thrown forward and onto the floor of the narrow cabin. He struggled to his knees, his shorts and briefs still stretched around him. Awkwardly he managed to slide them up to his waist. He crouched low and duck-walked toward the boat's stern. He felt another bump and braced himself on the companionway door. He thought of the old man at the dock and wondered if he'd blundered into a pod of Orcas. Then he heard what sounded life shuffling feet on the forward deck.

He peeked out of the cabin but before he could turn his head the first blow caught him squarely on the back of his skull.

"Bang the front of the head a little more. Like maybe he fell."

The accent was as thick as the black mustache. The man who owned both pointed at the back of the cockpit. His companion grabbed Michael Constantine and did as he was instructed.

"Let me see the face."

The second man pulled back on Constantine's shoulders. The flaccid neck muscles let the head loll to one side.

"One more."

Farouk Aziz, who listed his occupation as journeyman welder at a marine salvage yard in Tacoma, let go and the unconscious form of Michael Constantine fell forward and caught the edge of the compass with his cheek, opening a bloody gash.

"Better," the man with the mustache said. "Now, reattach the safety line."

As Aziz did so the man took out a small knife and sawed

through the nylon cord about halfway. He pulled on each side of the cut but the cord did not break so he sawed some more with the curved blade. He motioned to Aziz.

"Pull on your side." Aziz grasped the line with both hands about two feet from where it attached to Constantine's harness. The man gasped the line on the other side of the cut. Slowly the fraying cord unraveled and separated. "Good," the man said. "Now put the life jacket down below – like he removed it to use the toilet." Aziz disappeared with the vest. The man scouted the surrounding water. No other vessel was within two thousand meters he calculated. When Aziz returned topside the man pointed to the still motionless form. Then he nodded toward the stern. Aziz lifted Constantine by the back of his shirt and dragged him toward the transom. The man grabbed the short length of cord attached to the harness. "Push" he said.

Constantine's limp form tumbled into the blue-green water. The man used the safety line to hold it close to the boat's transom. "Tell me when it sinks," he said to Aziz. With little air in his chest cavity to provide buoyancy Constantine bobbed for several minutes then slipped slowly beneath the chop. Aziz watched as the safety line played out through the man's hands and disappeared over the stern.

In the distance the Port Townsend Ferry Steilcoom II was chugging on its mid-afternoon trip to Coupeville. Aziz and the man climbed into the Zodiac and untied it from the port-side cleat.

"No calls for three days," the man said.

Aziz nodded and watched as the white sailboat with the black stripe opened the distance between them. He strained to see the name written on the stern but could not make it out. It didn't matter, he thought.

It was a ghost ship now.

Collier leaned against the mast and felt the first breeze off Lake Union there had been all day.

"I wasn't sure you'd come," he said with a smile.

"I wasn't going to," Johanna replied. "It was the parenthetical 'S' that did it."

"The what?"

"The 'S' in parentheses after beer," she replied. Collier picked up the hand-lettered sign and looked at it. He gave her a questioning look.

"It told me two things about you," she said. "You probably have a college education or higher and you also have a sense of humor."

"You're not a profiler, are you?" Collier asked.

Johanna laughed. "No," she said. "Are you?"

"Not exactly. But I'm betting today wasn't the first time you rowed."

"Wow," she replied sarcastically. "You're right. Maybe you could be a profiler. Are you going to invite me aboard or was that false advertising? That's illegal, you know."

Collier smiled. This woman, he thought to himself, was absolutely stunning. He stepped to the port side railing and extended his hand. Johanna grabbed it and pulled herself onto the deck. The boat bobbed and dipped at the concentration of their combined weight in one spot but Johanna shifted effortlessly.

"You've spent a lot of time on the water," Collier said. "I can tell by the way you move."

Johanna glided to the opposite side of the cockpit in three steps and sat down. "I just have good balance," she said. "Comes in handy in certain situations."

Collier could not take his eyes off her. The tank top was emblazoned with the letters "SRC" and was matted with sweat to what he recognized as a sports bra. What was underneath that, he presumed, was very impressive.

"I'm up here," she said curtly, pointing to her face.

"Sorry," Collier replied, taking a seat opposite her. "I was trying to figure out what SRC was."

Johanna laughed. "OK," she said, "Nice recovery. As long as we're doing initials, Collier, what's the T stand for? Wait, let me take a guess." She leaned back and regarded him while he fished in the cooler for two bottles. "Thomas? No. Timmy? Not a chance. Teddy? God, I hope not." Collier twisted the cap off one of the ice-cold Curveball's and handed it to her.

"No," she said, holding the brown plastic bottle by its long neck. "I'm getting the sense it's something a little more, um, ostentatious?"

Collier almost dropped his beer when she said it. He twisted the cap off his own bottle.

"It's Trip," he said sheepishly. "You sure you're not a profiler?"

Johanna took a long pull on her beer and then surprised Collier by releasing a little belch. "Sorry," she said with a smile. "I'm pretty stinky after that row – sure you don't want to sit downwind a bit?"

"I'm good right here," he replied. "I was working on the boat most of today, so I'm not exactly springtime fresh either."

"OK, Trip Collier," Johanna said. "But that has to be a nickname. So what's your real first name?"

"You first," Collier said.

"No way," Johanna answered. "You're the one soliciting yourself to passing scullers, not me."

Collier drank from his own beer then wiped his lip with his forearm. "Soliciting?" he said. "OK, you're either a lawyer downtown or a U Dub law student. Right?"

Johanna laughed and took another swallow. "God," she said, "I really hope you're not a profiler. Our safety would be in great jeopardy."

Collier considered the comment and decided it wasn't the time to discuss his line of work. He was about to ask her for her name again when she spoke.

"So is it something horrid like Winthrop or Belvedere?" she asked. "Or is it more self-aggrandizing like Royal or pathetically pompous like Sterling?" Then she laughed again. "Yeah, I could definitely see that. Trust fund baby chilling on his twenty-two footer. I could totally see you as a Sterling."

"Twenty-four feet," Collier replied with a grin.

Johann leaned forward slightly. "Careful, Collier," she said. "I'm actually a pretty good judge when it comes to length." Then she sat back and stretched out her long, muscular legs. She had thighs that looked like they could crush a beer can, he thought. Collier could see his reflection in her wraparound sunglasses and realized he was staring at her. She didn't appear to mind. She tilted her head up slightly to catch the sun and he noticed the scattered freckles on her cheeks and neck. Her arms had great muscular definition and reminded him of the actress Linda Hamilton in her Terminator heyday. For a complete stranger to him and his boat she seemed oddly at ease.

Johanna reached behind her head and pulled off the scrunchy that held her ponytail. She fluffed out her auburn hair and it fell just on the tops of her shoulders.

"That's better," she said. "My dad always told me to take out my top-knot or I'd get a headache." She peered down the mouth of the beer bottle and shook it slightly. "So are you going to tell me or not?"

Collier drained the last of his beer and reached for another. "It's my real name," he said. "Triplett Collier. So, Trip for short." "That's it?" Johanna said. "Not Junior or the Third?"

Collier inhaled deeply. "OK. Triplett Lightfoot Collier, IV. Happy now?"

Johanna crossed her arms in front of her and almost doubled over. "See?" she said between chortles. "I knew it." Collier downed more of his beer and waited for her to stop laughing.

"OK, OK," he said. 'I did my part. Now it's your turn."

Johanna pushed her sunglasses up to the top of her head. Her eyes were almost the same color as the water, Collier thought.

"Not yet," she said. "I'm still deciding about you. Give me a little more back-story and we'll see." She sipped the last of her beer and motioned to him with the empty bottle for another. The ice rattled as he plucked one out, twisted off the cap and handed it to her. She tossed her empty into the open cooler.

"Why should I tell you anything?" he asked.

"Because this is fun," she replied. "And if you don't tell me, this will be the only fun we ever have." She grinned at him.

"OK, mysterious and slightly odiferous woman," he said. "I was born right here in Seattle at Virginia Mason Hospital. My father and my brothers are lawyers in the family firm in Redmond. They do a lot of work for Microsoft and Amazon. My grandfather was a lawyer as was my great-grandfather, although the origin of his law degree is a matter of some dispute." Collier paused to wipe the dripping bottle with his shirt. "My great-grandmother was descended from George Washington Lightfoot, an early settler of Mercer Island and the father of the Lake Washington Floating bridge. We've been here a long time and I," he paused and took a short sip, "I am the only adult Collier male who does not work for the family firm despite, shall we say, significant pressure being brought to bear. I graduated from Gonzaga University, undergrad and law school. And despite the objections of my father and siblings I am pursuing a career in government service here in Seattle. My family tells me on a regular basis that I am an idiot, wasting my law degree as a federal drone.

So I bought this sailboat with a portion the money my grandfather left me and named it accordingly."

Johanna rose nimbly and leaned over the boat's sloping transom to read the name. This posture and her tight Lycra rowing shorts gave Collier a view that made him shift in his seat and place his forearm across his lap.

"*Idiyacht,*" she said smiling. "That's priceless." She sat back down.

"OK," Collier said, "I've given you everything but two forms of picture ID. What about you."

Johanna wiggled her bottom on the seat and leaned forward, moving her beer bottle back and forth like a metronome. "All right,' she said. "Assuming it's all true, you did good." She shook her hair and eyed him for a few seconds. "I was born in Maryland to very middle class parents. I went to school in Baltimore and then in Des Moines. I'm in Seattle for advanced training which will be finished about this time next year. And today was not the first time I've rowed." She surprised him by standing up. "Thanks for the beers," she said. "I think that's plenty for today."

She stepped lightly toward the port side of the boat.

Collier raised up, arms loosely by his side. "Could I call you?" he asked. "Maybe we could meet sometime when we're not sweaty and dirty. You can pick the place."

Johanna was standing on the dock. She had dropped her sunglasses back down to her nose.

"I have to think about it," she said with a soft smile. "I'm assuming that was your cell phone number on the sign. I'll let you know."

"Come on," Collier pleaded. "Give me something. You're not in the Witness Protection Program, are you?" It occurred to him that he would have a better chance of finding her if she were. She paused and then used her hands to motion for pen and paper. Collier grabbed the second of his little signs and the felt tip marker he had used to make it. He handed both to Johanna. She made a few quick strokes and handed them back.

"I'll bet you're a really interesting woman," Collier said. Johanna had taken a step to leave. She stopped and turned around. The expression on her face, he noticed, had changed.

"If I do call you," she said, "And I'm not saying I will – but if I do, you have to promise me one thing."

"Sure," Collier replied. "What is it?"
Johanna cocked her head to one side.
"Don't ever say that to me again."

Chapter 7

THERE WERE ELEVEN CARS and twenty nine passengers on the *Steilcoom II* when it left Keystone, Washington on its return trip to Port Townsend across North Puget Sound. The ferry's master, Alonzo Parrish, had light winds and a rolling swell to contend with but otherwise it was a good day to be on the water, he thought. Pleasure boat traffic was light in the North Sound, which was surprising given the beauty of the summer day. The fog and dark clouds Parrish had dealt with on his four trips yesterday disappeared overnight, pushed out by a stationary high, according to the faxed weather advisory in front of him. Parrish should have been able to relax on a day like this but relaxation at the helm was not a luxury he permitted himself anymore. He'd been a ferry boat captain for thirty years with time served on The Staten Island, Golden Gate and, until two years ago, Philadelphia River Link ferries. Twenty eight years without an accident or a citation. Thirty spotless years as a ferry commander. He'd only taken the weekend job captaining the Duck Boat that plied the Delaware River loaded with tourists as a favor to its regular pilot who was recuperating from hip surgery. It was fun and he got to interact with the passengers, which made it even better. Better, that was, until a loaded barge had run them over a hundred yards from the Ben Franklin Bridge and the young kid had drowned. It hadn't been Parrish's fault. The Port Authority review board had cleared him. The barge hadn't posted a forward spotter which was a grievous violation. Although Parrish had returned to his ferry job, just being on the same river, in the same spot every day ate him up and he knew he had to leave. "Geographic cure," the company-provided therapist called it when he told her he was moving. Parrish hadn't cared. Google Maps said it was two-thousand-eight-hundred-and-ninety-nine miles to Port Townsend, Washington and its ferry dock and that seemed just far enough. So instead of strolling the deck and letting the mate steer, he sat at the bridge and scanned the blue-green expanse.

The little sailboat off to port was moving a bit erratically, he noticed, but it seemed to be keeping to a generally north-northeast line. Its jib was luffing a bit so Parrish grabbed the binoculars and glassed in its direction. He didn't see anyone in the cockpit but he could tell that the wheel wasn't moving. He guessed the pilot had gone below to get warm, get something to eat or, most likely in his experience, take a shit. Gauging speed and direction, Parrish did not think there was any chance of a collision. He'd used the giant air horn occasionally in the past, sometimes with humorous results. His favorite was when the naked couple had rushed up on deck of their little cruiser. Parrish could still see the woman, her big titties bobbing with the swell, giving him the finger as the ferry passed to starboard. The passengers, he remembered, had cheered. Parrish set down the large binoculars and looked at the chart splayed out in front of him. He grabbed a fine-point pen and made a little "x" where he dead-reckoned the boat's position, along with the time. He debated radioing a heads-up to the Coast Guard, whose Search and Rescue base was located on Seattle's Pier 36 on the downtown waterfront, right next to some of his favorite restaurants and bars. He was imagining steamed clams and cold beer when the mate tapped him on the shoulder.

"Need anything?" the younger man asked.

"I'm good," Parrish replied.

He promptly forgot all about radioing the Coast Guard.

It had taken Johanna twenty minutes to walk back to the Seattle Rowing Center on West Ewing Street where her car was parked. Rowers were still coming and going and the clatter of shells and oars being racked and unracked filled the slightly stale air of the elegant boathouse. Johanna went to the tiny locker and retrieved her keys. She was unsure if giving out even the cryptic bit of

information to a complete stranger had been wise. She had not
been in any sort of relationship for – she stopped and did the math
in her head – God, had it been ten years? By anyone's standards,
she thought, a drought of epic proportions. The thing was, she
really hadn't missed it. The physical, the emotional – she had come
to a kind of personal détente with her needs and desires. Sex and
love, she figured, they would always be there when she wanted
them. But for this period of her life, she decided, she was on hiatus.
It had worked well so far.

"Hey, J-Row!" a woman's voice called.

Johanna turned around.

"Oh, hi, Casey," she said. A blond woman in her early twenties
walked up to her. "How's it going?"

"Good," the girl said, using a tattered US ROWING towel to
wipe her neck. "Do you still have connections on the National
Team?" she asked. "I'm leaving for Princeton tomorrow for the
selection camp. The coach over at Pocock Rowing said she'd put
in a good word for me but something from you would go a long
way."

Johanna thought for a moment. The elite rowing community
was quite small and as a former Olympic rower Johanna still had
cachet even though she hadn't rowed competitively in over twelve
years. "I knew Mike Tate when he was at Cal," she replied, "but I
don't know where he is now. And I don't know offhand what his
deal is with the National Team."

"He's one of the coaches," the girl said. "I would really appreciate
it. You know how cutthroat it gets."

Johanna nodded. She knew that most rowers at this level would
do anything – and that truly meant anything – to park their
sculpted butt cheeks in the hollows of a sliding seat on a National
Team boat. Johanna pointed to the little but noticeable scar on her
own right deltoid. "Are they still doing muscle biopsies?"

The girl hiked up the sleeve of her sweaty t-shirt to reveal
a similar but much fresher scar. "They don't do it themselves
anymore," she said. "And they never tell you that you have to
have one. But word is no one without one of these little beauties,"
she tapped at the scar, "has a snowball's chance in hell of getting
in a boat. It cost me two-thousand bucks between the surgeon, the
pathologist and the muscle fiber analysis. And it hurt!"

Johanna arched her eyebrows. "What were your numbers?" she

asked.

"Seventy per cent slow-twitch," the girl replied proudly. "But my average muscle fiber-size is larger than normal, so that's a bonus. They're saying you might have to be closer to eighty within two years. I really need to make it this year."

Johanna nodded sympathetically. She was glad she was out of this particular rat race. The next logical step, she once concluded, would be the breeding of Olympic athletes. She personally knew of two former National Teamers who'd undergone genetic testing and then gotten married with the expressed intent of producing Olympic-class offspring. Johanna had often wondered how long it would be before elite athletes began asking for stud fees or offering their sperm and ova on e-Bay. She looked at the younger woman and saw herself at that age. "There's life after rowing, you know," she said to her. "Be careful how many deals you make with the devil."

The girl laughed. "Easy for you to say with your Olympic medals safely tucked away and your Sports Illustrated spread framed on your wall. Make the call for me, will you?"

"OK," Johanna said. "I'll track down Tate and pass the word that you're a comer."

A grin lit the girl's face. "Thanks, J-Row," she said and then looked at the black plastic watch on her wrist. "I gotta go," she said. "I have to get in three thousand more calories before eight o'clock." She turned and walked away.

Johanna navigated the two blocks to her car deep in thought. It was easy for her, she thought, to tell someone else to be careful. She had made enough mistakes to fill a book or two and only persistence and blind luck had kept her from being in a much different place than she was now. She hadn't looked at her medals in years but she knew they would be displayed proudly and prominently on the walls of her first office. Though her mother had been aghast that her pictures in Sports Illustrated had made her appear "basically naked", her parents had expensively framed the pages for her as a gift. She thought about the article's title, "Wrecking Crew", and often found it ironic that her choices, especially her adventure in in Des Moines, had nearly wrecked everything she had worked so hard to achieve.

Johanna had remote started and unlocked the Volvo. A blast of cool air greeted her when she opened the door. She sat behind the wheel and let the rush from the vents play over her. Her Cutter Clinic ID badge with its unsmiling picture hung from the rear-view mirror. J. Roberson, MD stood out in block letters; just below it was CTSurg in a smaller font. That was who we she was now and who she would be for a long time. But, she thought, she was still the product of all she had been before. The coltish teenager who took up rowing after being left off the travel basketball team in eighth grade; the preternatural high school and collegiate sculler; the Olympian and then the medical student; and, of course, the girl rescued hanging by a rope over a dam in her underwear.

Tires screeched on the street and snapped her from her musings. She looked at the crumpled white coat on the passenger seat and the stethoscope peeking from its side pocket. To almost everyone she knew she was Dr. Roberson now, not J-Row.

So why had she scribbled it on his stupid sign?

He'd started Googling before she was even out of sight, but the sun made the cracked screen on his much-abused smartphone hard to read. Trip Collier did a cursory survey of the deck, locked the companionway door and hopped down onto the dock. He debated heading to his office but decided to start on his home computer first. Holding his keys in one hand and the cardboard sign in the other, Collier made his way through the milling lakeside crowd in almost a fugue state. He missed the left turn for the walkway to the street and had to retrace his steps for almost a hundred yards. Arriving at the multiply dinged Nissan Sentra he unlocked the driver's side door and a rush of overheated air belched out at him. The dark leather seats looked like they could leave scorch marks, as did the black padded steering wheel. Collier leaned in gingerly and managed to get the key in the ignition. The engine cranked stubbornly then turned over. More hot air streamed out of the dashboard vents and Collier quickly pulled his head outside. He leaned against the rear fender and, using his shadow, centered the oversized phone in front of him and tried his search again. If he had taken her picture, he thought, he could have used Homeland Security's facial recognition software program to help track her down. He typed in the letters again. After noting that Google had returned twenty-four-thousand, six-hundred-and-eighteen results in forty-five thousandths of a second, Collier realized that none of them was what he was looking for. He exited the browser and put the phone in his pocket. Leaning inside the still baking interior of the car he reached into the back seat and pulled out a marginally bound Greater Seattle phone book. A few tattered pages wafted to the ground as he flipped through it, finally arriving at the R's. He scanned three pages without getting a hit so he tucked the sign in as a bookmark and lowered himself into the driver's seat

Four hours later only the phone in his apartment jarred his intense concentration. Collier had lost track of how many mouse clicks, keystrokes and phone book pages it had been since he'd sat down. When he picked it up she didn't even give him time enough to say hello.

"Tell me you're a hostage somewhere and maybe, maybe I'll forgive you," a barely pleasant female voice said.

"Sorry, Kelly," Collier replied. "I got caught up with some stuff at work and lost track of the time. I just got home a little while ago. Can I still meet you?"

"Well," the reply came, "I've been sitting here on this nice bench at 99 Union Street for over an hour. You're car didn't go into the garage and you haven't gone in the condo main entrance, so that's bullshit. You know, Trip, I'm thirty one years old. I had my first date at fifteen. And I have never, ever, been stood up before."

"OK," Collier stuttered, "I'm sorry. I have been here. But I have been working on something on the computer and I just-" he stopped. "I fucked up. I'm sorry." He walked to the window and peered down seventeen floors at the woman with the phone to her ear. "I'll buzz the door open for you," he said. It was apparently not the right thing to say because for the remainder of the conversation Collier held the cordless handset an inch away from his ear. After berating and comparing him repeatedly to Charlie Sheen, Kelly Arcavedo borrowed a line from a Netflix movie they had recently together to deliver the coup de grace.

"You're like that Facebook dork," she said. "The reason people don't like you, Trip, is because you're just an asshole." Then she hung up. Collier watched her stride purposefully away, disappearing down Union Street as the street lamps flickered on. He shuffled back to the contemporary glass-and-steel desk and pulled the illuminated keyboard toward him. He had written

down eleven numbers. Seven had the listing "Rowe, J," two
were "Rowe, J A," one "Row, R J," and one, a long shot, "Rown,
Jennifer." He debated the wisdom of calling from his office phone
in the morning but he knew that all the recipients' Caller ID would
display was "Unknown Number" and decided it was the safer bet.
Collier felt bad about Kelly. She was a nice person and he liked her.
But, he mused, he was never really intrigued by her.

J. Row, whoever she was, had piqued his interest in a way no
woman had in a very long time. He thought of the look she had
given him when he tried to compliment her. OK, he thought, she
doesn't want to be called interesting.

He wondered if she would appreciate intriguing.

Johanna didn't have any trouble tracking down Triplett
Lightfoot Collier, IV. In less than an hour she knew the year, the
day, and the hour of his birth and how much he had weighed.
She found Wikipedia entries on both sides of his family and the
website for his father and brothers' legal firm. Google Earth gave
her a surprisingly close-up aerial and street-view of his condo
building and a cursory check of real-estate listings told her his unit
was still worth a million on the current market, depressed as it
was. She found an old newspaper article describing his winning
goal for Gonzaga that beat Oregon State in the finals of the Pacific
Northwest Collegiate Lacrosse League playoffs. He'd been named
tournament MVP and PNCLL player of the year. The grainy
accompanying picture showed a grinning younger version of the
man she'd met with longish, tousled hair and a neatly trimmed
beard. His dated picture on seattlelwayers.com still had the beard
and a much more serious look but the "Contact Info" section was
blank. Johanna followed his internet trail until it ended two years
after graduation from Gonzaga Law School. After that, she noted,
he all but disappeared. His home phone number was unlisted.

She printed the lacrosse picture then cut it out and taped it to her
monitor. She looked at the digital clock in the lower right corner of
her screen. It was nearly ten. The row had been really good and she
was glad to feel physically tired in place of the emotional and static
physical drain surgery usually imparted. She got up from the desk,
walked into the darkened bedroom and crawled under the sheet.

She set the alarm for five-thirty. She was only assigned one case in the morning, she knew, but she would be on call.

Johanna stretched her legs and slipped her left hand beneath the waistband of her Nick and Nora pajamas. If she fell asleep right away, she thought, her next waking moments would be back on the job with all its worries and stresses. If she were asleep by ten-thirty, she calculated, she would still get seven solid hours of sleep – almost a luxury. She shifted her hips and palpated the prominence of her pubic bone. Then she felt for her femoral pulse. About sixty and regular, she noted with satisfaction

The little stirrings were like a greeting from an old, very good friend who had moved far away. She rested her hand and thought about it.

It had been such long time, she decided.

Maybe it was time to get reacquainted.

Chapter 8

"YOU SEEM VERY HAPPY today, Dr. Johanna."

Johanna tilted her head toward the scrub nurse, Evelyn Moya.

"Thank you, Evelyn," she said. "I got a great night's sleep and I do feel really good today." Johanna towered over the tiny Asian woman who needed three risers to put her close enough to Johanna's level to pass the surgical instruments efficiently.

Evelyn Moya had lived in Seattle for thirty-nine years but her parents had been Japanese immigrants and her speech patterns still retained many of the familiar rhythms, especially when she was nervous. "I think maybe you have a new boyfriend. You have that boyfriend-happy look today," she giggled.

Johanna felt her cheeks flush but shook her head. "Sorry, Evelyn," she said. "You know me. No husband, no boyfriend. Not even a goldfish. Two-0 heart please."

Evelyn handed Johanna a long needle-holder with a trailing black thread.

"You need a boyfriend," she said. "You're getting too much like the men surgeons here. You walk like them. You curse like them. You treat assistants like them. You were a sweet person when you first came here. I think you're still a sweet person, inside. You can still be a great surgeon without being, you know, a bitch."

Johanna stopped sewing. The heart of a seventy-nine year-old retired boat mechanic beat three inches below the cleaved and spread breastbone on which she now rested her gloved hands. The three other people in the operating room kept their heads down and feigned scribbling on whatever paper was closest at hand.

"I could be wrong, Evelyn," Johanna said in a measured tone, "But did you just call me a bitch?"

Evelyn Moya straightened her back. "No, Dr. Johanna. I just say how you change. Dr. Constantine gone next month and then you are the new chief resident. You are great surgeon. Everybody knows it. You can be yourself now. You need to be yourself." She paused. "Then maybe you get boyfriend."

The words hung as if suspended in the air. Johanna looked down at the operating table. The palpable tension in the room was broken only when she suddenly let out a laugh. It occurred to her that, except for the patient, all the people in the room, the nurse-anesthetist, the circulating nurse, Miss Moya, the perfusionist and herself, were women. If Dr. Taylor didn't come in and thus let her do the case by herself, there wouldn't be a male medical presence until she got to the CVRU where, on most days, half of the nurses were men. Perhaps the world had changed in the six years she had been a surgical resident, she thought. The anger Johanna initially felt pulsing up dissipated like a puff of steam. She turned and looked at Evelyn, who appeared to be holding her breath.

Then Evelyn spoke. "I leave if you want," she said. "Robbie or Helen can come and replace me."

"You stay right here," Johanna replied. "I'm betting Dr. Taylor's not coming in so I need the best help The Cutter has to offer." She picked up the needle holder and went back to suturing. "Give the heparin, please," she said to the anesthetist. "And see if that intern we had Friday, Annalisa, is available to come in and help us."

Evelyn Moya's surgical mask wrinkled with the breadth of her smile underneath it.

Seljuk el-Hamini laid a dressing over the three-inch incision and rolled off his sterile gloves. His hands were delicate, almost feminine, and he rubbed them together to disperse the talcum powder that had accumulated.

"Any word from Dr. Constantine?" he asked. "It is most unlike him to deprive us of his presence without notification."

"Dr. McCarthy's office is working on it," a nurse replied. "He technically belongs to the CT Surgery department so if there's an absence, they want to handle it."

"This is fine," el-Hamini replied. "It is nice to know I can still do these procedures by myself if I have to."

"It actually goes a little faster," the nurse, a petite black woman, replied.

"Ah, Constance, you flatter me. Contrary to popular belief, this is in your best interests!" El-Hamini laughed and looked at the clock embedded in the wall of the brightly lit procedure room. "How soon can we begin the next implantation? Another defibrillator if my ageing memory serves."

"It might be a little bit." The disembodied voice echoed from the speaker mounted to the right of the clock. El-Hamini looked through the thick glass below it at the Control Room supervisor who was speaking into a desktop microphone.

"And why is that?" he asked, untying and retying the braided drawstring on his scrub pants.

"They're waiting for his paperwork to clear. He's a protocol patient. Amanda is on the phone working on it right now."

El-Hamini slid off the bouffant scrub cap and smoothed his barely disturbed silver mane. "I will call the Admissions Department myself," he said and began to walk toward the double doors that guarded the room's exit.

"The problem isn't with Admissions," the voice replied. "She's on the phone with Homeland Security. We may have to cancel and reschedule him for tomorrow."

A tight smile over gritted teeth appeared on el-Hamini's face; he drummed his fingers on his thighs, took a sharp breath in and then exhaled slowly. "I am leaving on vacation after Friday, as you all know," he said. "Please give my apologies to the patient and prepare for a longer day tomorrow. We will anticipate young Dr. Constantine's presence as well. Can we have both rooms running in the morning?"

"Tipton-Kohler has three angioplasties scheduled," the supervisor answered. "I'll talk to him. He'll probably cancel two of them himself, like he always does. I'll get him to move the other one – his favorite procedures are the ones done by his partners."

There was laughter on both sides of the glass. El-Hamini smoothed the front of his scrub top and reached into the breast pocket for his watch.

"I will be in my office attending to paperwork," he said. "Please have Amanda call me if she cannot solve the problem herself."

"No problem, boss," the supervisor said. "Enjoy the afternoon off."

El-Hamini tilted his head and gazed through the glass.

"Alas," he replied, "There is no rest for the wicked."

"Was that my pager?" Johanna asked. She was watching Annalisa's painfully slow progress in suturing closed the long skin incision.

"I'm sorry I'm taking so long," the younger woman said.

"It's OK," said Johanna. "Doctors remember how fast they did something; patients remember how well they did it." She turned her head and winked at Evelyn.

"It was McCarthy," the circulating nurse said. "He wants you to go to his office as soon as you're done. Says it's very important."

A little knot announced its presence in Johanna's stomach. She drummed her fingers on the surgical drape.

"He just wants to talk to you about being the new Chief," Evelyn said confidently.

Johanna stepped back from the table and pulled her gown off. Then she slipped off the brown latex gloves with a practiced snap and tossed them into a large pail with a red liner. "Miss Moya will help you finish," she said to Annalisa. "I'll go to the unit and write the orders."

Johanna walked to the table at the rear of the operating room. She picked up the chart and her pager which, she noticed, had two small Post-It notes attached to it. She clipped the pager to the waistband of her scrub pants and peeled off the tiny paper squares.

"McCarthy's office," the top one said. She pulled it off and crumpled it. Then she looked at the second one.

There were three words and a little drawing on it:

BUY A GOLDFISH!, the note said.

"Have you talked to Constantine?" McCarthy asked.

He was seated behind an enormous teak desk. The late-morning sun shone through four narrow windows with integral miniblinds all cocked at an identical thirty-degree angle. The light bounced off McCarthy's wire-rimmed lenses and the blinds cut diagonal shadows across his face and chest. Johanna shifted nervously in her chair.

"I talked to him over the weekend," she said. "We had breakfast Saturday morning after Grand Rounds."

"And since then?" McCarthy asked, tapping a finger on his blotter.

"That was it," Johanna replied. "Why?"

McCarthy leaned forward, changing the pattern of shadows falling across him.

"Because he hasn't shown up for work today and we were wondering if he decided to skip the last few days of his residency. He already has his signed certificate as I'm sure you know."

Johanna didn't know that but any concern she had for Michael Constantine's whereabouts was, at the moment, submerged well below her relief that McCarthy wasn't asking questions about el-Hamini, his defibrillator patients or Constantine's suspicions.

"Mike wouldn't do that, Dr. McCarthy," Johanna said. "He was an altar boy until he finished high school. If there's anybody that follows the rules, it's Mike."

McCarthy nodded and sat back in his chair, the sun again reflecting off his polished bifocals and obscuring his eyes. Johanna tried not to squint.

"No one's answering at his apartment and he's not responding on pager or cell phone. Did he mention traveling anywhere when you spoke to him?"

Johanna shook her head. "He said he might go boating on Sunday," she said. "He's got a little day-sailer that he bangs around the lakes on. His farewell party is today after work over at the Tin Room in Burien. You probably got an-"

"Yes, I got the invitation," McCarthy interrupted. "I've asked them to reschedule it for Friday, his real last day." Then he stood up. "We'll keep trying to track him down. But I may need you to do me a favor."

Johanna stood so he would not be looking down at her. It was a trick Constantine had taught her. "Sure," she said. "What is it?"

"Until Dr. Constantine returns to work, I need you to take his place on Dr. el-Hamini's service. Just until his new Electrophysiology fellow starts next month. Seljuk is going on vacation at the end of this week, so it's only three, four days at the max. Can you do it?"

Johanna knew it was not a request. "Sure," she said, "but I'm on call today and I have cases scheduled the rest of the week." McCarthy waved his hand dismissively. "You can start tomorrow and I'll take you off the call schedule the rest of the week as a reward. Dr. Taylor can stand to do a few cases himself. I just hope he remembers how." He walked the short distance to the office door and opened it. "I'll tell Dr. el-Hamini you'll meet him in the device lab at seven-thirty tomorrow."

"Unless you hear from Mike, right?" Johanna asked.

"Just be there at seven-thirty," McCarthy said in a toneless voice. "I'll deal with Constantine."

Justin McCarthy had been chair of The Cutter Clinic's Cardiovascular Institute for less than a year. What he did not need right now, he decided, was anything resembling scandal associated with his little kingdom. The body that had washed up on the shores of Vachon Island, he knew after his conversation with Johanna, was possibly that of Michael Constantine. The Coast Guard was already searching for his sailboat. After listening to his conspiracy theory on Saturday evening, he'd asked Constantine if he had shared his concerns with any other members of The Cutter staff. He said he hadn't. Still, McCarthy wondered if he'd said anything to Johanna Roberson. She was a cool customer, he thought, but he hadn't seen any flicker of concern during their conversation. He decided to watch her closely once news of Constantine's loss was announced. McCarthy sighed, trying to remember when the last time his biggest worry was the welfare of the patients.

With the door closed, the only sound was a German clock ticking in the far corner of his spacious office. Seljuk el-Hamini looked at the framed picture of his wife and daughter. It was the last one he had taken, standing in front of the Departures drop-off at Seattle-Tacoma International Airport. Their trip back home was only supposed to have lasted two weeks. El-Hamini touched his finger to the date-stamp on the picture's lower right-hand corner. It would be two years tomorrow. He looked at his daughter's face and wondered what she looked like today. His wife's beaming smile – would it be as bright when next he saw her? He knew they were alive and, as far as he could tell, not terribly mistreated. Could it be that within a few short days he would be on his way to meet them? And what of his life after that?

He was startled when the cell phone in his jacket pocket vibrated. "Yes," he said when he had retrieved it.

"How many remain?" The voice was unexpected and instantly known.

"I was only able to complete one today. I will finish the rest this week," el-Hamini said.

"A slight adjustment," the voice said. "The new number is twelve and the last one must be ready by Thursday. This is still possible?"

"If the Homeland Security clearances are in order, I can perform three implantations tomorrow. If there are no complications I can discharge all three by Wednesday evening." El-Hamini wiped a bead of perspiration from his temple.

"See that there are no complications, brother," the voice replied. "They are, after all, actually quite healthy individuals. And quite in a hurry to fulfill their glorious destiny."

"And my family?" el-Hamini inquired with a tiny quaver.

"They are well and anxiously awaiting your triumphant reunion. A hero's welcome, so to speak. You have your ticket and your new passport, yes?"

"Yes." Both had arrived with some clinical papers in an interoffice envelope, a signal to el-Hamini that there was someone inside The Cutter Clinic watching his every move. His own flight was scheduled to leave from Sea-Tac on Wednesday at midnight.

"We will not speak again," the voice on the phone said and the connection was broken.

In a dingy apartment on the border of Seattle's original Skid Row neighborhood Tamal Hajiik rubbed at his large mustache. Across the room a younger, newly clean-shaven man leaned over a rickety double bed, carefully packing a Nike duffel bag.

"Make sure he gets on each of the planes," Hajiik said, still holding the TracFone. "Two stops – London and Vienna. Don't lose sight of him. His family will be waiting when you arrive in Damascus. Give them a few hours together."

The younger man zipped the duffel bag closed. "Then?"

Hajiik permitted himself only a few seconds of contemplation before replying.

"Kill them all."

Chapter 9

JOHANNA TRIED CONSTANTINE'S HOME number and his cell number again. She looked at her watch.

"I need you to do me a favor," she said.

"Sure," said Annalisa Dunker, who was seated next to her on the worn futon in the surgical residents' on-call room. They were watching Dr. Oz expound on the splendors of defecation.

"I need you to cover for me for a little while. Just take my beeper and answer the pages. If you need to get hold of me use my cell phone. I'm going to buzz out and see where the hell Constantine is hiding himself. Otherwise I have to play pacemaker jockey the rest of the week." She unclipped her pager and held it out. Annalisa didn't take it right away.

'What if there's an emergency or a bleeder?"

Johanna flipped the pager into her lap. "Don't be such a baby," she said. "I'm not going out for a nooner. I'll be back in ninety minutes, tops. If anybody asks just tell them I had a personal emergency outside the hospital but you can get hold of me immediately if necessary." Johanna stood up. "Come on," she said with a laugh, "You get to be in charge of the whole Cardiothoracic Surgery service. How many other PGY-1's can say that?"

Annalisa looked at the beeper as if it might be radioactive then clipped it to the pocket of her white coat. Johanna grabbed her car keys from the pocket of her own white coat and headed out the door.

The little apartment building in downtown Seattle's Belltown neighborhood fit right in with Michael Constantine's personality, Johanna thought. Interesting without being ostentatious; its charm almost understated. She slid out of the front seat and walked up the six immaculate cement steps to the foyer door. Peering inside through the leaded glass she saw a weathered divan and two mismatched wooden chairs. She tried the doorknob and was met with resistance. The glass panes around the door frame were done in the Prairie style of Frank Lloyd Wright and didn't enhance her view of the interior very much. Johanna knocked on the heavy glass several times without result. She looked for a doorbell or intercom but didn't see one. She was about to try another part of the building when she saw the lobby elevator doors open. An elegantly dressed black woman, who Johanna guessed to be in her early seventies, looked at her with alarm. Johanna rapped on the door again, lightly this time, and the woman took a few halting steps toward the door.

"I'm looking for Dr. Constantine," she said in a voice loud enough to be heard through the glass. "He lives in this building. Can you help me?" Johanna turned up her palms in supplication. The woman turned and got back on the elevator. Johanna's shoulders dropped in exasperation and she turned around. As she took the first descending step a young Japanese man alighted the bottom step. Johanna almost ran into him.

"I'm sorry," she said. The man looked up.

"Somebody sick?" he asked. "Are you an EMT?"

Johanna descended to the sidewalk so she would be at eye-level. "No," she said. "I'm a doctor and my friend who lives in this building is a doctor. He didn't come to work today so we're making sure he's all right."

Johanna watched as the gentleman quickly took in her appearance and watched as his eyes darted to her hospital name tag.

"You're a friend of Dr. Mike's?" the man asked. His speech was completely unaccented Johanna noted.

"Yeah," Johanna replied. "Mike Constantine is my chief resident. Have you seen him?"

"I talked to him yesterday," the man replied. "Do you want to try his apartment? Maybe he just overslept."

"Yeah, thanks," Johanna replied. The man walked up the remaining steps as Johanna followed. He put his foot against the bottom of the door frame and turned the knob without any difficulty.

"I thought it was locked," Johanna said.

"No, it just sticks unless you put pressure on the door." He waited until Johanna entered the little foyer and then closed the door hard behind her. "We told the landlord not to fix it," he said casually. "Helps keep the riff-raff out." Johanna followed as he walked to the elevator and watched as he withdrew a small key and inserted it just below the "Up" button. "Which floor does he live on?" the man asked. It sounded to Johanna like a test question.

"Four," she answered. "He's in Four-A."

Apparently satisfied, the man turned the key to the right and pushed the button which lit immediately. Johanna could hear the car rumbling in the shaft.

"My name is Carlton Yee," the young man said. "Mike is my neighbor." He proffered his hand and Johanna shook it firmly.

"Johanna Roberson," she said as the wood-paneled doors glided open. "Thanks for helping me. I don't think Mike's ever missed a day of work in the two years I've known him. You hear about people overcome by carbon monoxide in these old buildings."

"These apartments all have the old-style radiators," Yee answered as the doors closed and he pushed the large black button marked "4". Johanna momentarily debated the wisdom of being alone with a person she didn't know, especially having not told anyone where she was going. Several scenarios flashed through her mind including one in which the pleasant Mr. Yee had killed Constantine and was now planning a similar fate for her. She reflexively took a step back and palmed the keys in the large side pocket of her lab coat. There was a little "ding" as the car ground to a halt and the doors opened again. Johanna waited.

"Ladies first," Yee said, turning to her.

Johanna shook her head. "You go," she said. "You know the way." Yee stepped off and turned left down the narrow hallway.

"That's my place," he said as they passed a mismatched metal "4" and "D" on a burnished oak door. They walked silently on the carpeted floor until they reached 4A. Johanna knocked on the door.

"Mike? Mike? It's Johanna. Hey, Constantine, you in there?"

There was no answer. Johanna listened at the door but heard nothing. Yee, she noticed, had stepped around behind her. She tapped again on the door. "Mike, buddy," she said. "Can't miss your going-away party. Are you in there? Hello?" She flinched when she felt a hand on her shoulder. Yee took a step back.

"Sorry," Johanna said. "You startled me."

Yee appeared just as startled and Johanna relaxed a little. "I can call the building super," he said, "but he lives off site. I'm not sure he'd open it for you. Have you thought about calling the police?"

Johanna let out an involuntary breath at his mention of the police and suddenly felt incredibly stupid. "I probably would have to ask the hospital to do that," she said, tapping on her name tag.

"My dad's a judge here in Seattle," Yee said, "So I know a lot of the policemen. If you're really this worried, I could do it for you. You know, the concerned neighbor and all that?"

Johanna smiled at her own apparently misplaced paranoia. "Thanks," she said, "but Mike would kill me if this is nothing. He starts a new job at Harborview next month and I'm not sure a missing persons report would be getting off on the right foot. Know what I mean?"

Yee nodded. "Have you checked with the marina?"

Johanna looked at him blankly.

"I know he was planning on going sailing yesterday," he said. "He was asking me about boat ramps on the Sound."

"I thought he kept his boat on Lake Washington?" Johanna asked.

"He does," Yee replied. "But I guess he grew up sailing off the coast in New England. He said he wanted some bigger water."

"So where would he go to get on Puget Sound?"

"You can get there on the water from Lake Washington, but you have to navigate the locks and the drawbridges and it takes a while. I'm pretty sure he was talking about trailering over and dropping it in. I don't sail but I have friends who do. They recommended the Don Armeni ramps. You know where that is?"

Johanna shook her head. Yee pointed to the window at the end of the long hallway. "Take a left on Fifth and go till you get on the Alaskan Way viaduct. Take it to the West Seattle Bridge. Get off on Harbor and follow the signs for Alki State Park. The ramps are just past a restaurant called Salty's. Great view of the city from Duwamish Head. I think they're open for lunch."

Johanna had heard of the restaurant but had never gone there. "How long from here?" she asked, looking at her watch.

"Traffic'll be light," Yee replied. "Twenty minutes."

Johanna had just turned right off of the bridge when her cell phone rang. "Pit of Hell," a synthesized female voice said, phonating the contact identity Johanna had entered for the hospital switchboard number. She pressed the button marked with a tiny green telephone. "Roberson," she said.

"Dr. Roberson," a woman's voice said nervously, "This is Annalisa. One of the cardiologists just called from the cath lab. He said they have an aortic dissection they think needs to go to surgery. They want you to come see it."

"Where is it?" Johanna asked.

"In the cath lab."

"No, no," Johanna replied. "Where is the dissection?"

"He said in the aorta."

"Where in the aorta?" Johanna said, exasperated more with her own risk-taking at leaving the hospital than with the intern's befuddlement. "Ascending or descending?"

"He didn't say."

"Well, call him back. One we have to operate on; the other we don't. Which cardiologist was it?"

"Tipton-Kohler? Does that sound right?"

"Yeah," Johanna said. "Unfortunately. He's an idiot. Did you tell him where I was?"

"I said you were at the gynecologist's office."

Johanna laughed. "What made you say that?"

"He sounded like someone who wouldn't ask any more questions about it."

Johanna could see Salty's restaurant getting closer. "You're right about that," she said. "I'm pretty sure he sits down to pee." She could hair Annalisa chortling. "I'm only about thirty minutes away. Call me back as soon as you know." The she hung up.

The parking lot at Salty's was sparsely populated. She could see the boat ramps beyond and some empty boat trailers parked in another empty lot. She didn't see anyone to ask so she stopped in front of the restaurant, turned off her car and got out. There was a nice breeze off the Sound and downtown Seattle glittered in the sun across it. Johanna pulled open the outer door and stepped into a small hallway. She tugged on the inside door and stood by the "Please Wait to Be Seated" sign. An attractive dark-haired woman approached her.

"Sorry, hon," she said. "Lunch service is over. Bar's open, though." Then she cleared her throat with a bronchitic rasp and took in Johanna's hospital garb. "Probably don't want to drink on duty, though, right?"

"That's OK," Johanna replied. "I was wondering if there's anyone around at the marina. I need to ask about a sailboat that launched here yesterday."

The woman scratched at her ear with a stubby pencil. "It's not a marina, dear. It's just a boat ramp." She pointed out the large window that looked out on Elliot Bay. "There's an old fella that sits by the water and helps people launch and land with their trailers. Makes pretty good money at it, too, I think. He was in here for lunch so he might still be around. Just look for a little wooden stand."

"Thanks," Johanna said. She walked back out into the sunlight and shielded her eyes. The ramp was four or five hundred yards away. She decided it would be easier to drive over. As she remote started the old Volvo her cell phone rang again. She hit the "talk" button before the appellation had time to sound.

"Ascending," Annalisa said. "Eighty-two years old. You're on your way back, right?"

"Right," Johanna lied. "Shit. OK, just go down to the Cath Lab and act confident. Type and cross six units of blood, order a stat CBC and a cold agglutinin titer. Call the OR and tell them to open the instruments for an ascending aortic replacement with left subclavian cannulation and tell anesthesia and perfusion we might need deep hypothermia and circulatory arrest, so get the ice machine cranking. You got all that?"

There was a pause. "I'm typing it into my phone." Another pause. "OK, I got it."

Johanna started the engine, shifted into drive and pointed the car back towards Harbor Road and the West Seattle Bridge with a knot in her gut. "Who's on call for staff today?"

"It's Dr. Taylor," Annalisa replied. "He already called."

"Am I at the gynecologist?" Johanna asked.

"Dentist," Annalisa said. "Sounded like he might ask more questions."

Johanna accelerated up the ramp to the bridge. "Right on that one, too," she said. "Anybody hear from Constantine?"

"No, but I guess the party's on Friday now."

"Better for us," Johanna replied. "Let's just hope the guest of honor gets the message." She looked out her window at the expanse of rippling blue and green that stretched north to the horizon.

Big water, she knew from experience, was highly overrated.

Chapter 10

AMANDA WINGFIELD WAS IN a lather and Trip Collier knew why.

"It just took a little longer than I thought it would," he said. "I'll have them done by the end of the day and bring them over myself in the morning, OK?"

"Well, darlin', I had my rather magnificent ass handed to me by one of our doctors this afternoon, thanks to you. So forgive me if I'm just a little less than reassured."

Collier looked at the small stack of folders in the center of his desk.

"I have five ready to go."

"Just make sure I have the three that are on the schedule tomorrow. Can you promise me that?"

"What time do you get to your desk?"

"What time can you get them here? That's when I'll be at my desk."

Collier looked at his digital desk clock. "Just for you, Mandy, I will drag myself out of bed at an ungodly hour for a government worker and be at your desk promptly at seven o'clock. Deal?"

"Six-forty-five," Amanda replied a whit more pleasantly. "With a large decaf latte, two percent milk, one sweetener and a scone of your choice. Do you need to write that down, darlin'?"

"I got it," Collier replied, scribbling the particulars on the folder of one Halam Karshi of Yemen, which lay on the top of the little pile.

"Good," Amanda said, apparently satisfied. "Oh, and one more thing."

"Of course," Collier said with a laugh.

"I want it from Espresso Vivace. No place else. Are we clear?"

"Crystal," Collier replied, having just watched *A Few Good Men* on AMC a few nights before. "It's over on Broadway which means it'll be dark when I have to get up tomorrow. Satisfied?"

"I'll be satisfied when you tell me you're sorry for making my day miserable," Amanda replied.

Collier sighed. "I'm sorry, Mandy. That's the truth." He heard Amanda laugh.

"Trip, honey, I like movies too so I know you'll understand when I tell you this."

"Tell me what?" Collier asked.

"You can't handle the truth," she answered. Then she hung up.

It was almost one a.m. when the phone rang in Operating Room 44.

Johanna looked up from the table. "Platelets ready?" she asked hopefully.

The circulating nurse shook her head in the negative. "It's Dr. Taylor," she said. "Wants to know how we do?"

Johanna looked down into the chest cavity. Across from her Annalisa Dunker appeared on the verge of collapse. Johanna lifted up a large sponge packed around the heart. She watched for a moment and then pressed one of the suction catheters into service. It gurgled as the tip met the slowly upwelling pool of blood.

Johanna sighed. "Tell him I think we're getting there but we'll be drying up for a while yet." She took a new white sponge and pushed it into the chest. "Don't ever go into heart surgery," she said to Annalisa.

"Why won't it stop?" her assistant asked.

"All the platelets have been paralyzed so the blood can't clot," Johanna replied. "Thanks to our friend, Dr. Tipton-Kohler." A collective groan went up from the operating room.

"How did he do that?" Annalisa asked.

"Before he knew what was going on here he gave the patient gigantic dose of Plavix, a great drug which stops the platelets from sticking together. The right drug if this had been a heart attack and he'd had to put in a coronary artery stent. But instead of seeing the patient and figuring out what the actual problem was, he just dosed him and took him straight to the cath lab." Johanna picked up a corner of the sponge and peeked underneath then quickly pushed it back down. "Watched blood never clots," she said quietly. "Anyway, this poor guy had a classic presentation for dissection: ripping chest pain that went straight through to the back, hypotension, no EKG changes and a new heart murmur." Johanna shook her head. "Take a history? No. Do a physical exam? Nah. Just completely annihilate his clotting system, take him for a reimbursable procedure and then, after pulling the pin, hand this live grenade to us and go home. Asshole."

Annalisa yawned under her mask. The phone rang again.

"Platelets are ready," the circulating nurse said.

"OK," Johanna said. "Here's the plan. We give the platelets and if things look even remotely dry after that, we're closing him up and taking him to the Intensive Care Unit." She looked up at the clock on the wall. "One way or another we're pulling out of here by two a.m. Eight hours of this is enough for him and us." She pulled up the blood-soaked sponge and gave it to the scrub nurse who handed her a dry one. "Did they ever get hold of Constantine?"

"Not yet," the circulator said. "But there's a note here for you from Cardiology. Says that they're starting the device schedule early tomorrow 'cause I guess now they have three cases on. You're supposed to meet a Dr. Hamini at seven."

Johanna looked again at the clock and calculated what she might get for sleep.

Two hours, she thought. Two hours, max.

Trip Collier X'd out of the search program at a little after one-thirty having come up empty again. He'd poured himself two fingers of armagnac and it was beginning to make its sedative properties known. He clicked on the spyware icon, started the scan running and turned off the desk lamp. Bad guys, he realized, were fairly easy to find. Beautiful women without criminal records, to his dismay, were not. He wandered into the condo's spacious bedroom, knocked back the last of the smoky liquor and climbed into the unmade king bed.

He tried to remember the last time he had waited for a woman to call him. And what he would do if she didn't? He thought of his broken date and Kelly's scathing assessment of him. He was thirty-one years old, he thought, and still behaving like the spoiled undergraduate jock he'd once been. Collier laughed to himself. Undergraduate jock to post-graduate jerk, he mused. The mystery woman on his boat had pegged him in less than a minute. He thought of Ava Gardner's famous quote: "Deep down, I'm pretty superficial."

He closed his eyes but could not drift off. This woman, whom he'd met for less than thirty minutes, had left him mildly obsessed and entering the uncharted territory of self-awareness. Maybe it would be best if she didn't call. Then at least he could continue on his chosen path, the one of least resistance. A memory bubbled up from his college days of his favorite Jesuit professor, Fr. Joe Feeney, whose classes he'd taken for all three of his required Philosophy semesters. Over beers at an off-campus watering hole they'd been discussing Socrates, St. Thomas Aquinas and the notion of the examined life. It occurred to Collier that his chosen career was really nothing more than examining lives. He'd pried into hundreds, perhaps thousands of other people's lives – always looking for something that wanted to stay hidden. He wondered if, deep down, it was an ongoing excuse not to look at his own.

Collier bunched the bed pillow under his neck and hooked his arm under it. Maybe the unexamined life isn't worth living, he thought just before he crossed the watery border into sleep, because it really isn't much of a life at all.

Chapter 11

A THIN LINE OF drool trickled from the corner of Johanna's mouth, down her chin and on to the dingy pillowcase. A widening pool of it magnified the "y" on the block-stenciled "Property of The Cutter Clinic" imprint. The on-call room was warm and she reflexively brushed away the top sheet with her left arm. Across from her Annalisa Dunker lay passed out on the other small bed. An ancient nightlight cast a feeble yellow glow that barely reached the sleeping occupants.

When the phone rang Johanna woke with a start. She reached toward the flimsy particleboard night table and knocked the receiver onto the floor. "Shit," she muttered thickly and groped for the phone, finally reeling it in by its cord. "Yeah?"

Johanna rolled onto her back and kicked at the rumpled sheets. "How much the last hour?" she asked and waited for the answer. "Are we talking about blood or urine?"

She pushed herself up on one elbow and waited for her head to clear a little more. "OK," she said and rubbed at her temple, pushing moist and matted strands of hair to the side. "So eleven hundred total since he got back but only a hundred for the last hour?"

A female voice on the other end of the phone told her that was correct. Johanna shook her head. "Well, we're not taking him back for that," she said. "What's his 'crit?"

"The last hematocrit was twenty six," the voice replied.

"OK. So let's give him two units of blood and don't call me unless he's bleeding more than two-hundred an hour or if his

pressure gets unsteady. I think he'll probably be alright now."
Johanna reached to put the receiver back in its cradle then quickly
pulled it back. "You still there, Suzanne?"

"Yes, Dr. Roberson. Did you want something else?"

Johanna scratched her head and squinted at the clock she knew
was at the far end of the darkened room. "I can't read the clock.
What time is it?"

"It's a little after seven," Suzanne replied.

"Fuck!" Johanna said reflexively and dropped the phone down
hard on the cradle. Annalisa twisted in her bed. "Do we have to go
back?" she croaked from under a pillow.

"No, go back to sleep," Johanna replied. "I'm supposed to be
down in Cardiology right now." She limped stiffly toward the
tiny bathroom and flipped on the harsh fluorescent light. Then
she looked in the mirror. "Jesus, do I look like shit," she said to
her reflection. Johanna turned on the tap and rummaged in her
toilet kit for a toothbrush. After a cursory brush, rinse and spit she
grabbed a comb and went to work on her tangled hair.

"I hope Constantine had fun," she called to Annalisa as she
tugged on her mane. "'Cause when he gets back I'm going to kill
him before anyone else has the chance."

"There's no one aboard, sir."

"What's your position?" the Commander asked over the
crackling radio.

A young apprentice seaman had secured the bobbing sailboat
using the fore and aft cleats on its port side. The forty-one foot
United States Coast Guard Utility Boat bobbed synchronously on
the swell next to it, the mooring lines flexing and then snapping
taught with the periodicity of the two-foot waves. They were a
little more than a thousand yards off the edge of Deception Island
in the Puget Sound.

The Senior Chief Petty Officer in command of UTB 400414
looked at his GPS monitor. "Four clicks north-northwest of the
Deception Lighthouse, sir."

"That's a long way from home if it's the same boat the ferry
captain spotted," the Commander replied. "You report registration
number as WN 091101 NY, is that a copy?"

"Yes sir, that's a copy."

"Computer search says it was just sold last month. We're on the horn with the King County Recorder's office trying to track down the new owner. The previous owner is currently out of the country. Batten it down, bring it in and we'll go from there. Anything suspicious?"

The Senior Chief looked at the two seamen who had secured and searched the abandoned craft and were now standing back on the little bridge. They both shook their heads.

"That's a negative, sir. No contraband, no drugs, no weapons. No occupant ID's, either."

"Anyone see an EPIRB or an inflatable?"

"Negative on number one, sir. No distress radio beacon found on board. There is a six foot inflatable but it looks untouched. "

"Pictures?" the Commander asked.

"Say again, sir."

"Pictures, Russo. Did you take pictures? In the unlikely event that DHS or Seattle PD gets involved, they'll want pictures." Senior Chief Russo looked back at the seamen. One was reaching for the Canon digital and the other was already on his way down the scuttle ladder. "Getting those now, sir," he replied confidently. "Permission to drop the sheets for the tow once all the photographs are taken, sir?"

"Yeah, that's fine," the Commander answered. "Make some noise when you're in sight of the pier. Nobody boards until I have a look. Understood?"

"Copy that sir."

""I'm not going through what I did last time with those assholes at Homeland who think they're secret agents. If we were at war we wouldn't even have to talk to them."

"Roger, that. There's always hope for North Korea, sir," Russo replied. He heard the Commander chuckle.

"An identifiable enemy, Senior Chief," he said. "We haven't had that for a while."

"No, sir," Russo replied but the radio had gone silent. He looked aft and saw that the sailboat was now bare-poles and the seamen were standing by the mooring lines. Russo gave a thumbs-up signal and received two in return. He throttled up the port engine, one of a pair of Cummins diesels, and watched as the stern moved in a small arc allowing the crewmen to bring the sailboat aft. One of them skittered up to its bow and hitched the tow line into the D-ring in the prow. Russo throttled back and let the line go slack. He disengaged both props and the sailboat's bow gently nudged the UTB's transom allowing both seamen to come back aboard. As he gently put the engines back into gear he saw the Search and Rescue Helicopter in the distance. Russo glanced at the heads-up display and located the water temperature icon. Fifty-three degrees. Even in calm seas, he knew, the longest anyone would last in the water was about four hours before succumbing to hypothermia. The E-3 seaman had come back to the bridge.

"Was the swim ladder up or down," Russo asked.

"Up," the younger man replied. "You think six blasts?"

"I think six blasts," Russo replied, referencing the horn signal for Man Overboard. "With the ladder up and the smooth sides of these older fiberglass boats, unless a wave or a friendly orca lifts you up and drops you on deck, if you fall out you're not getting back on." He shook his head.

"These fucking day sailors," he said. "You're safer on a plane."

The smoldering carcass that had once housed the immortal soul of Farouk Aziz lay near the door of the little shack. The smell of burning flesh did not bother the man who stood next to it. For Hajiik it was not new. Nor was the odor of spontaneously evacuated bowels. But on this sunlit morning the combination of the two were briefly testing his own fortitude. He grabbed a scrap of wood and held it up to the still lit and hissing acetylene welding torch. The lumber caught with a glow and a crackle and he inhaled the woodsmoke, which temporarily calmed his rolling gut. He looked out the window and across the dirty stream to the Tacoma Marine Salvage & Reclamation Service. He had phoned in Aziz's absence two hours earlier with the pretense of a head cold. Since he could now clearly see Aziz's nasal sinuses through the scorched flesh and charred bone, he assumed the head cold had run its course.

When some of the smoke from the corpse had dissipated he used the torch to light an unfiltered Camel, holding it clumsily between the thick fingers of the welding glove. Then he went to work on the hands. As the digits melted and coalesced into a blackened mass he used a small stick to pick the gold ring from one of the long, thin bones. He let it cool and then slid it down the stick and into his pocket. Once the hands were done he reassessed the gaping neck wound. Using the welding torch to coagulate the flesh and liquid blood, he burned down to the bony vertebrae and vaporized the connecting ligaments. The white and jelly-like spinal cord peeked through the gaps. Grabbing a handful of singed black hair at the crown, he put his boot on the breastbone and pulled. Aziz's head separated with an audible pop.

Hajiik fingered his mustache. Prior to slitting Aziz's throat he had forced him to pull down his pants and now he stared at the circumcised penis that had betrayed his would-be betrayer. Had Aziz not elected to relieve himself over the side of the Zodiac and revealed himself as kafir, a non-believer, he would yet be alive. He sat down on a small wooden box and adjusted the gas mix until only a pure blue flame was visible at the tip of the torch. Slowly and deliberately he turned the exposed genitalia into a first molten and then fused lump of unrecognizable flesh. He turned off the gas at the tank and the torch went out with a sound like someone inhaling sharply.

Drawing long on the cigarette, the man his compatriots called "The Eagle" went over his mental checklist again. The young doctor was accounted for. Aziz, an unanticipated threat, was neutralized. El-Hamini and his pampered, turncoat family would never leave Syria. His roommate for the last three months would be killed in a men's room at the Vienna airport by an operative sent from Moscow. The loyal winery worker in the Willamette Valley had less than a day to live. He himself would be on an Air Baltic flight to Riga when the cataclysm occurred and a small branch of the Bank of Latvia would have his future in a closely guarded account. The President's personal deputy had arranged it himself. Whatever agency Aziz was working for would get their answer, he mused, but many hours too late. Perhaps then even his own sister, Rahim's mother, would finally understand and be consoled.

He doffed the heavy welding gloves and dragged Aziz's cooling hulk deep into the nearby woods. Several piles of fresh animal scat told him where to leave it. Then he collected enough deadfall to cover it completely.

Hiking back to the shack he rolled the disarticulated head into a cloth sack weighted with iron scraps. It was not a time for trophies, he thought. He walked along the stream for almost a half-mile until he found a deep, sludgy-looking pool. With a grunt, he heaved the sack out into its middle and watched it sink.

On the way back to the concealed vehicle he took in the rugged country around him. The peaks of the Cascades were still snow-capped and the green of the forests was almost too deep to be real. It was a beautiful country, he thought. Hand-made by God. If you spent your life in a desert, surely this is what Paradise looked like.

These people, and he believed they truly were infidels, they did not deserve it.

◆ ◆ ◆

There was laughter and the mix of several voices coming through the open door of el-Hamini's office. Johanna buttoned her long white coat, ran her tongue over her front teeth and walked in without knocking. She could see el-Hamini clearly. He was talking to a tall, red-haired woman in a smartly tailored suit. It was cut, she realized, to accentuate the woman's curvaceous backside. Next to her was a man in a blue blazer and khaki slacks. The woman's bouffant hairdo obscured the man's face. El-Hamini was already dressed in the azure scrubs of the Interventional Device Laboratory. A tuft of silver chest hair sprouted from the V-neck. He stopped talking when he saw her approach.

"Dr. el-Hamini," she stuttered. "I am so sorry. We were up all night doing an aortic dissection and I fell asleep in the call roo-"

The red-haired woman had turned around to look at her. Johanna glanced at The Cutter ID badge clipped to her lapel. "Amanda," read the top line while in a neat cursive script below it was printed "International Referral Specialist." As Amanda turned Johanna could see the clearly the face of the man standing next to her.

"Oh shit," she blurted out, "Not you."

There was a brief stunned silence which el-Hamini broke with his effusive laugh. "Well, good morning to you, too, Dr. Roberson. And I hope you are referring to me and not to either of our dear guests!"

In the haze of fatigue, sleep deprivation and surprise, Johanna was caught speechless, much to the amusement of Trip Collier who casually took a slug from his Vivace cup and smiled at her.

Amanda took a step back. "I know I've talked to you on the phone, honey," she said with a drawl that came from somewhere far below the Mason-Dixon Line. "I hope this doesn't mean I was nasty to you. I can be, shall we say, a bit direct when I need something."

Johanna had yet to utter another word. El-Hamini laughed again and seemed to be waiting for her say something. She darted a glance at Collier's government badge which was clipped to his breast pocket. A red laminated Cutter Clinic "Visitor" badge was looped on a thin elastic cord around his neck. She looked at Amanda.

"I, I..., no, I mean. No, I didn't mean you," she stammered. She felt her cheeks flush and knew Collier was zeroing in on her ID badge from behind his cup. There was more awkward silence. Then Collier spoke.

"I'm afraid this is my fault," he said contritely. "And I offer my apologies." He turned toward el-Hamini. "I met Dr. Ro..." - he darted a glance at Johanna's ID, "-berson briefly this weekend over at Lake Union. Actually, I tried to make her acquaintance but her keen intuition kept her from telling me her name. Thus, our mutual surprise at this unexpected reunion."

It seemed to Johanna that the last syllable hung in the air forever. Luckily, Amanda spoke up and saved the day.

"What Trip here is trying to say," she said to el-Hamini, "is that at some point this weekend he tried to hit on this lovely young doctor and she had the good sense to tell him to take a hike and now here he is, like the proverbial bad penny."

Johanna's expression was blank. She knew she had to say something. 'Well, yeah, but not exactly. But pretty close." Then she laughed and the tension broke. El-Hamini stepped forward. He reached down and handed her a steaming cup of the boutique espresso Collier had brought.

"Please, take this," he said. "Compliments of my new friend Mr. Collier and the United States Government. You deserve it more than I."

Johanna took the cup and moved it to her lips, inhaling the lovely aroma. She took two long sips and immediately felt better as the concentrated caffeine rushed to her head.

Trip Collier, she noticed, was trying desperately not to laugh.

An hour later, warm, soapy water dripped from both their arms. "So you have not heard from Dr. Constantine, either?" el-Hamini asked.

"No," Johanna replied. "I went to his apartment yesterday to see if he was alright but got called back in for that aortic dissection. His neighbor said he might have gone sailing."

"Whose case was the dissection?" el-Hamini queried.

"Tipton-Kohler's," Johanna said.

"Ah, yes," el-Hamini replied in a dispirited tone. "He's a complete idiot, as I am sure you know." He shook the water from his hands and used his knee to turn off the flow from the scrub sink's tap. Johanna did the same. The she followed him through the door and into the spacious interventional device suite.

"Then why is he still at The Cutter?"

El-Hamini shook his head slightly. "He is protected by Dr. Scongilli, our beloved chairman, to whose daughter he is married."

"Ohhh," Johanna said. "So there's really no hope of ever–"

"None whatsoever, my dear," el-Hamini said, cutting her off. Then he turned to look at her. "When a man knowingly protects a dangerous fool, he reveals himself to be even more of one himself. It is something to remember."

Johanna was not sure what to make of the statement so she nodded her head knowingly and took the proffered sterile towel. El-Hamini faced the anesthesiologist at the head of the operating table. "He is stable and sedated, I trust?" he asked.

The anesthesiologist shook his head. "Had trouble getting his blood pressure down, though," he said. "Didn't expect that with a twenty per-cent E. F."

El-Hamini clicked his tongue "Compensatory vasoconstriction," he said sharply. "Not surprising at all." Johanna caught the exchange but said nothing. "We have two more devices that we must do today, dear friends, thus I implore you to work carefully but swiftly so that we may all go home as early as possible." He put on his surgical gown and turned to Johanna as a nurse cinched the ties behind him. "As you are only with us for a few days and you have been up all night operating, perhaps you will allow me a pleasure I so rarely have anymore – that of doing the procedures today myself."

Johanna smiled under her mask. "I will learn more today by watching you," she replied deferentially. "Dr. Constantine calls you the Afghan Flash."

El-Hamini did not reply and Johanna was worried she he said something to offend him. She tied up her own gown, gloved and tucked in next to him, resting her hands on the draped and snoring patient. There were a series of whirrs and staccato clicks as el-Hamini positioned the bi-plane fluoroscope over the chest. Only a small circle of skin was visible under the right collarbone. Johanna twisted her shoulders under her heavy and uncomfortable lead apron.

"Two-percent Marcaine with epinephrine please," el-Hamini said and reached out his hand. The scrub nurse placed the barrel of a large syringe with a long needle in his palm.

"Two per-cent, with," she said as she did it.

Johanna watched as el-Hamini expertly infiltrated the anesthetic solution into and beneath the area of exposed skin in a wide arc just below the collarbone.

"With us for a few days," he had said.

Johanna wondered.

How would he know that?

Chapter 12

TRIP COLLIER WAS ASTOUNDED at the amount of readily available information he had been unable to find the night before. He really wanted to ask her about her adventure on the Des Moines River a few years back but decided he'd better start slowly. They'd both been collegiate athletes, he mused, so maybe he should start there. Lacrosse and crew – were there two more elitist sports on the face of the earth? Her accomplishments had far outstripped his own but there would at least be some common ground to keep an initial conversation going. He had been wrong about her on the boat. She wasn't just interesting or intriguing.

She was fascinating.

He was trying to find the photo spread in the Sports Illustrated online archives but wasn't having much luck. He was about to call the Seattle Public Library to see if they had hard copies going back that far when his desk phone rang.

"Recovered yet?" Amanda asked sweetly.

"Why whatever do you mean, Mandy dear?"

"Hey, I was right there next to you, sugar," she replied. "I saw your face. Baby boy, you are hooked through the gills."

Collier laughed. "I was just surprised, that's all," he said.

"You need to realize," Amanda replied, "I have gotten where I am by being a highly accurate judge of reactions in a male-dominated environment. You can bullshit me all you want, darlin'. I know what I saw."

"Like I said, I was just surprised. Do you think I've been sitting here all day just doodling her name?" He looked down at his several years out of date desk calendar and saw that he had done just that. Several times.

"No, I am calling to tell you that Dr. el-Hamini will be done in about two hours and thought maybe you could bring me a couple more patient clearances."

"I gave you everything I have done," Collier replied.

"Well, then, find some more," Amanda said sharply. "Dr. Harrington has two patients from Qatar waiting for natural orifice surgery. Maybe you could bring those."

Collier looked at the remaining stack of folders and smiled. "How long did you say?"

"Two hours," Amanda replied. "But you'd better leave now. There's a little wine shop on Third. I want a bottle of Bogle Phantom. It's an underappreciated red blend – you might have to ask for it. That's to make up for being such a natural orifice yourself to someone who's trying to help you out."

Collier thought of his brief conversation with Kelly. "That's twice in twenty-four hours," he said quietly.

"What's twice?"

"Nothing. You sure just one bottle?"

"Well," Amanda said, "You could pick up a couple more bottles of that very nice wine I mentioned if you were planning to, oh, I don't know, maybe make a nice dinner for a new acquaintance. In my experience, it's perfect for, shall we say, a private social occasion?"

"This is extortion, you know. I could have you-"

Amanda cut him off. "And I could report you for using your office and your government computer to snoop on one of our residents."

Collier looked at the web page open on his browser and laughed. "So are we even after this?" he asked.

"Not even close, honey" Amanda replied. "Do I need to remind you that it was my astute powers of observation and my tip to you which prevented that Turkish general from being asphyxiated by one of our Respiratory Therapists?"

"No," Collier said. "I remember quite clearly."

"And," Amanda continued, "If memory serves, that little incident earned you a Meritorious Service Commendation as well as a promotion from your previous and, no doubt, glamorous assignment inspecting cargo holds on container ships, did it not?"

Collier's nose wrinkled reflexively at just the reference to the stinking compartments he had wriggled into. "Bogle Phantom," he said. "Got it. See you in two hours."

"Be early," Amanda said. "I don't think you'll get another shot."

Johanna was asleep on her feet. The two cups of coffee she'd downed in quick succession before the start of this last case had only served to goose her kidneys and fill her bladder. El-Hamini was, she noticed, not even bothering to describe to her what he was doing anymore. His seemingly unflappable demeanor had soured with the lengthening afternoon and the self-multiplying delays. When one of the nurses had asked about rescheduling the third case for the following morning el-Hamini had all but bitten her head off. It was the crashing of the instrument stand that woke her up.

"Woman," el-Hamini said angrily, "You are trying my normally limitless patience." Johanna straightened her slumping back and tried to focus. It appeared that el-Hamini had taken the device the nurse had handed him and flung it, striking her Mayo stand and scattering some of the surgical instruments on the floor. El-Hamini stamped his foot.

"How many times must I repeat? We are participants in a tightly controlled clinical trial. We must use the devices specified by the protocol. Can you not understand this?"

The nurse who had brought the defibrillator into the room appeared close to tears. "I'm sorry," she stammered. "I thought that was the right one."

"It is not the right one!" His voice was rising slightly with each exchange. "Go! Find the right device. Now! It is because of you that we are here and not with our families."

Johanna watched the young nurse as she pushed the button that opened the pneumatic door and then heard her sob as it whooshed shut behind her. "Do you want me to go see if I can help her?" Johanna asked.

El-Hamini clenched his fists then tore off his surgical gloves. "No," he said forcefully. "Apparently if I want the proper device I must get it myself. There is some bleeding around the ventricular lead. Hold pressure until I return. And make sure not to disturb the other lead." He peeled off his gown, snapping the ties that held it closed behind him, threw it on the floor and stormed out.

"Well that's something you don't see every day," the anesthesiologist said laconically.

"It is if you're in the heart rooms," Johanna replied.

"Tell me about it," he said in a flat, Midwestern accent. "I used to do cardiac anesthesia at the mother ship in Indianapolis. Dr. Tobias, Dr. Whitney and that maniac Poole. They were all nuts. When I agreed to come out here it was only because they promised me I didn't have to do open hearts anymore. I'm too old for this shit."

Johanna was tempted to ask him if he had known Colin Walker but then thought better of it. She lifted up the little gauze Ray-Tec sponge and watched the oozing wound. "Do you think he'd care if I put a stitch around this lead?" she asked. "It's not going to stop on its own."

The scrub nurse didn't answer but quickly loaded a curved needle attached to a long blue suture and handed it to her.

"I've been working with him for years," the scrub nurse said. "I've never seen him act like this. Must be something else going on."

Johanna put a quick figure-of-eight stitch around the shiny silver pacemaker lead. "I'll bury the knot in the pectoralis minor muscle," she said. "He won't even see it." She snipped the protruding wisp of polypropylene thread just as el-Hamini re-entered the room.

He opened a cardboard package which Johanna noticed had writing in both English and Arabic. He peeled back the outer wrap exposing the top of the clear, sterile molded plastic inner packaging. "Here, take the device," he said, pushing his arm toward her. She grasped the package and laid it on the patient's chest. "Start connecting the leads in the manner I showed you," he said curtly. "I am going to use the gentlemen's room and then I will scrub back in." He looked up at the clock above the door. "I want this man out of here and back on the nursing floor by five-fifteen. And I want him discharged by afternoon tomorrow." Then he turned and walked out.

Johanna pressed her thighs together and tried not to think of her own swelling bladder. "Maybe he'll be better after he pees," she said. Everyone in the room laughed.

Everyone except Johanna.

She thought about Constantine and what he'd told her. She wondered if that was the something else that was going on.

El-Hamini closed the door to his office and sat down at his desk. Cradling his head in his hands he tried to think of a way out of this basket of snakes in which he was trapped. He was not a deeply religious man and he had never cared for politics. When his wife and daughter had been taken he'd been sure it was only for money. Money he would have gladly paid ten times over. The note he received tucked in an office chart had told him the day and the hour when he would be contacted. Up until the time the man on the phone began to speak he still assumed it was going to be about the terms of the ransom. After the call had ended it had taken him almost half an hour to stop shaking. At first it had sounded preposterous; then merely crazy; then outlandish but possible. But as each step unfolded and he was drawn in more deeply he realized it could actually succeed. When a front page article in the Wall Street Journal had detailed how easily explosives disguised as printer cartridges had been smuggled into the cargo holds of passenger planes he had given up hope of derailing the plan.

El-Hamini picked up the walnut picture frame and looked again at his wife and daughter. Their cheeks were pressed together and smiles lit their faces.

How often he had wanted to alert the American authorities. But how? Someone was obviously watching him even within the supposedly secure confines of The Cutter Clinic. Was it one or were there many? Were they listening to his phones, reading his e-mail? How could he be sure? The Seattle Police and the FBI, he knew, had offices within walking distance. The State Department had a post within The Cutter itself. Yet each time he let his mind entertain the thought he was pulled back to the final moments of that first phone call. The man had spoken slowly, almost gently as he described the agonies that would be visited upon his family and himself. First, the slow beheadings of his cherished – one made to watch the other to magnify the horror. Then, after his own abduction, he would be forced to watch the hideous video of it again and again until he pleaded, and the man promised he would beg, for the same fate.

A tear fell on the glass and zigzagged lazily until it reached the frame. El-Hamini set the picture down and wiped at his eyes. A life devoted to helping and healing would be remembered only for senseless death and destruction. Surely The Prophet, he believed, had never intended for His words to unleash this kind of madness.

He sat back in the leather chair and felt a sort of calm descend upon him. His part in all of this was now done. Once the last of today's patients left the hospital it would be out of his hands. He could plead – what was it the attorney had called it in his only malpractice suit? Plausible deniability?

He dismissed the notion and exhaled slowly. There was no way out and he knew it. The snakes had writhed and coiled and knotted themselves around him. This image was forming in his mind when a knock on the door dispelled it. El-Hamini cleared his throat and dabbed at his eyes again. "Yes, come in," he said with more vigor that he actually possessed. A shadow cast by the light in the outer office preceded the entrance of his visitor.

He forced a smile when he saw who it was.

"The three patients from today are all doing well," Johanna said. "The two from yesterday were ready to go, so I discharged them and dictated their summaries. They seemed like they were in a hurry to get out." She was trying to gauge his mood as she spoke, he realized. "Can I do anything else before I leave?"

El-Hamini dropped his shoulders and smiled, this time genuinely. "No, my dear, and thank you." Johanna took a step closer to the desk. "I am sorry for my behavior today," he continued. "Sometimes our plates are, as you say here, too full?" Johanna nodded. "We will spend time tomorrow discussing something educational. I promise."

"No word on Mike Constantine?" Johanna asked. A little shiver danced up el-Hamini's back.

"I'm afraid not," he answered. "At least not that I have heard from Dr. McCarthy, anyway. Shall we start at nine tomorrow? I will treat you to breakfast if you promise not to report me for today's resident work-hours violation."

"You're at the end of the line on that one, I'm afraid," she said.

Johanna turned to leave when he spoke again. "If you don't mind an old man asking, is it true what Amanda said about that nice Mr. Collier? He doesn't seem like the type to be a, a – what word do you say here – a masher?"

Johanna laughed at the dated colloquialism. "No, I don't think he's a masher. We just met out of context, I guess. I mean, if you can't trust Homeland Security, who can you trust? Right?"

El-Hamini paused before replying. "I suppose that is true. Now, please go home, go to sleep and we will start fresh in the morning. I must say, though, that in the few brief minutes of our mutual company, the young man did appear quite taken with you." He intertwined his fingers on his desk in front of him and looked at her. "We must have love in our lives," he said, "or we are but empty vessels, aimlessly adrift."

"Thanks," Johanna said. "I'll keep that in mind. I'll make rounds and then meet you at nine in the staff dining room. Do you want me to close the door?" El-Hamini nodded and she glided out, pulling it shut softly behind her.

Out his window he could see the flashing strobe at the top of the Space Needle. A light in the distance, he'd once been told, meant there was always hope. He placed his elbows on the desk and rested his chin on his hands, feeling his wedding ring rubbing against the stubble. He thought about Johanna and wondered if his own daughter might one day be like her. Then he thought about Triplett Collier and the Department of Homeland Security.

"A light in the distance," he said softly as the evening sun filtered in. "A light in the distance."

Amanda Wingfield tucked the bottle of wine in her eco-friendly tote bag and looked at her watch.

"I thought you said to be early," Collier said.

"Good things are always worth waiting for, sugar," she replied.

"I never really thought about your last name." Collier pointed at her engraved desk nameplate. Amanda shrugged.

"Alas," she said, "my late daddy was a surgeon with literary pretensions. I believe he found the pen more interesting than the knife, actually. Always scribbling away at one manuscript or another for as long as I could remember. I think that he was never published was his greatest disappointment."

"I'm sorry he's no longer alive," Collier said.

"Me too," Amanda replied wistfully. "He was just such a wonderful man, gone before his time."

"Cancer?"

"Drunk driver. Coming home late one night after an appendectomy. Did you know they don't even do them as emergencies anymore?" Amanda dabbed at an eye. "Anyway," she said, straightening her shoulders and composing herself. "It could have been worse. He didn't name me Laura."

Collier smiled. "I wasn't a big Tennessee Williams fan. Had to read him for one of my English requirements at 'Zaga but that's about it." He was about to continue when Amanda looked up.

"Get up. Quick!" she said. "Act like you just got here." She began shuffling the folders on her desk. Collier rose and stood by her credenza. He felt the riffle of a tiny breeze as Johanna pushed open the heavy glass door.

"Well, isn't this just the strangest of coincidences?" Amanda said brightly

Collier looked at Johanna and smiled.

They stood side by side in the marble and granite hallway just off The Cutter Clinic's main foyer, neither having spoken since leaving Amanda's office.

Johanna broke the silence.

"I don't always look like cat vomit, you know."

"I'm sure you don't," Collier said. "That's why I waited for you. Would it be OK if I walked you to your car? Seattle is the sixteenth most dangerous city in the United States."

"It's not even dark yet," Johanna replied. "Do I look vulnerable to you?"

Collier smiled. "Of all the adjectives I could come up with, Dr. Roberson, vulnerable would not even make the top one hundred."

"Good answer," Johanna said. "One I would not have expected from a Gonzaga Laxhead."

Collier picked up his pace slightly to keep up with her. "Former Laxhead," he corrected. "Or maybe recovering laxhead but, fortunately, never a laxaholic." Johanna kept walking, her little overnight bag dangling at her side. "Unlike you," Collier continued, slightly out of breath, "my athletic pedigree ended with graduation." Johanna turned her head and looked at him.

"Googling me on government time, were we?"

"I was on break," Collier replied. "Apparently you were-"

"Checking the sex offender registry," she said, interrupting him.

"Just in case." They arrived at the gleaming steel and glass atrium at the main entrance of the hospital. Johanna stopped. "I can take it from here," she said. "Unless you think I'm a threat to national security or you plan to elevate your game to stalking me. Which you might be doing already, for all I know."

Collier laughed and put his hands in his pockets. "I would really like to see you on a social basis," he said. "I'm a pretty good cook and a reasonable judge of wine. If you'd feel safer on neutral territory, I know six great restaurants that are local secrets. If that's still too forward, I will buy you burnt coffee and stale Danish in the hospital cafeteria." He brushed a tuft of brown hair off his forehead. "I would just like to see you sometime where we can both act like normal people. You're not secretly married or leading a double life of some kind, are you?" Johanna stared at him for just a moment then let it pass.

"Maybe I'm a lesbian," she said.

"Not that there's anything wrong with that," Collier said.

Johanna laughed out loud. "Which season?" she asked.

"Season Four," Collier replied. "I have them all on DVD. I love Seinfeld"

Johanna pulled her bag up to her chest and ran her tongue inside her lips. "OK," she said. "Call me tomorrow through the hospital switchboard. Just ask them to page me. I don't really cook and I know even less about wine, but you're definitely not getting off with caffeinated swill and a day-old donut. Let me think about the venue, OK?" She wondered exactly what the inside of a million dollar apartment looked like.

Collier smiled and took his hands from his pockets. "Deal," he said. "What time should I call?"

"Somewhere between ten and eleven should work," she replied. "But sometimes it takes a while to get to a phone so just stay on the line."

"Operators are standing by," Collier said with a grin. "You might just like me. I'm really not a bad guy."

Johanna took a step. "Well, you're not a registered sex offender. Let's start with that and see how it goes." Without another word she walked away and though the massive glass doors that parted silently on her approach. The evening breeze was cool and felt good on her face. She'd had three hours of sleep in the last forty-one, she realized.

So, she wondered, how come she suddenly didn't feel tired?

Chapter 13

THE COAST GUARD OFFICES on Pier 36 were still bustling despite the late hour. Fleet Week and Seattle's annual SeaFair celebration were less than a month away.

"Something I can help with, Commander?" Senior Chief Russo asked.

"Just trying to finish this report," the Commander replied without looking up from the wireless keyboard on his lap.

"Any line on the new owner?" Russo asked.

"No," the Commander replied. "Hull still had the old stickers on it. The King County Recorder's Office was hit hard in the last round of layoffs. They're six weeks behind in data entry. Anything from SPD?"

Russo looked at the printout in his hand. "The Missing Persons Unit handles about two thousand reports a year, three quarters of which are juveniles. I had them run anything over the last seventy two hours that involved a person or persons over twenty-one. Got three pops."

"Any likelies?"

"Hard to say. Three very different people."

The Commander looked up. "Anyone that might be able to afford a used sailboat?"

"One maybe. A doctor at The Cutter Clinic. The other two don't look like the nautical types."

"Who called it in?"

"Two calls, actually. One from a neighbor and one from the hospital's Human Resources Department."

The Commander kept typing. "Air SAR reports no PIW," he said, pronouncing each word as he entered it. "Water temp 52 degrees; if MO scenario may not have recovery for some time if at all. Potential vessel owner identified. Case referred to SPD MPU. No further USCG involvement unless directed by SPD or Harbor Patrol. Vessel impounded pending further authorization for seizure or transfer to other law enforcement agency." He pounded the terminal period dramatically. "Our work here is done."

"The three of us are betting six blasts," Russo said. "That your take on it?"

"Looks like," the Commander replied. "Most likely he took his life jacket off to catch some rays. Probably had his harness on. Then, who knows? A rogue swell or a big wake. Hell, maybe even an Orca pod. Safety line snaps and one second later he's a Person In Water with no way to get back on deck. Gets pretty cold pretty fast out there if you're in the drink, even on a hot day."

Russo nodded. "I'll tell MPU it's a high likely. They can start knocking on doors."

"What was his name?" the Commander asked.

"Constantine. Dr. Michael Constantine. Heart surgeon, according to this."

The Commander rubbed his temple with his index finger. "Constantine," he said, and then looked at Russo. "A famous name. You familiar with it?"

"Like the movie," Russo replied. "With that guy from The Matrix. Has the power to tell the devils from the angels. That one?"

"I was thinking a little further back," the Commander replied. "Roman emperor in the Third Century. The dawn of Christendom. He established a capital in what is today Istanbul, Turkey. It was first called Byzantium then, much later, Constantinople in his honor. A thousand years later it would fall to the Ottoman Turks and mark the beginning of the Muslim advance against Christianity. Nearly a thousand years after that and here we are, still fighting the same war."

"So this isn't the guy from The Matrix?"

The Commander shook his head. "No, Russo. This isn't the guy from The Matrix." Russo shuffled his feet while his superior officer pondered the thought.

The Commander clicked on the "cc" line on his screen. He typed in the letters "Se-" and the e-mail program thoughtfully completed

the line with "-attle Police Department." Then he clicked "Send."
"Nowadays it's Homeland Security's job to tell the devils from
the angels," he said. "I'm just glad it's not mine."

Johanna tried Constantine's number again and, for the third
time, got his answering machine. His cell was going right to voice
mail. She tried his pager and even sent him an e-mail. It wasn't
dark yet but she was having trouble keeping her eyes open. The
little burst of energy she'd had upon leaving the hospital and Trip
Collier had lasted only long enough to get her home. Crawling
into the unmade bed with her scrubs on she reached under her
top and slipped off her bra. Then she checked to see that her alarm
was set. She laid her head down and within a minute was more
unconscious than asleep.

Even though two hours had passed, it seemed to her that she
had drifted off for only a few moments when the phone rang. The
room was now pitch black and she groped for the receiver.

"Johanna?" a man's voice said. In her fugue state it seemed
familiar but she couldn't place it right away.

"Johanna, this is Justin McCarthy."

"I'm not on call tonight, Dr. McCarthy," she said slowly, almost
drunkenly.

"I know, Johanna," McCarthy replied. "That's not why I'm
calling."

"Did a patient die?" she asked as she began to fall back to sleep.

"No, the patients are fine," he said evenly. "Johanna, I need
you to wake up. I need to ask you again about Mike Constantine."

Chapter 14

DESPITE THE BUSTLING OF people in white coats and the clanking of breakfast cups and saucers they sat in silence. Johanna stirred some half-and-half into her steaming cup and watched it disperse. Finally she spoke.

"Did you hear it from Dr. McCarthy?"

"Yes," el-Hamini replied. "He called me at home early this morning. But then he called back to tell me he was – thankfully – mistaken. Is Dr. Constantine a close friend of yours?"

Johanna shook her head. "Between the on-call and the long hours in the O.R, and the stress, the cardiac surgery residents never really get a chance to bond. I think that's probably on purpose. We're basically indentured servants. The last thing they want is us banding together." She blew on her coffee and took a sip. "One of us is always on call, so we can't even go out for a beer together. I just keep hoping it's just a mix-up and that he'll show up today or tomorrow or the next. It just seems hard to believe that somebody could just be," she paused, "gone."

El-Hamini nodded slowly. "When I was a young man going to the medical University in Baghdad it would sometimes happen to students in our class." Johanna tilted her head and leaned forward as he continued. "One day they would be in the seat next to you or borrowing your notes and the next," he spread his hands, "poof – you never saw them again."

"Kidnapped?" Johanna asked.

"If they were lucky," el-Hamini replied solemnly. "It was quite important not to ask any questions unless you wished your own seat to also soon be empty."

"So you just pretended nothing was wrong?"

"You must understand, no words, no conversations, perhaps even no thoughts, could you ever be assured were completely private. I was Afghani and so I just assumed I was always being watched. But it could be anything. You might make a joke about a politician or a general or the government. Or your brother or your father had an enemy. It didn't matter. Your life was not guaranteed from one day to the next. You, growing up in this country, can never know what fear and uncertainty will cause you to do." He took a sip of his own coffee and appeared lost in thought. "Or not do," he finally said. "If you were single it was your father, your mother or your brother who was at risk. If you married, your wife and child became targets. If you had an education or, God and Allah forbid, an independent mind, anyone you even spoke to put you at risk. I was never so happy as when I came to this country."

"I saw a picture on your desk," Johanna said. "Was it of your wife and daughter?"

El-Hamini froze momentarily, as if desperately unsure how to answer.

"Yes," he replied in a low tone. "They are traveling out of the country at the moment. I hope to meet them when I leave later this week on holiday. But enough about me," he continued and tapped the table with his spoon. "I hope you will tell me more about this Triplett Collier. I may wish to speak with him again. Perhaps we can all have lunch if you two become friends."

Johanna was perplexed and her face showed it. She shifted gears and decided to approach her nagging doubts about Constantine's suspicions as gingerly as possible.

"Can you tell me more about this defibrillator protocol you're involved in? I noticed that the patients are all fairly young and all men. What are the inclusion criteria, exactly?"

El-Hamini fumbled with his spoon and did not meet her gaze.

"Yesterday's were the last of the protocol patients," he said, almost in a whisper. "The study is now closed." He bumped his coffee cup and some of the brew spilled on the table. "The results are blinded. Even I do not know which patients received the experimental device. They were all made to look the same to reduce any possibility operator bias."

"Who funded the study?" Johanna asked. "Usually it's one of

the companies that make the devices." She thought el-Hamini was becoming increasingly nervous with each of her questions.

"Even that I do not know," he said, clearing his throat. "Again, completely blinded."

Johanna was about to press the issue further when she saw a heavyset man in an ill-fitting suit jacket heading toward their table. A Cutter visitor badge hung around his neck and some other official looking credentials were in his outstretched hand. El-Hamini, she noticed, became almost rigid in his seat.

"Johanna Roberson?" the man asked. His Asian features were subtle but noticeable. Johanna nodded.

The man flipped closed the laminated creds before she had time to look at them. El-Hamini bore a distinct look of relief.

"Travis Hsu, Seattle PD MPU." He pronounced his last name like "she".

"MPU?" Johanna asked.

"Missing Persons Unit, doc," Hsu replied. "We heard you were at Michael Constantine's apartment yesterday and would like to talk to you. Got a couple minutes?"

"Sure," she answered. "Do you want to go-"

"Officer, sit here," el-Hamini said and slid himself out of the little banquette. He looked at Johanna. "Take your time my dear. I will page the P.A. and you can join us on rounds when you are finished." He took a step to let the larger man wriggle his girth into his spot. Then el-Hamini strode purposefully toward door at the far end of the dining room.

If he'd left any faster, Johanna thought to herself, he'd have left skid marks.

Collier checked the time. He'd gone through several decision algorithms already.

Ten o'clock? Too desperate.

Ten-twenty? Better, but still kind of pushy.

Just before eleven? Too nonchalant.

He finally decided on ten-thirty-six exactly, figuring it seemed more random and not quite as anal-compulsive as ten-thirty. He checked his watch again. He had nine minutes to think of what he wanted to say.

♦ ♦ ♦

Johanna watched as Detective Hsu scribbled on the little notepad in front of him.

"I know this will sound silly," he said, "but he didn't have any enemies that you know of, right."

"Everybody liked Michael," Johanna answered. "The staff guys, the nurses, even the housekeepers – everybody. I can't think of anyone you could even say he had a conflict with." Hsu scribbled some more but did not look up.

"Girlfriends?"

"We're on call every other night, detective. Not exactly a schedule conducive to romance."

Hsu nodded. "Not having an affair with any of the staff surgeon's wives or maybe a married nurse, I assume?"

Johanna didn't answer and Hsu looked up. "I know," he said, seeing the expression of disbelief on her face. "But in my experience doctors and nurses are no different than any other cross section of humanity. A little smarter maybe, better educated, with more money to throw around – but at the end of the day, just as down and dirty as anyone else."

"No," Johanna said. "I can say unequivocally that Mike was not having an affair with anyone's wife."

"I'm sure he wasn't," Hsu replied, closing his notebook.

"What do you think?" Johanna asked.

Hsu paused, apparently considering his reply. "I always worry more when a solid citizen goes missing," he said. "It doesn't mean he's not passed out in a Vegas hotel room with a stripper, but it's lower on the list."

"Lower than what?" Johanna persisted.

Hsu smiled. "Lower than accident, misadventure or foul play."

Johanna bit her lip. The urge to tell him about Constantine's suspicions was like a sneeze she was trying to hold in.

"Yes, Dr. Roberson?" he asked.

"Nothing," Johanna said. "I'm just very worried, that's all." She wasn't sure if Hsu was buying it. He reached into his jacket pocket and withdrew a small business card which he held close in front of him.

"You can call me anytime if you think of something that might help us, or, hopefully, if you hear from Dr. Constantine. OK?"

"OK," Johanna replied. "I will." Hsu held the card a moment longer. Johanna wondered if he was giving her a chance to reconsider. Then he laid it on the table and slid it toward her. She noticed for that, for a large man, he had beautiful hands.

"My cell number is on there," he said. "Don't hesitate to use it."

"Thanks," Johanna said, taking the card and dropping it in her breast pocket. "I won't."

"Won't use it or won't hesitate?" Hsu asked with a smile as he slid his bulk out and stood by the table.

Johanna smiled back. "Won't hesitate," she said firmly. "And would you be able to let me know if you find out anything – good or bad?"

"I will let you know if anything definitive develops," he replied. "Thank you for your time and cooperation, Doctor." Johanna watched as he walked away. She almost called after him but then her pager went off. She slipped it out of its plastic holder and looked at the number and then at her watch.

She really didn't feel like talking.

Chapter 15

Outside Dundee, Oregon

THE WILLAMETTE VALLEY WAS in full bloom. It was a down time at the winery but still there were visitors every day and business to attend to. The elevation made the days cooler and the heaviest work was shipping the stored cases to restaurants and suppliers. Work in the vineyards themselves never ceased, what with spraying and pruning and grafting to be done. But that was another world as far as Henry Cardoza was concerned. As he walked in the cool shade of the warehouse he pondered the coming days and his role in them. He had meticulously followed the shipping and receiving schedules on the in-house computer system. He had checked and rechecked the airline schedules and kept a sharp eye for any changes in cargo protocols. With the cordless wood burning tool he'd purchased at a local Hobby Lobby, he had marked the shipping crates with his own identification system. The refrigerated trucks were due in from Salem in the morning and he would personally see to the loading. If he stayed late tonight, he knew, no one would think twice. He was not, after all, the Employee of the Month for no reason. The replacement bottles he had carefully placed in the marked crates were indistinguishable from the ones with actual wine in them. The volatile liquid would be much more stable at a cooler temperature he knew. The weather forecast for the day the cases would be loaded into the cargo holds was for above average temperatures in everyone of the departure cities. Cardoza took this as a sign that even nature was following

His will.

He nodded to a passing forklift driver and walked from the warehouse into the small break room. Opening his tiny locker he lifted up the concealing debris and looked at his passport and itinerary. In less than forty-eight hours, he knew, he would be on a flight home to Tehran where his brothers-in-arms would welcome him as a hero. Henry Cardoza would evaporate as quickly as he'd been created and only Roozbeh Abbasi would remain to bask in the glory of successful *jihad*. He closed the locker and spun the combination dial. Another worker he did not recall having seen before entered through the heavy door and took a seat at the scuffed and pitted Formica table.

"Another beautiful day at Eagle Ridge Winery," Cardoza said, taking off his hat.

"Yes," the man replied with a pleasant smile. "A day truly meant for an eagle."

Trip Collier felt like he was fourteen and asking Marie Sheehan to the Sophomore Cotillion all over again.

"Sounds like maybe I caught you at a bad time."

"No," Johanna replied, "I'm just processing some worrisome news."

"I'm sorry for that," Collier said. "Would it be better if I called back?" There was a long pause and Collier felt his stomach floating somewhere between his hips and his shoulders as he waited for her reply. Sure, he half-expected, how about never? How does never work for you?

"Um, no, that's OK. I've got a few minutes before I go to the lab."

Collier had to stifle exhaling with relief. "Is it OK to ask what the worrisome news is? Feel free to say no."

There was another pause.

"My senior resident, Mike Constantine, hasn't shown up for work for two days." Johanna answered. "I just spent half an hour with a detective from the Seattle Police Department, so I'm a little rattled, I guess." Collier sensed the uncertainty in her voice.

"Was the guy from Homicide or MPU" Collier asked instinctively.

"Missing Persons is what he said."

"Well, that's a step in the right direction," Collier replied. "Who was it?'

"Detective Hsu. I think that was his name."

"Travis," Collier said with a laugh. "I know Travis. Would you believe he was once a D-1 linebacker?"

"No," Johanna replied. "Where?"

"Seattle University. Yet another waste of a Jesuit liberal arts education."

"He was pretty nice," Johanna said. "Dr. McCarthy, our chief, called me late last night. There was a body washed up somewhere on Puget Sound. He thought it was going to be Constantine, but it wasn't."

"Why we would he have thought that?" Collier asked.

"I don't know. I was asleep when I talked to him. Anyway it wasn't, so they're still trying to track him down. He told a neighbor he might go sailing on Sunday but that's the last anyone's heard from him."

Collier started making notes on a DHS tablet while she talked.

"How are you doing?" he asked.

"Well, I guess since he's just missing and not presumed dead, I'm doing OK. You're kind of in law enforcement. What do you think?"

Collier had been hoping she wouldn't ask. "Too early to jump to a conclusion," he lied. "If you want, I can call Travis and ask him to move this one up on his list."

"I'm really worried that something bad has happened," Johanna replied.

"Why would something bad happen?" Collier asked, trying to sound less like an investigator and more like a concerned friend. There was a longer pause this time.

"I, I don't know. Some things that probably aren't related. I don't know. I'm just really worried."

Collier decided not to push any further. "OK," he said, "I'll call Travis and nudge him a little. He'll want to know why – is it OK if I tell him we're friends?"

"I guess that depends on how honest you want to be, Agent Collier."

Collier laughed. "How about non-hostile acquaintances?"

"Better go with friends," Johanna said. Collier sensed a little lightening in her mood and decided to take a chance.

"Any interest in dinner tonight? I could see if Detective Hsu has come up with anything during the day and update you. I mean, unless you're on call or something." Collier held his breath.

"They let me off call the rest of the week so I can fill in for Constantine. Dr. el-Hamini is getting ready to leave the country in a couple days so we probably won't be doing much." Collier had yet to exhale. "Yeah, OK. Dinner is OK. You said you knew some good places?"

'I know some great places. OK if I pick or do you have a preference in cuisine?"

"No," Johanna replied. "You pick. I'm tired of making decisions. Let me know and I'll meet you there." Collier let out a deflating breath.

"I'd be happy to pick you up."

"That's alright," Johanna said. "Just in case something comes up and they call me in."

Collier was about to mention that she'd just told him he wasn't on call but thought better of it. "Deal," he said as brightly as he could. "I'll call you back around four with the details."

"If I don't pick up just give the operator the place and the time. I have an alpha-numeric pager so she can put it in there."

Collier was puzzled by her wariness but pressed on. "Alright," he said, "But you have my cell. If you want, just call me at the end of the day and I'll tell you myself."

"You're the boy," Johanna replied. "You can call me."

Collier smiled. "I'd like to hear your take on being a college athlete," he said.

"Ditto," Johanna replied. "So, why'd you lose the beard?"

"The girl I grew it to impress said it made me look like an apostle," he replied. "Not exactly what I was going for."

Johanna laughed. "I bet not," she said. "I'll wait to hear from you."

Collier heard the line click off. She was meeting him for dinner, he thought. It was a better outcome than he had expected.

Johanna's pager vibrated again and she looked at the number. Somebody wanting something, she thought. Another problem to solve; another fire to put out. It never stopped. She remained seated, oblivious to the bustle around her. She quickly calculated, she hadn't been on an actual date in ten years. And now she had one. Her pager went off again but she ignored it. A million thoughts swirled in her head but only one burned brightly enough for her to identify it:

What exactly was happening to her?

"It makes me concerned."

"I understand this," replied the voice on the telephone. "But all is in place. I don't believe he could stop it if he tried. And, I assure you, Dr. el-Hamini will not try."

"But until the explosions actually occur it's always possible."

Abdul Abdallah had been cleaning physician offices at The Cutter Clinic in Seattle since it opened. Of course, he'd filled out the employment application as Arthur Billings, the birth name of his former self. Having left college in Ithaca, New York following a disastrous second semester in his sophomore year he had drifted aimlessly. Only after he had embraced Islam did his life make sense to him. He thought he would follow the path the pop singer formerly called Cat Stevens had walked. But his new brothers, even at the first, had shown unusual interest in him and what they deemed his "potential". Within a year he had found himself at a camp in Quetta. In less than eighteen months he had become completely "radicalized", as the infidel press described individuals such as him. With his American identity and documentation still intact he was recruited for a "glorious mission" that, to his initial dismay, would not require him to blow himself up. He had found little glory in the last two years of emptying wastebaskets and polishing desks. The tiny microphones he planted and the occasional message he anonymously delivered did little to spark his enthusiasm. Only in the last few weeks was he given any details of the objective. Its audacity and magnitude rekindled his dedication. When he returned to his brothers in Quetta, several weeks from now to avoid suspicion, he would be welcomed as a hero. They would not need to know he had waged *jihad* with a maid's cart and a can of Pledge.

"I'm worried about the people around him."

"The threat has been eliminated," replied the voice on the phone.

"Do you believe there are others?"

"I'm worried from the conversations that the new woman doctor is much too inquisitive. She was a friend of the other one. I think he may have gone beyond el-Hamini before he was taken care of."

"He knew nothing of the real plan," the voice replied. "It is flawless and will remain so. What other doctors are you listening to?"

"I have placed a microphone in McCarthy's office," Arthur Billings replied. "He's an adulterer and uses alcohol freely. I'm worried that Constantine may have said something to him that would draw attention to our plans."

"As I said," the voice replied. "It is too late. In three days the world will understand the length of our reach and the depth of our patience. Continue with your work, brother."

"I want to ask – is there a chance I can return to my new homeland sooner?"

"You will be home soon enough," the voice replied.

Tamal Hajiik set the phone down and, as was his habit, stroked his mustache with the thumb and index finger of his right hand. Pushing against the grain he smiled at its thickness and breadth. It was, as Saddam had once told him personally over cigars and hundred-year-old cognac, truly big enough for an eagle to land upon.

The noise in the DHS office just outside Collier's made him plug his opposite ear with his index finger and then press the phone even closer.

"So are you tapping that yet?"

"You could say it's still pretty early in the relationship, Travis," Collier replied.

"Collier, you're a dog. You always have been. Everybody knows that. If you don't want to tell me, that's fine. But I don't believe you're not sniffin'."

"You've met Johanna, right?"

"Yeah, man. She's the whole package. A lady doctor – that's quite a step up for you, Collier, isn't it?"

"She was an Olympic medalist. Did you know that?"

"No kidding. What sport?"

"Rowing."

"Damn. She could stroke my oar anytime she wanted."

"Yeah, OK, Travis. Let's call it good right there. Can you help me or not?"

There was a pause and Collier could hear Travis Hsu shuffling papers. "Nothing else has turned up yet. This guy's pretty low risk for FP."

"What about him going sailing? Anything there?"

There was another pause. "Yeah," Hsu said. "You know, I kind of forgot about the sailing thing. There was a floater last night but the coroner says it's female." More papers shuffling. "Wait. There's a copy of a report here from the Coasties. Give me a second." Collier rubbed at a spot on his office desk while listening to Hsu make unintelligible sounds into the phone.

"Well?" Collier asked.

"They found an empty sailboat drifting off Deception Island Light yesterday."

"Out in the Sound?"

"Yeah. Looks like. I think she told me this guy kept his boat on Lake Washington, though."

Collier tapped his pen on the desk. "Could've trailered it, Travis. Or gone through the locks. They must have the hull number or registration."

"Says previous owner OOC and new owner YTBD."

"What?"

"'Out of country' and 'yet to be determined'."

"They could have just said that."

"The Coast Guard is still the military. Their reports usually have more abbreviations than words."

"Acronyms," Collier corrected. "When it's all initials it's an acronym."

"Whatever," Hsu replied. "I'll call the CG Commander back this afternoon and see what they have. There's a neighbor of this guy I have to run down, too."

"Any chance you could fax me the report? We're not under attack today, as far as I know. I might have a little time to help you out."

"Thanks, but you know I can't do that," Hsu replied.

"Call it interagency cooperation," Collier said.

"See if the lady doctor has a discreet friend and I'll call it whatever you want. You know, maybe a gymnast?"

Collier could picture Hsu's leer through the phone. "You haven't changed, either, Travis. Call me if something pops, OK?" "I will. You sure you're not out of your league here, Collier?" "I'll let you know if I need help. Thanks, pal." Collier hung up the phone. He would have no trouble calling the Coast Guard Station on any number of pretenses. His gut was telling him that Constantine's story was not going to have a happy ending. Maybe it would be best, he thought, if he didn't ruin dinner.

Justin McCarthy was seated behind his desk. Again the afternoon sun shone across his face and bounced off the lenses of his rimless spectacles, obscuring his eyes. Johanna wondered if he had arranged his office this way intentionally.

"That's quite an interesting theory. And potentially quite an explosive accusation, you'll have to admit," McCarthy said in a measured tone.

"I'm not making an accusation, Dr. McCarthy," Johanna said in a voice that belied her anxiety. "'Mike Constantine thought there was something rotten in Denmark. All of a sudden he's a missing person. Yeah, probably not related, but hard to ignore. He didn't mention anything about this to you?" She saw McCarthy shift slightly in his chair. It was maddening not to be able to read his face. The glint off his glasses made her squint every time he tilted his head.

"Not a word," McCarthy replied. "You said he privately reviewed patients' echo studies and then came to this conclusion?"

Johanna understood immediately – the best defense was a good offense.

"I think he did it as part of his rotation," she said a little more forcefully than she would have liked. "He was assigned to the service. If you're wondering about a HIPPA violation, I think he's safe."

McCarthy shifted again, uncomfortably. "The rules for private patients who bring their own studies are open to interpretation. We didn't perform the echo, so technically it's not part of The Cutter's patient record. Do you see what I'm getting at?"

Johanna saw exactly. She rose from her chair and buttoned her white lab coat.

"You haven't shared this with anyone, I assume," McCarthy said.

"No. Just you."

"And Dr. Constantine?"

"As far as I know, just me," Johanna replied.

"Let's keep it that way for now," McCarthy said. He kept his head in the shaft of sunlight. "As you can imagine, any truth to this would severely damage The Cutter's image both here and abroad. And, as you're well aware, being the new player in town we're in a very competitive market situation. On the other hand, a false or even an honestly mistaken accusation of this magnitude would probably end the accuser's career, at least in cardiac surgery."

"Could always retire on the whistle-blower's settlement," Johanna replied and then wished she hadn't. She looked at the scrolled wood nameplate at the front of the large desk. "I didn't know your first name was actually Justinian."

"Yes," McCarthy replied. "He was an emperor if I remember correctly."

"That's right," Johanna said as she edged toward the door. "Do you know what he was famous for?"

McCarthy allowed a thin smile. "I'm afraid I don't, Dr. Roberson."

Maybe it was from sitting in the bright sunlight, Johanna thought, but she could make out a thin line of perspiration at his brow. She moved until her body blocked the light streaming in behind her so she could see his face before replying.

"He put up a wall," she said.

Scrolling through the contact numbers on the screen, el-Hamini could not find one that looked like it would connect him directly with Agent Triplett Collier. He glanced nervously at the doorway and finally jotted down two of the numbers. He didn't dare call from his office even if it was on the cell phone, he reasoned. El-Hamini knew he was being watched. He assumed it would be more intense as the fateful day approached and that perhaps he could identify and thus avoid whoever was surveilling him. He slipped the paper with the numbers on it into his pocket. The number of Cutter Clinic employees who were Middle-Eastern was enormous and the number that passed in and out of his department's suite of offices every day was daunting. It could be any one of them, he knew.

El-Hamini was worried about Johanna. She'd helped him implant two routine pacemakers earlier in the day. He'd tried to make the small-talk with her but it had been forced and he sensed wariness on her part. He considered trying to contact Collier through her but feared for her safety if he did. How much he ached for his own wife and daughter when he was with her!

His fingers tapped lightly on the desk as if he were playing a musical piece on an imaginary piano. Could he stop this madness without sacrificing his beloved ones? There had to be a way! What would his life be, even with his family, if they knew he was the author of such death and destruction? Would they able to live with it? With him?

He was staring at the now blank monitor screen when movement at the door startled him and he almost cried out. A dull-eyed American boy pushed a cleaning cart in and then stopped.

"Sorry," he said flatly. "I can come back later."

El-Hamini composed himself. "That's alright," he said. "I'm ready to leave." He snapped his briefcase shut, grabbed it by the handle and walked out.

He couldn't shake the feeling that there was something else he had wanted to do.

Chapter 16

THE CROWD AT THE Wild Ginger was larger than Trip Collier expected for a Tuesday night. He thanked the hostess and sat down at the window table. On Third Street he watched the milling pedestrian traffic. A frail-looking Japanese woman was pushing a battered grocery cart filled with what looked like all her belongings. She stared straight at Collier then flashed a toothless grin. Three gang-bangers walked up and stood menacingly near the old woman as she fiddled with a balky wheel on her overburdened cart. Collier banged on the window and waved his DHS creds. The youngest of the three, who couldn't have been more than twelve, flashed several gang signs then gave him the finger as the group walked off. Collier flagged a passing waitress.

"I hate to do this," he said. "But is there any chance you could find me a table away from the window? I'm meeting a friend and I'm thinking this might be a little-"

"Distracting?" The young woman said with a smile.

"Yeah, distracting," Collier replied. The waitress looked around at the bustling restaurant.

"I just cleared sixteen," she said. "It's a four but it'll be quieter and you'll have more room. It's a little out of the way, though."

"Thanks, I really appreciate it," Collier said as he stood. He looked at his watch: seven-thirty. He didn't expect her to be on time. He followed the waitress to a darkened area just off the main dining room. She motioned to a table and he sat down.

"Your guest won't be able to see you back here. What does she look like?"

"Tall, athletic build with light brown hair. She'll stand out."
The waitress smiled. "Lucky you," she said handing him the wine
list. "Dates are always impressed by a big tip. Try to keep that in
mind." Then she turned on her heel and was gone. Collier checked
the leather-bound Wine List for the Bogle Phantom Amanda had
recommended but decided to wait until they ordered their meals.
He checked his pager to make sure it was on "Vibrate" then picked
up the menu which, he thought, had the best selection of pan-Asian
fusion cuisine in the city. He checked his cell phone for missed calls
or texts. There were none. He'd given the hospital operator explicit
instructions on what message to type into Johanna's pager, going
so far as to have her read it back to him. Collier tapped the menu
nervously on the polished table top. He thought about Kelly and
having stood her up. Now here he sat desperately hoping the same
thing didn't happen to him. He wasn't a big fan of karma.

"You look like you're having a *petit mal* seizure."

Collier looked up. Johanna was dressed in a slacks and a tailored
blazer. A white silk shirt with long collar highlighted her tanned
features. She was smiling at him and he wondered if she could see
the relief on his face.

"The waitress told me you said to look for someone short and
dumpy," Johanna said as she pulled out the chair on the opposite
side of the table. Collier belatedly stood up. "Sit down, Collier,"
she said. "Trust me. Chivalry, at least in surgery, has been dead for
a long time." She looked around the table. "No wine?"

"I was waiting for you," Collier replied. "Where did you park?"

Johanna shook her hair and swept it off her neck. "I took a cab,"
she said. "If I'm going to be off-call, I'm going to have a drink."

Collier looked for their waitress. "I can take you home," he
offered.

"Or, I could take cab or an Uber," Johanna replied brightly.
"One thing at a time. OK, Collier?"

"OK." He caught the waitress's eye and held up the wine list.

"Start you off with something to drink?" the girl asked, pulling
an order pad from a front pocket in her apron.

"We'll have a bottle of the Phantom," he said, handing her the
large placard. He looked at Johanna. "Red alright with you?"

Johanna nodded. "Better for your heart," she said and picked up
her menu.

Arthur Billings left the vacuum running and sat down at the desk. With his Pledge-soaked rag he bumped the wireless mouse and watched as the monitor came to life. Keeping the rag on his hand he clicked the "Back" arrow, spending several minutes trying to memorize each screen. It was clear now. The Eagle would have to listen to him. He was going to save the day, he knew. They would have to let him go home now.

♦ ♦ ♦

"Don't let me drink too much," Johanna said. "I'm out of practice. What's good?"

"It sounds trite, but really, everything is wonderful. You can't make a wrong choice."

Johanna sipped from her wine glass without looking up from the menu. "Did you talk to detective Hsu?" she asked.

"I did. He was going to follow up on the sailing angle. And a neighbor he was going to talk to."

Johanna put down her menu. "Yeah, that's the guy I met when I went to Mike's apartment. He thought Mike might take have taken his boat over to Puget Sound."

"Where did he usually keep it moored?" Collier asked.

"Lake Washington, I think. I guess he would have had to put it on a trailer to get to the Sound."

Collier shook his head. "Not necessarily. He could motor through the Ballard Locks but that would take a while. Travis said he would check with the Coast Guard to see if they had anything." He looked at his own menu and avoided eye contact with her after he said it. When he glanced back up he noticed that Johanna had emptied her glass. Collier took the bottle and refilled it halfway.

Thanks," Johanna said. "This is good – what is it?"

"It's called Phantom. From a family winery in Clarksburg, California, or so it says on the bottle. It's a blend of three red varietals and-"

"You can stop there," Johanna interrupted. She drank half of what Collier had poured. "It's really good – spicy, almost. That's all I need to know."

Collier put his elbow on the table and rested his chin in his hand. "Well, alrighty then," he said with a laugh.

Johanna grimaced. "I know," she said. "I'm too direct. It's an occupational hazard. Just about all the surgeons who trained me have been brilliant, high-powered but seriously dysfunctional men. Cardiac surgery, unlike the rest of medicine, is still primarily a testosterone-fueled specialty. I've had to, shall we say, adapt?"

"I'll keep that in mind," Collier replied as the waitress sidled up, pad in hand.

"Are you ready or do you need a few more minutes?" the waitress asked, making it clear that she was ready for them to order.

"You go first," Johanna said.

Collier peered at the menu again. "I'd like to start with an order of the Chicken Satay. Then I'm going to have the Wild Ginger Duck."

"Very good," the waitress said and angled toward Johanna. "And for madame?"

"I'd like the Laska to start and then the Pad Thai, but only if the prawns are fresh."

"They came in today," the waitress replied.

"Oh," Johanna said, "And can you ask the chef to make both of them hot?"

The waitress paused. "Do you mean hot, hot-hot, or Thai hot?"

"Definitely Thai hot," Johanna replied.

The waitress nodded approvingly. "Will you be needing a second bottle of the Bogle?" she asked. Collier looked at Johanna, who smiled and shrugged,

"Sure," he said. "But don't bring it until you serve the entrées."

"Gotcha," the young woman said, taking the proffered menus. "I'll be back with your appetizers."

Collier leaned toward Johanna, his eyebrows raised. "Thai hot?" he asked.

Johanna laughed. "I'm an Olympic Class date, Collier," she said. "Try to keep up."

◆ ◆ ◆

"It is always better if you wait for me to contact you," the voice on the phone said with a trace of impatience.

"I did not feel this could wait, brother," Arthur Billings replied, his cheeks flushed and his pulse pounding.

"Your dedication is worthy but you must not allow it to cloud your judgment. Not when we are so close to the hour of victory over the non-believers. Where are you at this moment?"

"In the office of the traitorous dog el-Hamini," Billings replied.

"Is there a safe place I can find you?"

"I can be home in two hours," Billings said. "You must know where my apartment is."

"Apartments can be watched. Is there a private place there at the hospital where we can meet unobserved?"

Billings touched his brow with the sickly-sweet smelling cloth. "The loading platform on the eastern side of the Clinic. There is a metal door just off the far-right truck bay. I will leave it propped open with a rag. I'll be inside waiting for your arrival."

"We will be alone, then? No one will observe us speaking?"

"It will deserted by nine p.m. Come after that."

"You will not be missed from your duties?" the voice asked.

"My shift ends at eight-thirty," Billings replied.

There was a pause. "Very good. Make sure to – what is it you say here – time out?"

"Clock out," Billings corrected.

"Yes that's it. Clock out. I will meet you at nine-fifteen. And brother?"

"Yes?"

"I think you can plan on being home sooner than expected."

The phone in Arthur Billings' hand blinked and told him the call had ended. He sat at el-Hamini's desk trying to calm himself. He had to make clear what he'd heard the woman doctor tell McCarthy. And what he'd found on el-Hamini's computer. He rose and looked at his watch. He wondered how long it would take him to pack for his trip. Then he emptied el-Hamini's wastebasket and turned off the brass desk lamp. He pushed his cleaning cart past the secretaries' desks and out into the dimly lit hallway, his heart lighter than it had been in months.

"Room for dessert?" their waitress asked.

Johanna shook her head. "But I could go for a little cognac." She looked at Collier. "Are you up for it?" she asked. "My treat."

Collier knew that Johanna was, at the very least, mildly intoxicated. But she seemed to be enjoying it so much he decided against saying anything. She wasn't driving, he told himself.

"Have you ever tried armagnac?" he asked. "It's cognac's snootier cousin. A fourteenth-century Cardinal once declared that it had forty separate virtues." He looked at the waitress. "You do have armagnac, right?"

The waitress looked offended. "We have a 1973 Marie Duffau at thirty-five dollars a glass or a fifteen year old Sempe' at twenty dollars."

Collier cocked his head at Johanna. "Your call."

"My call? You're the one who suggested it."

"Yeah, but you're paying for it."

Johanna laughed. "Then let's get the good stuff."

"So, two glasses of the Marie Duffau?" the waitress asked. Collier nodded.

"I want to pay for those separately," Johanna said. The waitress smiled and left for the bar. Collier thought he heard Johanna slur the 's' just a little. He wondered how early she needed to be up in the morning.

Arthur Billings sat on an empty drum that once contained industrial cleaning solution. The Cutter Clinic had developed a revolutionary system of robotic stock retrieval for everything from operating room supplies to toilet paper. The pudgy-looking wheeled contraptions followed coded magnetic tracks in the warehouse floor to their various destinations. Billings could see three of them from where he sat. They were motionless, each with a blinking, emerald-green light indicating its "ready" status and a cocked boom arm capable of lifting anything from a box of tongue depressors to a pallet of hundred-pound linen supplies. He watched the back of the metal door for movement, periodically scanning the large warehouse for signs of anyone who might disturb their meeting. He had never met The Eagle but he knew from his brothers in Quetta what to expect.

When the door opened Billings tensed and gripped the rolled rim of the drum with both hands. The man he saw push through the door, however, was not six-foot-six, nor was he as broad as a camel's back. The figure who approached him was slightly round-shouldered and was, at best, five-foot-ten or eleven. A hood concealed his face as he walked in shadow along the far wall. Billings hopped down from the drum and stood beside it. The man pulled back his hood as he neared. The eyes that met Billings' own momentarily transfixed him. There was a burning intensity in them that could not be easily ignored. The beaked nose would have dominated the man's face were it not for the impressive mustache that seemed to cascade from his upper lip like a black waterfall. As he came closer, Billings could see several scars over the left eye and on the right cheek.

"Salam, Abdul Abdallah," the man said.

"Salam, oh great brother of brothers," Billings replied.

"So tell me what is so important."

Billings was so intimidated and excited by the man's presence that he fumbled with his words at first. A hand placed gently but firmly on his shoulder slowed him down.

"The woman doctor, Johanna Roberson. She spoke privately with McCarthy today. She suspects that el-Hamini is placing the devices in men who do not need them."

The man pulled his hood back up and nodded, indicating for him to go on.

"She said that Constantine suspected this and shared his worries with her. She believes that el-Hamini does this in collusion with doctors in our homeland to make them all money."

"And what did McCarthy say?" the man asked, using his whole hand to stroke his mustache.

"He said this would be a damaging problem if it were true."

"Did he then call anyone else to report the woman's suspicions?"

"Not from his office. He made several phone calls during the rest of the day but this was not discussed."

The hood caused a shadow to fall across the man's face that deepened the appearance of the facial scars. "And then I looked at el-Hamini's computer," Billings continued. The hooded man's eyes registered surprise. "He left it on," Billings said quickly and then went on to describe the Homeland Security web pages he had seen.

"And the good doctor made no calls that you know of?"

"No," Billings replied. "I was listening while I cleaned the hallway. He made no calls and then left. Do you agree now, brother, that we must act?"

"Completely," the man replied and reached for something beneath his jacket.

When Tamal Hajiik was a medical student in Lebanon he had wanted to be a surgeon. He was first in his Anatomy class at the Arab University of Beirut's Faculty of Medicine. He never shared the reticence his classmates displayed for cadaver dissection and had often gone to the lab late at night to probe further into the complex construction of Allah's greatest creation. The chronic exposure to the formaldehyde fumes had spurred him to grow his abundant mustache, which he would dab with a strong aromatic before each session. It had also caused his conjunctiva, the membranes covering the whites of the eyes, to become chronically inflamed giving them, to this day, a red and rheumy appearance that was variously interpreted as indicative of disease or alcoholism. It was while he was serving as a consulting specialist at Baghdad's largest hospital that he'd been asked to join Saddam Hussein's retinue of personal physicians, a position he enjoyed for nearly three years. That all ended the day the bombing began. He had attended to Saddam's insane son, Uday and had been at his side when he died, working desperately to revive the critically wounded scion. Uday had been in bed with two women when the shell hit. To hide this fact Saddam had ordered Hajiik beheaded along with the other officers present at Uday's inglorious demise. Only a chance meeting with the oily and chronically duplicitous minister Tariq Aziz had allowed him to escape the palace and flee to Syria before Baghdad fell. It was in Damascus, four years later, when the stash of funds he'd escaped with were running low that he had met the Russian envoy. It was a stroke of luck he was willing to assign to either God or Allah. At first, the envoy – Petyr was his name - was interested only in Hajiik's stories of the sadistic Uday's unique tortures and methods of execution of those who displeased him. Petyr was willing to provide hot meals and generous amounts of alcohol in exchange for increasingly lurid details. When the tales of beheadings, castrations and disembowelments ran thin, Hajiik moved on to highly embellished stories of Uday's sexual perversions, which interested Petyr even more. Hajiik was able to parlay these twisted tales of Arabian nights into almost three weeks of free food and drink and a billet in Petyr's apartment. As

the Russian drank more, the talk turned to politics and the real
reason for the envoy's presence in Damascus. Before long, it was
Petyr who was doing most of the storytelling. Hajjik began to
realize the crucial part that *jihad* against America played in
the degraded superpower's plans for a return to glory and,
more important, parity on the world stage. Clearly the Russians
needed the United States to be engaged in as many conflicts as
possible on as many fronts as possible. Perhaps, the envoy
suggested, another successful attack on American soil would be
the key. If the blow was staggering enough, he went on, what
better time for the Russian government to offer to stand with
the Americans and pledge that together they would stamp
out the scourge of international terrorism. All the election
indiscretions would vanish. The enemy of my enemy becomes
my friend. Hajiik marveled at the beauty and simplicity of the
plan. Create a hole and then offer to help fill it. But, Petyr
cautioned, it must be a large hole - one that required help on such
a global scale. But, could such an attack be arranged, Petyr had
asked. With the last Syrian Pounds in his possession, Hajiik
plied his new comrade with more Arak and began to sell
himself as someone who could get such things done. Hajiik
greatly exaggerated what had been his quite inconspicuous role
in Saddam's inner circle. The Russian responded by showing him
the card of an *apparatchik* and began to reveal details of a
network based in Pakistan who bowed each evening not to
Mecca, but to Moscow. By the time Petyr boarded the Aeroflot
Sukhoi Superjet 100 at Damascus International, Hajiik found
himself an accidental terrorist. Religion was a waste, Hajiik
decided at that point, useful only as a tool to recruit the easily led
into performing unthinkable acts. Only political power and the
money that came with it really mattered. Now he somehow
needed to deliver a blow that would set the American
government reeling so badly that it would be willing to accept a
helping hand – even a Red one. The Pakistani cabal, he
discovered, had already done much of the recruiting, aided by
cells in Yemen, Jordan, Bahrain and even the United Kingdom.
Their original idea had been to implant the actual explosives into
the bodies of the willing servants. It was Hajiik, with his
medical background, who had upgraded and refined the plan
and who, by doing so, had become its avowed mastermind and
chief perpetrator. He was still surprised at how quickly he had
taken to the savagery of the *jihadis* and, in a complete turnaround,

how he'd gone from someone who had taken an oath to preserve life to someone who now took lives personally and randomly.

These were the recollections that occupied Hajiik's mind as he struggled to stuff the lifeless form of Arthur Billings into one of the empty drums.

Hajiik did not usually care for the bayonet. Its three-sided design left a wound that would not close. But he reserved the dagger for fellow Muslims and select Christians – the former for the honor, the latter for the ignominy. He remembered from his medical studies that if a chest wound was larger than the diameter of the windpipe, air would flow preferentially through the hole, collapsing the lung and suffocating the victim quite efficiently. For this purpose and on this occasion the bayonet had served nicely. He'd taken the precaution of making appropriate sized holes in both sides of Arthur Billings' thorax. The boy had deflated like a child's balloon, the panicked look of asphyxia still frozen on his face when Hajiik banged down the lid.

Chapter 17

IT TOOK JOHANNA ALMOST a full minute to determine that she was in her own bed and that her head hurt. She reached tentatively with her left hand and groped around on the mattress behind her. There was no other body. Then she felt under the covers. Her slacks were off but she had her panties on. The crotch was smooth and dry she noted with some relief. She reached up and found that her blouse was on and buttoned and that she still had the little tortoise shell clip in her hair. With some effort, she dragged the clip out and dropped it on the floor, bringing a measure of relief to her aching head. She squinted and lifted her chin to make out the numbers on her digital clock-radio. It was four-fifty-eight. *Ante Meridian,* she sincerely hoped.

The light was creeping in through the half-tilted venetian blinds. Johanna pushed the covers down and slid one leg off the bed while simultaneously pushing her torso up with one arm. Then she brought the other leg over until both feet touched the wood floor. She felt a little woozy but was able to stand by steadying herself on the night table. She lifted up the sheet and comforter and found her slacks bunched underneath at the bottom of the mattress. There was a light on in her living room but she needed to pee badly and that, she decided, took immediate precedence.

She flushed and stood at the vanity mirror surveying the damage. Her mouth tasted like kitty litter and she had a vague recollection that she may or may not have smoked a cigar. Johanna grabbed the toothbrush and ran the water. It took four doses of orange-flavored Listerine and another brushing before she was ready to tackle her hair. Then she heard a sound from the living room. Pulling a cocoa-colored robe around her she padded to the bedroom door and peered out.

Trip Collier was asleep on her loveseat. His tall frame was somehow compacted onto the two cushions and his head rested on his folded blazer. Both his shoes, she noticed, were parked neatly near the front door of the second floor apartment. The filtering light showed the stubble on his cheeks and she watched as his jaw muscles moved involuntarily. Johanna decided she would take a hot shower and make herself presentable before addressing the hazy events of the previous evening. Thank God she didn't have to operate today, she thought.

In the tiny bathroom the sound of the hair dryer drowned out everything else. Johanna brushed her hair and slipped into a clean bra and panties. She donned the robe and walked back into the bedroom. The door was closed, something she did not remember doing. She chose khakis and a medium weight pullover from the narrow closet and, after checking herself in the mirror, decided it was time to face the proverbial music. She had a rough idea of how much they'd drank and was surprised she felt as good as she did. When she opened the bedroom door the aroma of fresh coffee filled her nostrils. Collier was at the refrigerator hunting for something. Her footfall on the hardwood floor got his attention.

"Took me a little while to figure out your coffee maker," he said. "Hope you don't mind."

Johanna sat on a wooden stool in the little breakfast nook. "OK," she said. "Help me out. How did we end up back here?"

Collier smiled and handed her a steaming mug. "We took a cab from the restaurant. After the armagnac – a smashingly bad idea in retrospect – I wasn't going to chance driving home. I thought I would just have the cabbie wait until you got inside but then you sort of passed out on my shoulder."

Johanna blew on the hot liquid and took a sip. "I told you I was out of practice," she said. "Why were we drinking armagnac in the first place?"

"Technically it was your idea," Collier replied. "You wanted to order cognac. I suggested the alternative so I guess I have to share culpability."

"How much wine did we drink?"

Collier held up two fingers.

"Ooooh," Johanna said with a grimace. "Why did you let that happen?"

Collier set down his cup. "Honestly? Because you looked so relaxed and happy. Like maybe you were just Johanna Roberson, normal adult female for a few hours. I didn't see the harm."

Johanna took a longer sip. "I'm surprised I don't feel worse," she said.

"I drugged you."

"You what?" Johanna replied holding the mug away from her face.

"Don't worry," Collier said. "It was just four Advil. Plus two large glasses of water, a One-a-Day with Iron from your medicine cabinet and a big glass of orange juice. The Gonzaga hangover prevention invention."

"Well, it apparently worked. Why did you sleep on the couch?"

"If that's a couch then I should be in the NBA," Collier said. "It's more like a chair with grander aspirations."

"Actually it's a loveseat."

"Well it didn't love me. I'll probably need a chiropractor to fix my back." He made an exaggerated stretching motion. "Sorry about tucking you in with all your clothes on. I did take your jacket off, though. It's hanging in your room somewhere. Anyway, you were all but unconscious and I didn't want something bad to happen. We had a guy at the lax house who passed out on his bed during a party and choked on his own-'

"He aspirated," Johanna interrupted. "I get the picture." She rubbed at a spot just above her eyebrows. "Well, thanks for being such a gentleman. I owe you one."

Collier took a big slug from his cup. "I can get a cab from here back to my car. I just hope they haven't towed it. What time do you need to be at the hospital?"

Johanna looked at her watch. "El-Hamini doesn't have any cases scheduled today and I'm still off-call, so, maybe eight, eight-thirty? I'll drop you off at your car. We'll have time to finish our coffee unless you need to be in earlier."

Collier shook his head. "I don't have to clock in anymore," he said. Then he put down his mug and looked at her. "Do you remember what you were telling me about Dr. el-Hamini?" He watched as Johanna's face went blank.

"I don't remember much after the Pad Thai arrived to be quite honest," she said. "Was I talking about him?"

Collier drained his mug and put both hands on the table in front of him.

"It was quite a story. I'm sure you have a lot of confidentiality restraints just like we do and I respect that. But if any of it's true, I think you need to avoid putting yourself in a bad spot."

"Exactly how much did I tell you?" she asked.

Collier reached for Johanna's mug and stood up.

"Enough to make me worried," he said. "And in my line of work, that's saying something." He refilled both cups and set them down.

"One more thing," Johanna said, a puzzled look on her face.

"What?"

"Did, did I smoke a cigar?"

The dark blue Dodge Charger had been in either his side or his rear-view mirror since just north of Portland. Traffic on Interstate 5 was moderate and Tamal Hajiik had set his cruise control at a sedate sixty-three miles per hour. His handheld GPS told him he was seven miles from the Washington border so he was not totally surprised when the headlights finally started flashing and red and blue lights appeared in the grill. Hajiik considered feigning ignorance and trying to make it across the Columbia River Bridge but quickly dismissed the notion. He slid the dagger from underneath his bulky sweatshirt and forced it between the passenger seat and the center console. Then he flipped on his right turn signal and pulled onto the paved shoulder, slowly gliding to a stop. He shifted the battered Nissan into "Park" and waited, motionless. When the rap on the driver's side window came he tilted his head up. The trooper tapped again, slightly harder this time, and made a circular motion with his index finger. Hajiik reached for the handle and rolled down the window.

"Do you know why I pulled you over sir?" the trooper asked.

"I'm sorry I don't, officer," Hajiik replied as meekly as his simmering rage would allow.

"I saw you talking on your cell phone back there. Oregon, like Washington, requires any cell phone use while driving to be hands-free. Are you aware of that, sir?"

"I am sorry, I was not. I was only checking for messages on my phone. I don't believe I was talking to any-"

"May I see you license and registration, sir?" the trooper said, cutting him off. Hajiik noticed the man's right hand was planted firmly on the stock of his holstered service revolver.

"Might I unbuckle my safety belt?" Hajiik asked. "My wallet is in my back pocket."

"Yes, sir. Just do it slowly. I'll also need proof of insurance."

Hajiik clicked open the belt which retracted so quickly that the flange banged against the inside of the door. The trooper braced reflexively and reached one arm into the car.

"I am sorry," Hajiik said. "I would like to purchase a new car but my present circumstances don't allow it."

"License, registration and proof of insurance, sir. Now, please."

Hajiik reached slowly into his back pocket and withdrew his wallet. He fished out the Washington driver's license and handed it to the trooper.

"Are you the owner of this vehicle, Mr.," he paused and looked at the card, "Aquila?"

"I am ashamed to say that I own this piece of junk, officer. The registration and insurance card are in the glove compartment. I will get them now."

The trooper made no reply and Hajiik reached across and popped open the glove box. The officer, he noticed, had crouched down so he could see what Hajiik was reaching for. Hajiik grabbed the only items in the dusty compartment and handed them through the window.

"Please remain seated in your car, sir. I'll be back in a few minutes."

Hajiik watched the trooper in the mirror as he walked back to the idling cruiser. Then he turned up the radio. A benighted fool named Hannity was ranting about a mosque in New York City. Hajiik loved American talk radio. It stoked hatred like petrol on a flame. In his imaginings, the pompous and self-righteous Hannity and all his ilk would all be seated in first-class cabins babbling to captive seatmates when the holocaust engulfed them. It seemed to Hajiik that the so-called "masterminds" of the 9/11 attack, as the radio men called them, had found little to deter their plans despite the egregious mistakes they had made at every step. Better that they were all martyred, he thought, as suicide missions required only a feeble mind and a pliant will. They had attacked not a sleeping giant, but a passed out and drunken one – intoxicated with its own arrogance and assumed of its invincibility. His own plan, he knew, would become legendary, having been carried out with the enemy not only awake but on high-alert. The only shame being that he would never get the credit. He had made good time on the drive from the Dundee winery and had been in the process of calling el-Hamini when he'd first spotted the police car. The trooper, he knew, would find little of interest in the Miguel Aquila known only to the Washington Department of Licensing and GEICO Insurance. Arab, Italian, Greek, Indian, African, Mexican – it usually didn't matter. Most Americans couldn't recognize the differences and were, in his experience, concerned only with whether a stranger was "like me" or "not like me." The genetically coded instinct to differentiate "self" from "non-self", as his Virology and Immunology professor had once taught him.

The crunch of boots on gravel redirected his attention. A thick pad was thrust through the window, the trooper pointing to it with his pen.

"I'm giving you a citation for talking on a handheld device while driving. The fine is one hundred and forty-two dollars plus costs. If you wish to plead 'guilty' just sign on this line and send your copy in with payment. If you wish to plead 'not guilty' your court date and location are listed on this line. Do you have any questions?"

"None, officer," Hajiik replied. "I will try to be more careful in the future."

The trooper tore off a pink carbon and handed it to Hajiik along with his license, registration and insurance card. "Have a good day, Mr. Aquila. And don't forget to buckle your seat belt before you get back on the road."

Hajiik pulled on the balky belt and reattached it to the buckle. He checked his mirrors and pulled back into the flow of mid-morning traffic. He was tired and needed sleep. Once Billings had been disposed of he had left immediately on the almost four-hour drive south to the Willamette Valley, arriving at the deserted winery a little before two a.m. Abassi had assured him that all the cargo deliveries were on schedule and that all the incendiary devices had been placed within them. Abassi was rummaging in his locker for his identification papers when Hajiik had struck him. His shoulder still ached from having to drag the unconscious man to the grape press. Unfortunately, Abassi had awakened just enough to realize what was about to happen to him, so Hajiik neatly severed both of his carotid arteries in an act of mercy for his comrade. He felt sure the heavy press would obliterate any traces of those interventions.

The Columbia River yawned below him, green and sparkling, as he considered what to do next. He reached over and retrieved the dagger. Seeing no cars on either side he pricked the flesh on his arm until several drops of blood stained the blade. Hajiik thought about the girl and the risk she presented. Then, in accordance with custom, he wiped the blood from the dagger and tucked it away.

Chapter 18

WITH NO EARLY CASES to do, Johanna had appreciated the chance to pull herself together. She watched el-Hamini approach and tried to look chipper.

"Good morning, my dear," el-Hamini chirped. "It's nice to have a day out of the lab, don't you think?" The sunny hospital corridor gleamed from a recent high-gloss waxing.

"Yes," Johanna replied. "It's good to have a day to catch up."

El-Hamini smiled but his face, Johanna thought, appeared lined with worry.

"You look tired, Dr. el-Hamini," she said.

"It's nothing," he replied. "Just trying to arrange all my affairs before I leave the country. I have not been home for some time, I'm afraid."

"Where exactly is home?" Johanna asked.

A wistful look came over his face. "I was born in Farah, in the western region of Afghanistan. My father was an electrical engineer there. Oh, my dear girl, in that time it was a wonderful place to be a child. The Russians ignored us and neither the Taliban nor the murderous fanatics of the calphate could even be imagined then." He shook his head. "So much has changed. So much has been lost."

"Are you going back to Farah, then?"

"No," el-Hamini replied. "I am going to Damascus where I will reunite with my dear wife and my lovely daughter. I worry about them in such a dangerous place." His voice quavered and Johanna thought he might be tearing up. El-Hamini cleared his throat and continued. "My daughter, Saaleha, she is tall and beautiful like you, though much younger. She also wants to be a doctor."

Johanna laughed. "Well, tell her not to go in to heart surgery. Too many years. Too much stress. Make sure she has a normal life."

El-Hamini crossed his arms in front of him then brushed off each sleeve as if trying to rid himself of whatever he was thinking. Abruptly he changed the subject.

"Amanda tells me that perhaps you will be seeing that nice Mr. Collier?"

Johanna looked dumbfounded. "Amanda told you that?"

Now el-Hamini laughed. "If your government were smart," he said, "they would utilize the dear Ms. Wingfield for their intelligence instead of your FBI and your CIA. I can assure you she has at least as many contacts and, how would you say, listening posts?" Before Johanna could answer, he continued. "I should very much like to speak to Mr. Collier before I journey abroad. If you see him would you ask him to contact me?"

Johanna wasn't sure how to respond. "Sure," she said uneasily. "If I see him I'll ask him to call your-"

"My cell phone," el-Hamini replied, withdrawing a business card from his blazer pocket. "The number is written on the back. I am leaving soon, as you know. So my questions for him are a matter of some urgency. Tell him to call anytime. We are out of the lab today. Perhaps that would be convenient?"

Johanna hoped her confusion was not obvious as she took the card and placed it in the breast pocket of her lab coat. "OK, she said hesitantly, "If I see him I'll give this to him."

"Very good," el-Hamini replied. "Are you going to the reception this evening?"

"What reception?"

"Perhaps I have spoken out of turn. But my understanding was that invitations were extended to attending staff and Chief Residents."

"I'm not a Chief Resident until next week," Johanna said.

El-Hamini looked troubled. "Yes, I understand. But in Dr. Constantine's absence, perhaps you will be asked to fill in. Is there any news from him?

Johanna eyed him carefully. "He's officially missing but the police are working on it. "

"Yes, that officer who was at breakfast yesterday. What did

he think?"

"He didn't think anything," Johanna said coolly. "He's the one trying to find him." She sensed that el-Hamini wanted to say something else but had stopped himself.

El-Hamini straightened his shoulders and buttoned his jacket. "We have only a few patients to see on rounds," he said. "Once we're done the day is yours to do with as you please." He took a step forward. Johanna waited then followed a half-step behind, still trying to figure out what exactly was going on.

The medical library at The Cutter Clinic was as ornate and well-appointed as a luxury hotel. Two hours later Johanna sat in a burnished leather chair at a teak study carrel. Seated in the carrel next to her she recognized one of the General Surgery residents, asleep after a night of being on-call. His head lay on an open textbook, a thin trickle of drool meandering down his chin and staining the page. She wondered if in talking to McCarthy she had made a serious mistake. At institutions like The Cutter, she knew, palace intrigue at the staff level was rife and often cutthroat. The informal residents' credo was "trust no one." She had now violated Rule Number Two, she realized. The sleeping resident next to her started to snore. Johanna reached over and slid the textbook an inch to the right, unobstructing the young man's airway and restoring quiet. It was then that her pager went off. She recognized the number as McCarthy's office.

"So what do I wear?"

"Snappy casual," Justin McCarthy replied. "Just don't show up in scrubs."

"Thanks, Dr. McCarthy," Johanna said. "I figured that much."

"Oh, and Roberson," McCarthy said. "Have you ever met Dr. Poole?"

"No, but a surgeon I rotated with in Des Moines trained under him in Indianapolis."

McCarthy chuckled. "Well, I don't know what he told you, but if I were you, I'd consider bringing a date."

"A date?"

"Alright, a guest, then," McCarthy said. "It might save you the trouble of finding yourself in, how can I put this? – an awkward situation."

Johanna's shoulders slumped as she tried to process what she was hearing. Then her back straightened.

"Ohhh," she said. "OK, I got it. Really? The Surgeon General would-

"In a heartbeat," McCarthy said. "He was a mentor of mine so I don't want to say any more."

"Thanks for the heads-up," Johanna replied. "So, Space Needle at seven-thirty, no scrubs and bring a date. Got it." The call ended. Johanna walked back into the medical library and roused the still-slumbering resident. "It's after twelve," she said, "You can go home now." He tilted his head and she watched as the glazed look on his face slowly dissolved.

"You're Roberson, right?" he asked, blotting the saliva on his chin with the sleeve of his lab coat. "I'm thinking about doing a Cardiac Surgery fellowship here when I'm done. What do you think?"

Johanna laughed. "I'd stick to hernias and hemorrhoids if I were you," she said. "This shit will kill you."

Trip Collier still had the remnants of his headache and Travis Hsu wasn't making it any better.

"Heard you and your new friend closed down The Wild Ginger last night," Hsu said. Collier punched the "down" arrow on the volume control button on his office phone and held the receiver a little further from his ear.

"Am I now a person-of-interest for some reason?" Collier asked.

"Collier," Hsu said in mock exasperation. "I'm married and have two rug rats under the age of four, man. I have to live vicariously through your exploits. You're the Great Gaijin Hope for the rest of us, buddy."

"Gaijin is Japanese. I thought you were Chinese."

"Depends on the day and who's asking," Hsu answered.

"Anyway, thanks, pal," Collier replied. "I'll try to live up to that honor."

"So?" Hsu asked.

"Why don't you tell me what you've got on our missing Dr.

Constantine," Collier said.

Hsu laughed. "Quid pro quo, Clarice. Quid – pro – quo."

"OK, Hannibal. We had dinner. We drank a little. I took her home. Nothing even remotely exciting after that except for this headache and that was almost gone until I started talking to you."

"Hmmm," Hsu replied. "Then this parking ticket I'm looking at was probably issued to a different Triplett L. Collier. Seems this other Collier dude left his car parked on Union Street in a metered spot from somewhere after six last night until sometime after seven this morning. Freaky coincidence, huh?"

Collier looked at the pink copy of the ticket which was tucked into a corner of his desk blotter. "OK," he said. "Neither of us thought it was a good idea to drive. We took a cab which dropped her off and then took me home. Is that all, Lieutenant Columbo?"

"Another funny thing, then," Hsu said. "The Parking Control officer says this other Triplett L. Collier guy was dropped off by a woman in a nice car shortly after she wrote the citation. It just gets curioser and curioser, doesn't it? But she did say the guy was good-looking, so that goes against it being you, I guess."

Collier knew he was busted. "I slept on her couch and took a cab back to my car this morning. Want me to sign a statement?"

"Nah," Hsu replied. "I just like busting chops on a federal agent. Evens the playing field a little, don't you think?"

"I think you should tell me if you've got anything on Constantine."

"I talked with the neighbor who, by the way, had my gaydar pinging the whole time. Anyway, Constantine was asking him about where he could put his boat in on the Sound. This guy, the neighbor, thinks he might have tried the Don Armeni boat ramps over at Duwamish Head. I'll go over their later today and look for a car or a trailer."

"What about the sailboat?" Collier asked.

"The Coasties say they're done with their part. They want us to take the boat off their hands but we don't have any place to put it. The impound yard says they don't do boats without trailers. So until we can crack the bureaucratic backlog at the King's County Recorder's office or until the boat's previous owner reenters the country to tell us who he sold it to, we can't confirm."

"Confirm what?"

"Collier, everything I got tells me this is Constantine's boat. The CG Commander says he was probably on deck without a PFD and maybe hit a swell or got whacked by the mast."

"You mean the boom," Collier interrupted.

"OK, Popeye, whacked by the boom. Anyway, they figure his lifeline snapped and he went overboard. With the swim ladder up you'd have a hell of a time climbing back on, I guess. Especially in four foot seas, which is what the Sound was running all weekend. The boat was thirty years old. Good chance so was the lifeline. I don't want to tell your girlfriend any of this until I'm sure. The regs say I have to tell next-of-kin first, anyway, so don't you say anything, OK?"

Collier rubbed at his temple. He thought of how many times he'd sailed alone without a life jacket or a lifeline. "She's not my girlfriend," he finally said.

"Not yet, Collier. Not yet. I bet you can fool her for a while. She must be pretty smart to be a heart surgery doctor, though. She'll figure you out eventually."

"Thanks for the vote of confidence," Collier replied glumly.

"I just call 'em like I see 'em, dog. Enjoy it while it lasts."

"Well," Collier said, "Thanks for the update. I figured this might end badly."

"You mean Constantine or your relationship?" Hsu interrupted.

"Very funny. Constantine. The classic tragic accident, I guess."

"Nothing to suggest anything else so far," Hsu replied. "Hey, do you still have your thong collection?"

"Goodbye, Travis," Collier said and hung up. His speakerphone beeped and he tapped the little button with the megaphone icon on it.

"Did you remember you have a JTF meeting at one-thirty?" the secretary asked.

Collier worked his mouse and clicked on his calendar. "I see it," he said. "Dare I ask? Which joint task force is this?"

"DHS, FBI and SPD – anti-terrorism, it looks like."

"Is it here?" he asked.

"No, are you kidding? It's always on Bureau turf – eighth floor, Abe Lincoln Building. Maybe they'll have food."

"Yeah, maybe," Collier replied. "Who's the Bureau guy on this one?"

There was a short pause. "Charley Higgins," the secretary replied.

"Oh, good," Collier said. "I like Charley. He's the only guy there who likes to talk sports. Remind me at one o'clock and I'll walk over." He pressed the button again and the speaker went quiet. He knew Johanna would be asking about Travis Hsu. He would have to be careful. He did not want make a habit of lying to her. He was about to get up when his phone beeped again. He didn't recognize the outside number but decided to pick it up anyway.

"Collier, DHS," he said gruffly.

"Oh, hi. Um, it's me. Johanna. Roberson."

"You had me at Um," Collier replied.

There was silence on the line and Collier suddenly felt very stupid for having said it. Then he heard a chuckle.

"I guess that's better than 'show me the money'," Johanna said. "Listen, I'm sorry to do this," she continued, "but do you have any plans tonight?"

Collier could not suppress a grin. And his head, he realized, no longer hurt.

As he waited outside the apartment building, Tamal Hajiik reflected that of the many people he had killed with his own hands, there had been very few women. Some of his brothers, he knew, relished the opportunity when it presented itself and Hajiik had always deferred to their greater enthusiasm. He had, of course, attended a few of the obligatory hangings and stonings of murderous or adulterous wives. Often the aggrieved husband, if he wasn't deceased, was given the honor of removing the chair or throwing the heaviest rock; otherwise the honor went to the surviving son or daughter who, sometimes, had to be forced into performing the act. Hajiik had participated in several stonings but, to his knowledge, he had never hurled the fatal chunk of brick or cinderblock. He didn't care for stoning, particularly. All the digging and burying the condemned to their waist or their neck, only to have to excavate the corpse when the bloody deed was finished. He also did not believe executions required group participation and he detested his younger comrades' obsession with video and cell phone cameras. They collected the gruesome images the way American boys collected baseball cards. It was not the manner of death that interested him so much as what was to be gained from it. The crazed and cowardly Uday had tossed enemies, real and perceived, feet first into an industrial shredding machine while Hajiik had stood by his side. A true sadist and sociopath, Hajiik had quickly determined, the young man accomplished nothing beneficial and only infected those around him. His death was, he thought, perhaps the one positive result of the American invasion. As for beheadings, Hajiik thought they should only be carried out by someone skilled at the art. He had tried to teach the younger brothers why the ritual was important, but their blood lust was overwhelming. Addicted to violent video games from young ages, each one tried to outdo the next in their savagery and brutality. Beheadings were not an act, he tried to tell them. They were a message. Even the Mexican drug cartels understood that. But the rise of the caliphate had taken it beyond even Hajiik's level of comprehension. He doubted that not since the Nazi SS troops had redefined the term atrocities had pure psychopathy been on such brutal display. He had steered clear of the caliphate believing it was, at its black heart, clearly apocalyptic and thus of only fleeting historical import. They would end up like Robespierre, another champion of murderous purification – resting headless in the common grave of the past.

Hajiik looked at his watch. If she did not come out before nightfall, he would have to go in and get her. He rarely felt sympathy but he knew her death was necessary only as an insurance measure, as her colleague's had been. It didn't matter to him who they were or what they believed. They threatened an event that would, Hajiik believed, set in motion a change in the world order. Unwitting brethren, he knew, would also be sacrificed along with infidels of every variety. The deaths of innocents, even the horror of the carnage was not really the issue. The actual toll would be a fraction of the World Trade Center and Pentagon attacks. But its audacity and the fact that the events would all occur beyond the supposedly impenetrable security screenings had occurred – this would shake the puppet government of the Zionists to its core. This would instill in the people of this supremely arrogant country something far more potent than fear. It would instill doubt. And doubt, he knew, was not just immobilizing, it was paralyzing. Across the land the sleepers would awaken and fill the void. America's already stressed military would be thrown into yet another fray. Hajiik had decided to craft a false trail that would place responsibility for his attack squarely on Yemen with hints of Pakistani complicity. The Americans were surely weary of the still-smoldering conflicts in Iraq and Afghanistan, and the bellicosity emanating from the Korean Peninsula. A new attack in their homeland would handcuff their leaders and Putin's window for Russian ascendancy as brother-nation-in-arms would be wide open. There were enough madmen still in power to keep the "world's policeman" busy for years to come. Throw in the regrouping Taliban, the caliphate's ghastly thugs and the Saudi's penchant for playing both sides of the board, and this one act of destruction would ripple through world history for the rest of the twenty-first century. So lost was Hajiik in these thoughts that he did not see the official looking sedan that pulled up and parked at the corner. Nor did he see the young man who alighted from it and walked briskly up to the front door of the apartment building. Only when the door opened and they stepped out did he become aware of what was happening.

"We're going in that?" Johanna asked, her tone incredulous.

"What?" Collier replied, taking mock offense.

"I mean, seriously, it looks like I'm being taken in for questioning, that's what."

Collier looked at the dark green Ford Crown Victoria with the DHS logo stenciled in yellow on the passenger door.

"Isn't there some, you know, penalty for private use?" she asked.

"That's government envelopes," Collier retorted. "Have you ever tried to park down there? I figured we'd be able to roll right up to the door in this." He looked almost proud.

Johanna shook her head and started walking. She looked over at Collier. "Is that what you call 'snappy casual'?"

"Jeez," he replied. "First my car, now my clothes. You asked me on this date, you know."

Johanna stopped at the curb. "Collier," she said, "This is not a date. You are escorting me to an obligatory social function. In this!" She pointed at the car, shook her head again and opened the door before he could do it for her. Collier waited until she got in then closed it. Peering in the window he could see she was trying not to laugh. He walked around behind the sedan, fishing his keys out as he did so.

"Sure looks like a date to me," he said as he approached the driver's side door.

Hajiik waited until the car's brake lights brightened at the corner. He shifted into gear and pulled slowly away from the curb. It appeared as if they were heading for Interstate 5. He checked the gas gauge and hoped they weren't going too far.

Chapter 19

"I LOVE THE SPACE Needle," Collier said. "It's always been my favorite place in Seattle." They were on the elevator en route to the Observation Deck where cocktails would be served.

"I'm sure it's a guy thing," Johanna replied as the car whisked them upward. "Skyscrapers, rockets, phalluses. It's all the same."

"No, that's not it," Collier said. "I like the Space Needle because it makes no pretensions. It's just what it is. There is not a single bolt, girder or tile in this thing that's been yuppified, typified or gentrified like the rest of the city. I mean, for God's sake, there are latte' bars and boutiques on Old Skid Road."

"Don't you mean Skid Row?"

"No, I mean Skid Road. When the city was a logging town they used to haul timber down it from the mountains to the sawmills. 'Skidding' the logs they called it. So the road, naturally, was called Skid Road. Only after the loggers moved out and the factories moved in did it become a neighborhood of flophouses, warehouses and seedy taverns. That's when it turned into Skid Row."

"Wow," Johanna said as the doors parted and the snow-capped peak of Mount Rainier filled the horizon.

"Me or the view?" Collier asked.

Johanna didn't answer. She walked to the railing in front of the large glass windows and stared out, transfixed. "I can't believe I've lived here all this time and never been up here," she said. "This is incredible. How high up are we?"

"Five-hundred and twenty feet," Collier answered without hesitation. "The red aircraft warning beacon at the very top is six-hundred and five feet. Long way down."

"I guess," Johanna said. She was walking slowly along the perimeter of the deck's enclosed portion. She saw several groups of people who she recognized as Cutter physicians, but none that she knew personally. They came to an exit door. "Can we go outside?" she asked.

"Unless you're afraid of heights," Collier replied. "I'm a believer in never looking down."

"I love high places," Johanna said with a giggle. "Have you ever been to the Indian Watchtower at the Grand Canyon? It's at the eastern end of the South Rim. Most tourists don't even know about it. This is just as amazing, though." Collier pushed open the door and held it for her. Johanna strode directly to the outer railing and looked down. "This is so cool," she said. "Anybody ever BASE jump from here?"

Collier held onto the rail and looked straight ahead. "There have been several parachute jumps and a few successful suicides, all from the O Deck." He noticed that Johanna was leaning over without holding on. "You might want to lean back a little," he chided.

""I have good balance, remember?"

"OK, Dr. Wallenda," Collier said.

"They died, you know," Johanna said somberly. "The Wallendas." She had turned around and was resting her back against the guard rail. "It happened before I was born but I watched a documentary about it. They were doing a seven-chair pyramid on the high-wire, their signature trick. One person at the front faltered just a little bit and they all fell. I remember because they said a reporter who was there wrote that they fell so gracefully it looked like they were flying." She had a far-away look in her eyes. Then she turned and walked until they were looking out over Puget Sound. Again she leaned over and looked down.

"I'm guessing you're not a risk-averse individual, then," Collier joked. Johanna looked right at him.

"There's really no point in being afraid," she said in a soft voice. "Most of the time you'd be better off thinking about how to get out of a difficult situation rather than worrying how you got into or how bad it is."

Collier was about to ask exactly what it was they were talking about when he heard someone call her name. A well-dressed man in a khaki suit and a pinstripe oxford button-down walked up to them. "Dr. Roberson," he said cheerily. In his left hand he held of plastic cup of what looked like Chardonnay. He did not extend his right hand in greeting. The man stood with his back to the inner deck. The evening sun shone brightly off the lenses of his glasses and Collier could see only a bright blur where his eyes should be. He wondered, briefly, if he was doing it intentionally.

"Dr. McCarthy," Johanna said. "This is Trip Collier, my guest. Trip is with Homeland Security here in Seattle."

McCarthy nodded. "Good to meet you," he said, again not extending his hand. Collier thought this odd. "Dr. Poole is running a little late, but I expect him here within the half-hour. He'll be going directly to the reception. We've reserved the Seattle and the Puget Sound Rooms on the Skyline Level. It's a hundred feet lower, but the view is still spectacular."

"Actually, it's about four-hundred feet lower," Trip said, deciding to mark some territory. "But you're right about the view."

A tight smile appeared on McCarthy's face. "So," he said. "You must work, where, at the airport, then?"

Collier exhaled in what was nearly a snort. "No, doc, that's TSA," he said. "At DHS we try to find the bad guys before they get to the airport." McCarthy took a sip of his wine, his expression unchanging.

"Well, OK, then," Johanna said, interrupting the nascent verbal pissing match Collier seemed eager to continue.

McCarthy turned only slightly to address Johanna. "Then we'll see you down at the reception in a bit?"

"We'll be down in a few minutes, Dr. McCarthy," Johanna replied through what sounded to Collier like gritted teeth.

"Wonderful. I'll introduce you to Dr. Poole myself," McCarthy said. "He has a special interest in how female residents are faring in our cardiac surgery training programs." He turned back in the same miniscule arc and looked at Collier. "Nice meeting you Mr. – Collier was it?"

Collier smiled warmly. "It's Trip, but you can call me Agent Collier if you'd like." McCarthy's rictus never changed. He exhaled sharply through his nose, nodded and walked away.

Johanna waited until McCarthy had gone back into the enclosed portion of the deck.

"Are you insane?" she said in a stage whisper. "Why did you

do that?"

"Because he's obviously a dick," Collier retorted.

"Yeah," Johanna said, "Well that dick is my boss. No, he's not just my boss; he's the Chief of the department I work in. That dick decides what cases I get assigned to, how much operating I get to do, how much call I take, when my vacation is, whether or not I graduate from the fellowship next year and whether or not somebody will hire me. So let me ask you again. Are you insane?"

"See?" Collier said, straightening his shoulders. "Even you think he's a dick. And you introduced me as your guest?"

"What did you want me to say?"

"I don't know. Good friend maybe? Non-hostile acquaintance. But guest?"

Johanna grunted. "Well I was going to say you were a paid escort or maybe my gay brother but either one of those would have dressed better!"

Collier realized he was holding his breath. Then he laughed out loud. To his relief, Johanna started laughing, too. It took them a little bit to stop.

Johanna spoke first. "Will you promise to behave yourself the rest of the evening?" she asked. "We will be meeting the Surgeon General of the United States, you know. I'm pretty sure he outranks you."

Collier desperately wanted to share his Colonel Sanders simile but decided it really wasn't the time. "OK, I promise," he said contritely. "Just as long as you introduce as something other than your guest."

Johanna started walking along the outer perimeter. As the downtown came into view the breeze ruffled her hair and the waning sunlight caught it, transforming the appearance of one color into several shades of auburn and copper and highlighting her profile. Collier drew in a breath. She was truly beautiful, he thought. Then she turned to him. "Be careful or I'll introduce you as my friend from the TSA," she said with a sly smile. They went back inside. A knot of people were clustered around a backlit wine fountain. "Is it too soon to drink again?" Johanna asked. "Something tells me we're going to need it."

"You can, I can't," Collier replied. He flashed open his jacket to show her his satellite pager. "It's only twice a month. Not so bad."

She grabbed a squat plastic glass, filled it and took a small sip.

"Do you work at the airport – you have to admit, it was pretty funny."

"Yeah, not so funny when I pull you out of line for a pat-down." Johanna dropped her chin and raised her eyebrows. "We're doing OK so far, Collier," she said. "But it's still pretty early." She took a step. "Don't even think about it."

"Think about what?" Collier said, striding to catch up.

"Touching my girl junk," she said with smile.

Hajiik watched the well-dressed crowd as they waited patiently for the elevators. There was an Arab restaurant not far from where he stood, across the boulevard from the Space Needle. He knew the cook there well. All he would need, he decided, was a white cloth busboy's jacket of an appropriate size. He had plenty of time. Perhaps enough for a quick meal. Kibbeh nayye with real Lebanese bread. Then he would go to work.

Chapter 20

"LADIES AND GENTLEMEN," a voice intoned over a tinny speaker, "the Surgeon General of the United States." An unfamiliar Sousa march began to play as Lloyd Poole strode in. Khaki suit, oxford button-down, blue tie, Collier noticed. As he looked around he saw that most of the male physicians in attendance had some variation on the same theme: khaki and navy blue, button-down collars, penny loafers or TopSiders, stick-up-the-ass posture. It was as if the L.L. Bean catalog had thrown up, Collier mused. He noted one physician who stood out in comparison – an athletically built, middle aged man wearing a string tie with a large turquoise slide. He sported an open-collared shirt and tooled western boots with silver tips. Collier asked Johanna about him.

"That's Dr. Tuggle, the trauma surgeon." she whispered. "He's from Texas. He does it just to piss the rest of the staff guys off. He calls them all drones."

Collier laughed. "I like him the best so far," he said. Johanna elbowed him in the ribs as Lloyd Poole passed by smiling and shaking hands like the President on his way to deliver the State of the Union Address. Poole looked at Johanna and smiled. Collier thought he was going to try to come over and talk to her when McCarthy steered him to the little makeshift podium. Poole tapped on the microphone and the crowd quickly quieted.

"Let me start by saying it's wonderful to be here at one of the leading medical institutions not only in the western United States, but in the whole Pacific Rim." He paused and there were a few seconds of awkward silence. He was apparently waiting for applause. McCarthy quickly obliged and the crowd politely joined in. As Poole droned on Collier began instinctively surveying the crowd. He had been paid a recruiting visit by the Secret Service during his senior year at Gonzaga but a penchant for alcohol-fueled civil disobedience had kept it from going any further. There were a large number of Asian physicians he noticed. Not surprising, he supposed, when you were trying to lure patients from as far away as Hawaii and the Far East. As he continued to scan the room he noticed that the women physicians also had their own version of the dress code. All wore slacks or pleated Khaki trousers, like Johanna. There was not a skirt in sight. And all were either wearing women's pinstripe oxford shirts or, again like Johanna, dark long-sleeved sweaters or blouses with mock turtleneck collars and, maybe, a simple pendant or necklace worn on the outside. Collier searched for any distaff iconoclast with a pair of Doc Martens or knee-high lace-up Converse All-Stars, but found none. A second burst of applause alerted him that the Surgeon General's speech was apparently over.

"I have to use the little agent's room," he told Johanna. Then he noticed that Poole was making a beeline toward her, ignoring glad-handers along the way. Johanna hooked an arm around his elbow.

"You stay right here, Collier," she said under her breath as Poole approached. McCarthy was trying to catch up to him, with limited success. Collier figured Poole for a youthful looking sixty-three, give or take a year. He had sandy hair that was graying throughout and a manner that struck Collier as imperious. His front teeth had been veneered and were just a shade too white. He walked up to Johanna and extended his hand.

"You must be the young woman Dr. McCarthy has told me so much about," Poole said. To Collier's ear it was the polished tone of a political animal and, Collier assumed, a habitual sexual harasser. "Johanna, isn't it?"

Johanna smiled uncomfortably and extended her hand. "It's a pleasure to meet you. I've known some of your former residents and they always said how much you personally influenced their training."

Poole nodded approvingly. "Justin McCarthy was brilliant even as a fellow. I had no doubt he'd be a Chief before long. That he's at a Cutter institution is more than I could have hoped for. Who else might you know that I had a hand in training?"

"I worked with Colin Walker when I was a medical student in Des Moines. Do you remember Colin?"

Collier watched as Poole's face seemed to freeze for just an instant, like when a satellite television signal got interrupted. The practiced smile quickly returned.

"Of course I remember Colin. Not in the same league with McCarthy of course, but I understand he's done well for himself in a, shall we say, smaller market."

"Dr. Poole, If I needed heart surgery tomorrow I'd go back to Iowa and have Colin Walker do it," Johanna said calmly. "I think that says a lot for how he was trained." Now it was Poole who looked uncomfortable, Collier thought. McCarthy was still two or three people away. "I'd like you to meet my significant other," Johanna continued. "Dr. Poole, this is Triplett Collier. He's also in government service." Johanna pulled him forward. Collier smiled warmly and extended his hand.

"Homeland Security," Collier said. "With all the foreign patients in and out of The Cutter Clinic, we might have to open a field office right there in the hospital pretty soon."

"It is truly an international referral center, now isn't it?" Poole replied in a stentorian tone. "And we must strive to safeguard our foreign visitors as carefully as we do our own citizens."

"That's what they say at Guantanamo," Collier replied cheerily. He winced when Johanna stepped on his toe. McCarthy finally arrived and shouldered in next to Poole.

"I see you've met Dr. Roberson," he said excitedly. "She'll be our first female graduate this time next year. We're hoping she might consider sticking around." The look on Johanna's face told Collier this was definitely news to her. "Dr. Poole was hoping you might have some time later this evening to meet with him and discuss the role of women in the cardiac surgical workforce."

Poole cleared his throat. "Unfortunately, Justin, my itinerary has been curtailed and I'll have to take a rain check on that." McCarthy looked momentarily crestfallen but recovered quickly. "Is that Maghdi Ravazi over there?" Poole asked. "I really need to say hello. If you will excuse me." Poole turned on his heel and headed for the opposite side of the meeting room. McCarthy shrugged and then followed him dutifully.

"So in ten minutes I've gone from guest to significant other?"

Collier asked Johanna. She slugged down the rest of her wine.
"Yeah, well, consider it a battlefield promotion," she said. "Don't
let it go to your head. Did you see how quickly he took off?"
"Yeah, what was that about?"
"He made a rapid assessment that my F.Q. was extremely low."
"Your F.Q.?" Collier asked, drawing out the unfamiliar initials.
"You figure it out, spyboy," Johanna replied. Collier looked
bewildered and fell silent. "There's I.Q. and then there's F.Q."
Collier shrugged. " My Fuckability Quotient," she said finally.
"Oohhh," Collier replied. "Right. F.Q. So can I go to the bathroom
now?"
"Right after you go and get me another glass of wine."
"Fine, but who is this Colin Walker guy? The SG looked like
he'd seen a ghost there for a second."
"It's a long story," Johanna replied. She unhooked her arm from
his. "Maybe someday I'll tell you."

"You there. Grab that tray! Hurry!"
Hajiik looked at the little man with the high voice. The Space
Needle was monogrammed on the breast of his Cascade-green
vest. Clearly a homosexual, he decided. They were everywhere.
No wonder this country was rotting at its core.
"You do speak English, don't you?"
Hajiik nodded and picked up the large tray loaded with wine
glasses. The *foufou* pointed at the service elevator. "Take
them to the bar in the Puget Sound Room. Then come back
for more plates." Hajiik avoided eye contact and did as he was
instructed. Alone in the service elevator he contemplated the
best strategic move as the car crept slowly upward. The doors
opened and he walked out, bumping into a man in a rumpled
sport coat in the process. "Excuse me, sir," Hajiik said.
"My fault," the man said. "Just trying to find the men's room."
Hajiik hurried away, scanning the floor plan as he did so. He
thought the man had looked at him strangely and for perhaps
just a second too long but he did not turn around to see if he was
watching him. As Hajiik approached the milling and clustered
guests he kept his head down but his eyes darted, searching in
the sea of faces - searching for her.

"Christ, you need a GPS just to find the head on this level,"

Collier said. "Here, I brought you another Chardonnay."

The woman he tapped on the shoulder turned around. "Well, I don't know who you are, but thank you," she said and took the glass from him.

"I'm sorry," Collier stuttered. "I thought you were someone else. Enjoy the wine."

She was tall and attractive but she was not Johanna. The event room was poorly lit and all he had seen was her height, khaki slacks and a dark sweater. The Secret Service had apparently been right about him, he thought. Collier got another wine from the fountain and weaved in and out of the crowd looking for Johanna. Total strangers nodded to him and a few shook his hand. The din was a little louder as the attendees' conviviality rose along with their blood alcohol levels. Finally he caught sight of her, talking animatedly with a much older, elegantly dressed woman doctor who had an uncanny resemblance, Collier thought, to Meryl Streep. He stood silently next to Johanna for almost a minute.

"Oh, hi," she said. "I thought maybe you got lost. Collier, this is Dr. Dani Rivers. She's the head of Congenital Heart Surgery and she is a rock star. Dr. Rivers is the role model for every woman surgeon in the Pacific Northwest."

" I don't know about that. I'm just glad there are more of us now," the older woman said. "It was tough being the only girl at the dance for so long." She started to say something else when Collier saw Johanna turn away suddenly. Someone was calling her, he realized. "Well, enjoy the party," Dani Rivers said and then glided away. When Collier turned around he saw who Johanna was speaking to – it was el-Hamini.

"Ah, Agent Collier! What a grand coincidence. I was hoping to speak to you again. If Dr. Johanna would excuse us for just a moment perhaps we could find some place a bit less hectic to talk." Johanna gave Collier a puzzled look then shrugged her shoulders and sipped at her wine. "I assure you, my dear," el-Hamini said. "We will return in two shakes of a camel's tail."

"Let's go up to the O Deck," Collier suggested. "I could use some air."

In the swift ride up to the Observation Deck el-Hamini remained silent, occasionally smiling and nodding. He fidgeted with the chain around his neck and Collier could clearly sense that he was nervous about something. When the doors opened he waited for Collier to exit and then followed closely behind. They walked through the enclosed area and then out through one of the doors. They were on the city side and the lights of Seattle shimmered in the summer night. A couple walked by them and el-Hamini uttered a few pleasantries as they passed. He waited until they were out of sight around the circular walkway and then turned to Collier.

"I am sorry to take you away from your lovely new friend," he said quietly. "But there is a matter of some urgency I would like to discuss with you." Collier reached in his jacket for his notebook and pen. El-Hamini took a pastel handkerchief from his pocket and dabbed at his forehead. "I hardly know where to begin," he said.

"Anyplace you want, doc," Collier replied. "The beginning is always a good spot."

El-Hamini grasped the railing tightly and drew in a breath. "Very well, the beginning then. Two years ago, Agent Collier, my wife and my daughter traveled back to our home-" Then he stopped, his halting words interrupted by a chorus of screams from somewhere directly below them.

Chapter 21

COLLIER PUNCHED THE "DOWN" button a third time then spied a sign for the stairs. He pushed open the door and descended the metal steps two and three at a time, stopping only to regain his balance when his momentum threatened to send him tumbling headlong. It took him several minutes to descend over four-hundred feet. As he grew nearer he could hear the waxing and waning sounds of people in the banquet rooms. There were no longer screams but rather an almost wavelike chorus of what sounded like moans.

When Collier finally reached the SkyLine Level he had to hunt in the circular hallway for an entry door. Finally locating one he pulled it open and burst in only to find himself facing an empty space. He quickly realized that he was in the Lake Union Room, the only one not in use. He ducked right and followed the now continuous murmuring. Entering the Seattle Room he saw nothing but backs. Pushing his way through he finally pulled out his credentials and yelled, "Federal Agent. I need to get through!"

The crowd began to part. As he neared what looked like its front row he asked what was going on.

A man of about seventy stepped back to make room for him. "There was girl out on the ledge," he said, a panicked look on his face. "I think she fell!"

Hajiik was in the freight elevator by himself. It seemed to take a long time to descend the relatively short distance. When the doors parted he was confronted by the foufou. "Where do you think you're going?" the man said. "Nobody leaves till after clean-up, remember?" His attempt to sound menacing would have amused Hajiik at any other time, but not at this one. Hajiik reached beneath his shirt for the dagger but kept walking. Three of the actual hired busboys were having a smoke by the street. Hajiik doffed his jacket and dropped it behind some shrubs before they saw him. He did not look up nor back and within a minute had melted into the small knots of pedestrians milling around the base of the tower.

At first he couldn't figure out how she had gotten out there.

As he wriggled himself through the gap between the glass pane and the concrete wall, Collier started taking off his leather belt. Johanna was clinging to a section of metal piping that must have been much stronger than it appeared. She had one arm wrapped around its narrow circumference and with her other arm she had a lock on her wrist. Collier stared down at the hundred foot drop and felt a wave of nausea pass through him. He swallowed hard to contain it. He could see no place to plant his feet, so he kept his pelvis wedged into the small opening. He extended his left foot to the edge of the metal frame that enclosed the banquet level. When he shifted his weight the bar that Johanna was holding on to creaked and inched downward a few millimeters.

"Shit!" she gasped. "Don't do that!" She looked up and into his face. For someone in such a precarious state she didn't have the terrified look Collier was expecting.

"I'm not even going to ask-"

"Good!" she snapped. "Just get me back up!"

Collier could see that there was no way she could regain the narrow concrete ledge by herself. By hooking her arm and clamping on to her wrist she had created a loop that was keeping her from falling but, he realized, she couldn't do anything else. The metal piping creaked again but he didn't see it move this time. In the distance he thought he heard sirens.

"Better think quick," Johanna said while exhaling. "This thing I'm holding on to feels like it's made of tin foil."

As if on cue, the metal creaked again and this time Collier saw it drop a little. He took his belt and passed the tongue through the buckle. He slipped the post into the third perforation and tugged until it stayed set.

He slid down in the narrow space until he was crouching.

Johanna's sleeves had been pulled up and he could see the cords in her muscled forearms straining. In the light of a full moon the vein on one arm stood out, distended, in stark relief. "Got a plan?" she asked in a chuffing breath.

"I'll get the loop I made in this belt out to where you can grab it. I made it big enough so you'll be able to put your whole hand through it and grab the strap, Then let go with your other hand and I'll pull you up."

"Did you say let go? Are you kidding?"

"I used to do a little guiding on Mt. Rainier when I was in college. I know this will work. I've done it before." Collier felt the crowd moving on either side of him trying to peer out the windows. Johanna looked up at him with an expression that pleaded for a different plan. "It's going to take a little commitment," Collier said evenly.

He laid the belt on the thin rim of concrete. The belt was stiff enough that he was able to inch it toward her. Her face was a mask of concentration. Collier pushed until the loop was almost touching her. Johanna stretched her fingertips until they were just grazing the leather. Collier nudged the belt forward. He could see Johanna's breaths coming in quicker succession with the effort. Finally she snaked the tips of her middle and ring fingers just inside the loop. Rhythmically extending and relaxing her hand she was able to work the loop to the level of the first joint in her middle finger. Collier tried to push the belt further to help her but a hump appeared in its middle and only grew the more he pushed. He could see that the locking grip she had on her wrist with her other hand was starting to slip.

"You almost have it," he said although he could see it wasn't true.

Johanna's teeth were clamped tightly together and she was breathing rapidly without opening her mouth. Her fingers continued to strain; the effort looked excruciating. They almost appeared to be in spasm. The metal tubing groaned and sank further below the concrete lip. Johanna's gaze was riveted on the loop in the belt. She looked like she was trying to will it to move further.

"Loosen your grip on your wrist a little and slide your arm up – you only need an inch," Collier said.

She shot him a look that under different circumstances he would have interpreted as "eat-shit-and-die" but then she nodded her head. Collier watched as her captive forearm inched upward. She grunted and the loop fell over her free hand.

Collier knew her muscles would soon fatigue beyond the point where she could keep them contracting. "Grab the loop and let go," he said gently. "I will not let you fall."

Time seemed to expand and she looked directly into his eyes for what seemed like minutes although he knew only seconds were passing. He watched her exhale slowly then take in a deep breath. Collier braced his aching hip bone against the glass and shifted his weight back in anticipation. The tongue-end of the belt was wrapped once around his right hand. He reached as far forward as he could with his left hand and squeezed the leather tight. Johanna looked at him once more then focused her gaze on the loop. In what seemed like time-lapse photography he watched as her fingers let go of her wrist. The arm she had looped around the metal piping slipped downward. He watched the belt slip over the concrete lip and suddenly felt no resistance. For an instant he was certain she had fallen.

Through the passenger window of his sedan Hajiik watched as the strolling tourists gathered in clumps, their necks craned upward toward the towering and illuminated edifice. How she had not fallen immediately was impossible for him to understand. He thought he could see movement above and a shuddering gasp came from the transfixed bystanders. A siren sounded somewhere in the vicinity. Hajiik shifted out of "Park" and drove slowly away.

Collier's arms were on fire. A young doctor in the crowd had gamely tried to belay him by encircling Collier at the waist but it was only serving to limit his ability to breathe. Collier felt his head start to ache. His inability to exhale fully was trapping the blood above his neck. He was letting out a steady guttural moan when he saw Johanna plant one and then both elbows on the thin rim of concrete. A rush of adrenaline shot through his system and he pushed up with his aching quads until he was almost standing. The young doctor had fortunately figured out his mistake and now had both hands locked on the waistband of Collier's pants. As Johanna's torso cleared the rim he let go of the belt with his left hand and reached for her. She extended her arm and locked her hand around his wrist. With a heave he pulled her up until she made three-point contact. The strain on his arms lightened. Collier let go of the belt completely and grabbed Johanna by the front of her slacks and pulled her toward him. He un-wedged himself and backed up. Her slimmer frame slipped through the opening and pitched forward, knocking them both to the ground. A wave of applause burst from the crowd as they closed in around them. Collier got up and pulled Johanna up with him.

She was spent with the effort and leaned on Collier. Questions flew at them from all directions as Collier elbowed them toward the elevators. Just as they entered a clearing in the throng a voice called out.

"There's someone hurt over here!"

Two Cutter doctors were crouched over an unconscious woman slumped against a support column. One of them was fanning her with a menu card. Collier wanted to keep Johanna moving but he stopped when he got a good look at the woman on the floor. He recognized the lanky frame, black sweater and the khaki pants right away.

Collier grabbed Johanna around the waist and pointed them toward the elevators.

"We need to get out of here right now," he said.

Chapter 22

"SO YOU WERE NEVER a guide on Mount Rainier? Like not even once?"

They were sitting on the leather couch in Collier's apartment. Johanna had her knees pulled up to her chin, her fingers interlocked just below them. A lightweight comforter was draped loosely around her. It was the first she'd spoken since Collier had hustled her into the car and driven off before the SPD and the Fire/Rescue squad had arrived at the Space Needle. The flickering gas fireplace was comforting even though she could hear the air conditioner running.

"Unless it's been in an airplane or a tall building, I have never been more than a thousand feet above ground level. Sorry. I needed you to buy in."

Johanna smiled but remained still.

"You have to say something about it," Collier said quietly. "You have to tell me what happened."

Johanna stared for a while at the fireplace. Then, without moving her head, she let her eyes take in her surroundings. The downtown lights glittered in the glass of the balcony door. The décor, which she recognized as post-modern, seemed a little at odds with the owner. She had expected an upscale man-cave. This, she mused as she completed her survey, was more like a mansion-cave. Her shaking had subsided and the shock of the experience was starting to melt away. She watched the fire's reflection dance in the snifter of dark liquid Collier had poured for her.

"Not armagnac, I hope," she said, again without moving her

head.

"Medicinal brandy," Collier replied. "Like they do in the Navy."

Johanna finally moved and reached for the glass. Picking it up, she swirled its liquid contents then held it as if to make a toast. "Anchors aweigh," she said and took a sip. The liquor lit her mouth on fire, but only for an instant. She marveled at its smoothness as she swallowed. "How old is this?" she asked.

"Older than we are," Collier said. "Combined."

Johanna nodded but continued to stare straight ahead.

Collier was seated next to her but, she noticed, he had maintained a respectful distance and had not tried to touch her. "You didn't go out there, did you?" he asked.

Johanna knew she needed to say it, but then it would become real again She took another sip of the brandy and set the glass back on the glass coffee table.

"Of course I didn't go out there," she said softly.

"I was pushed."

Tamal Hajiik sat alone in the darkened apartment. The end of his cigarette glowed brightly with each draw. Outside on the dirty street dogs barked and metal trash cans banged. He thought he had spied el-Hamini at the Space Needle. The good doctor was no longer answering his cell phone, nor was Hajiik's former roommate. He did not think the plan could be derailed at this point, yet a gnawing doubt that he had learned never to ignore kept him from packing his bag just yet. He considered the best case scenario. The girl, although not neutralized, still believed the devices were part of a money-making scam. The Cutter Clinic would have no interest in moving quickly to investigate something that would tarnish its integrity and reputation. El-Hamini, one of only two people other than himself who would not be on the planes when they exploded, would not talk, he felt assured. Not with the blade already at the necks of his wife and daughter.

He puffed on the cigarette until he could feel burning paper and tobacco on his fingers. Then he stubbed it out in his thickly calloused palm and considered the worst case scenario. He thought of what Saddam had taught him. The Glorious Leader had been a murderous psychopath and a malignant narcissist but, as was often the case in such individuals, a brilliant tactician. "Never leave anything to chance," he'd told Hajiik in a drawing room at the Baghdad palace. "Hope for the best; plan for the worst. Kill anyone who is in the way."

Collier grabbed the remote and tapped the up arrow on the volume key.

"Excitement tonight down - or should I say up? - at the Space Needle, Diane."

Johanna was in the bathroom and Collier could hear water running. He upped the volume a little more.

"That's right, Tom. Sources tell News Center Nine that an unidentified woman narrowly escaped a gruesome death tonight at Seattle's most iconic landmark. The woman, who declined medical attention and fled before she could be interviewed by police, was pulled from the ledge of the Needle's SkyLine Banquet Rooms, one hundred feet above the concrete pavement. How or why the woman got out on the ledge remains a mystery. It is unclear at this time as to whether alcohol was involved and an aborted suicide attempt has not been ruled out. The Needle was the site of a private reception hosted by The Cutter Clinic for visiting U.S. Surgeon General Lloyd Poole. Poole had left the reception by the time the incident occurred. The woman was apparently pulled to safety by another guest who also left the scene before assistance could be rendered. A second woman inside the banquet room was also reported injured during the reception. It is not known whether the two incidents are related. We'll have more tomorrow on 'Good Morning Seattle'."

Collier heard the bathroom door open and switched off the power.

"Am I on YouTube yet?" she asked.

"No, but you made the late news. No cell phone video, apparently. At least not yet."

"We can only hope," Johanna replied. She fluffed her wet hair with the thick towel. "I'm judging by the lack of feminine amenities that you don't host a lot of sleepovers." She was dressed in faded gray sweat pants and a blue hooded sweatshirt with "Gonzaga LAX" still faintly legible across the which had several bleach splotches scattered across the sleeves. "Just tell me this thing has been washed in the last month, please."

Collier smiled. "I do my own laundry so I can vouch for it," he said. "I really don't think you should go back to your apartment."

Johanna sat down on the couch and continued drying her hair.

"I'm a big girl," she said without much front. She tugged on the front of the sweatshirt, enthusiasm. "I think I'll be alright. Besides, my pager and my cell phone are there. Can't live without those, you know."

"I'm not trying to be cute," Collier replied in a sterner tone, "but I really think you should stay here tonight. You take the bed. If I can sleep on that thing you call a couch, I can sleep on this one. I have slept on this one. We'll go get your stuff in the morning and then figure out where you should go."

Johanna dropped the towel in her lap. "What do you mean, go?"

Collier sat next to her. "Johanna, I think you may have stumbled into some serious shit here. I think it's obvious that whatever is going on, it's worth it to someone to protect it. And apparently violence is going to be part of the equation." He paused. "The other woman doctor has a skull fracture and is in The Cutter ICU."

Johanna looked at him with a puzzled expression. "What other woman doctor?"

Slowly, Collier explained how he'd mistaken the woman for Johanna. "It's like she was, I don't know, your body double," he said. "My guess is whoever did this made the same mistake I did, realized it and kept looking until he found you." Johanna's shoulders sagged.

"What did Dr. el-Hamini talk to you about?" she asked.

"Do you mean what did he start talking to me about? I don't know. It was a little strange. He said he wasn't sure where to start so I suggested he start at the beginning. Then he begins by telling me about his family."

"I know he's meeting them when he leaves the country in a day or two," Johanna interjected. "They left on vacation ahead of him."

"Way ahead, I would say," Collier replied. "He said they left two years ago."

Neither of them said anything for a few seconds. Then Collier continued, "Anyway, that's a far as we got. I heard the ruckus from below and headed straight for the stairs. I don't know if he stayed on the O Deck or not. I didn't see him again, but then, I wasn't exactly looking for him, you know?"

"I'm glad you got me out of there so fast but why didn't we wait for the police?"

"Judgment call," Collier replied. "As soon as I saw your stand-in on the floor I figured we were dealing with somebody who meant business. There was no guarantee he or she wasn't still there. You didn't see anything?"

Johanna shook her head. "It felt like it happened in a millisecond. It was so freaking hot in that room. I stood by that open space because it felt like there was some air blowing in. I was looking at the lights and next thing I know I'm hanging on to that pipe. If my shoe hadn't caught on the ledge I think I would have just gone over head first." She gave a little shudder and looked at Collier. "What are you thinking?"

Collier cracked the knuckles on each hand and stared at a point on the floor. Finally he raised his head and looked at her. "What I do all day is run conspiracy scenarios, OK? So bear with me because it's an occupational hazard, like your being," he paused, "blunt. When I look at somebody who wants into the country I start asking myself 'Is this just some good-hearted moderate trying to escape his crazy and unstable country? Or is he part of something? Does he have a pack of Daesh trading cards in his pocket or an autographed picture of Bin Laden in his wallet? Is he here to do us harm?' And I have to err on the side of caution. I have to think the worst. We all do. That's why there hasn't been another major attack on our soil since 9/11."

"You just told me how you think but not what you're thinking."

Collier inhaled deeply. "OK, but as my old college roommate Mike Belz used to say, I'm just thinking out loud here." He tapped his fingers on his knees. "Let's assume that you, and Constantine before you, have accidentally tripped over this big-money pacemaker scam el-Hamini's running with God, or should I say Allah-knows-who. "

Johanna perked warily at the mention of Constantine. "Do you know something about Mike you're not telling me?" she asked.

"I know he's still missing," Collier replied. "Just hear me out." He took a sip of the beer he had opened for himself, dabbed at his lips and continued. "He figured it out, from what you let slip at the restaurant last night. And he told you and now you think he was right. So you try to tell that dick McCarthy who maybe tells somebody else, maybe he doesn't. My bet is no – he looks like someone who would never risk his own neck to do the right thing. But The Cutter is like any other big bureaucracy. Winston Churchill said that the only way two people can keep a secret is if one of them is dead."

"It was Benjamin Franklin," Johanna said. "And it was three people and only if two of them are dead."

"I hate Liberal Arts majors," Collier said with a laugh. "Especially when they're smarter than me. But do you see what I'm getting at? There are always more people involved than you think. It's like a dandelion – the roots go deep and in a lot of directions."

Johanna picked up her brandy and swirled it in front of her.

"Let's say this scam is worth, at minimum, millions of dollars over the long run," Collier continued. "Maybe it's tens of millions. You have to ask yourself: who's making the money? El-Hamini? Certainly. The Cutter Clinic? Got to be. Person or persons unknown? Without a doubt. So there are now a lot of people with a lot to lose. If The Cutter lets it get out, their reputation goes down the toilet. They're the eight-hundred-pound gorilla in Seattle right now for sure but, trust me, they are a very unpopular monkey. The media and the other hospitals would be like piranha at a feeding frenzy. So what do bad people do in this situation? They try to get rid of anyone or anything that threatens their enterprise. It's been that way for a hundred years here. The loggers did it, the sawmill owners did it, the pulp processors did it, and the lumber barons did it best of all. Medical fraud runs about sixty billion dollars a year in the U.S. Sixty billion. You think someone wouldn't take you out over even just a piece of that action?"

Johanna pondered the question. "I guess, but there's one thing that doesn't make sense to me?"

"What's that?" Collier asked, finishing the last of his beer.

"I think the scam, assuming that's what it is, only involves a small number of patients so far."

Collier torqued his mouth up on one side. "Like how small?"

"I don't know, but from what Constantine told me, maybe six or eight since he went on the service. It doesn't look like a high volume operation."

"Maybe not yet. Like I said, I'm just thinking out loud here. And the other thing is the big difference in who we're dealing with."

"What difference?"

Collier laughed. "These guys are crooks, Johanna. It's not like they're terrorists."

Chapter 23

SELJUK EL-HAMINI WAS BY nature a tidy person. It was difficult for him to create the disarray that he felt would be necessary. He did not wonder if he would come, only how soon it would be. His cell phone held eleven missed calls from his "brother." There were no texts or voice messages, thankfully. El-Hamini had glimpsed him at the Space Needle. He was pleased that Johanna was safe but he felt sorrow for Dr. Durkin, who now lay unconscious in the Neurosurgery ICU. All because of him and his – he didn't want to say it but there was no other word for it.

"My cowardice," he whispered to the empty room.

El-Hamini went to the bathroom closet and assembled the appropriate pill bottles, their contents clearly marked on the printed labels. Then he opened his medical bag, the one his father had given him as a gift at his graduation. He withdrew the vials he had secretly pilfered from several medication carts on the various wards. Digging further he found the small "butterfly" needle with it short length of tubing and needleless hub. Just below it was the Velcro tourniquet. These he placed on his night stand. He took out several small syringes he had taken from a supply cabinet in one of his exam rooms. He filled one with saline from a small bottle. The other he used to carefully withdraw what he hoped would be an adequate dose to do what he needed it to do.

The small cup of black tea he had poured himself was only half full. He would finish it after he had inserted the intravenous catheter in his own arm, a harder task than it looked. He had meant to bring extra IV needles in case he failed on his first attempt but in his haste had forgotten to do so. Sitting on the edge of the bed he put the tourniquet around his bicep and tightened it, letting his arm hang down. He made a fist several times then held his wrist under the light looking for what he always referred to as the "intern's vein." The several large glasses of water he had downed since his arrival at home helped pop the vein into stark relief. El-Hamini took several breaths to steady his nerves. Then he poked the intravenous needle into the engorged vein. A flash of blood appeared in the tubing. Carefully, so as not to dislodge it, he peeled off the adhesive backing on the plastic wings and pressed it against his skin where it stuck firmly. He undid the tourniquet and flushed the little catheter with three cubic centimeters of the sterile saline. He breathed a sigh of relief.

Gently, el-Hamini arranged the collection of vials in a decidedly haphazard array. He pushed the plunger of the larger syringe all the way to the bottom and laid it on the bed. He downed the rest of the tea in one gulp. Then he laid down on the bed.

And waited for him to come.

Hajiik had never been to el-Hamini's home. There had been no need, until tonight. He had parked many blocks away and taken a circuitous route to his destination. He surveyed the neatly trimmed hedges and the manicured lawn and shrubs. He obviously had a gardener, probably an Arab one, he thought. He slipped into the darkened yard and saw the open basement window. Waiting until a car on the street passed he slipped noiselessly through the aperture. Small green and red power lights glowed in the darkened room. Hajiik waited for his eyes to adjust then walked slowly toward the stairs.

Not daring to close his eyes, el-Hamini watched the security system panel on the wall nearest to him. He had disabled the automatic call to the police as well as the blaring siren and the automatic lights. Laying in the dark he waited for the sound. For two years the steps had not creaked under anyone's weight but his own; the doors had not squeaked and the water had not run unless it was for him. Then he saw the electronic display begin to flash. It was, he knew, the motion sensor on the main level that had activated. He drew in a breath and reached for the smaller syringe. Its blunt plastic tip entered the diaphragm on the plastic hub of the tubing with a tiny "pop." Another breath. Counting the seconds. Then another. As he breathed out he heard it – the creaking riser on the fifth step. He inspired deeply again and then exhaled as far as he could. He pushed the plunger on the syringe and felt the burn in his arm. Pulling out the small syringe he quickly replaced it with the larger empty one. He prayed he had timed it correctly.

The bedroom was dark but the door was open, Hajiik noticed. He waited just outside but heard nothing. The dagger was still sheathed, his fingers rested on the belly of the handle. Now in his stocking feet he made no sound as he entered. He turned to the right and saw him – asleep! His fingers wrapped the handle. He took two more steps and sensed something was wrong. The traitor's chest barely moved. In the glow of a nightlight he saw the vials and the prescription bottles. He let go of his grip on the dagger and picked them up. Ambien, he saw. Ten milligrams. Thirty had been prescribed and the bottle was empty. So were two identical bottles. Hajiik threw them on the floor and picked up one of the glass vials. Potassium chloride. Ten milliequivalents in every milliliter of fluid. Another empty vial lay on its side. He saw the intravenous needle in the limp arm and immediately understood. The coward had taken a lethal dose of sleeping pills and then injected himself with more than one hundred milliequivalents of straight potassium, enough to stop the heart within seconds. Hajiik felt at the neck. There was no pulse. He stepped back from the bed. Instinctively he reached for the dagger meaning to take some measure of what had been denied him. Then he stopped. If suicide was his choice, then so be it, Hajiik decided. It was the end that mattered, not the means. His rage cooled quickly and he let go of the dagger, having not unsheathed it. There was no requirement to draw blood, he knew. Not from this one. But something was tickling inside Hajiik's brain; He grasped the dagger's handle. Suicides could be faked, he knew. A few pokes with the blade and he would know for sure. He was about to unsheathe it when he heard a car door slam and voices out on the street. Hajiik scanned the room and backed away from the bed, brushing his footprints out of the carpet. He exited as silently as he had come in.

Chapter 24

JOHANNA HAD FINISHED HER brandy and was staring at the glowing fireplace.

"What do you know about Constantine," she said quietly. "And don't lie to me, please."

Collier had poured himself a short brandy and reached to refill Johanna's glass. She covered the mouth of the snifter with her hand. Collier set down the heavy cut-glass decanter and looked at her.

"I talked to Travis Hsu," he said slowly. "The Coast Guard found an abandoned sailboat floating in the Sound. They haven't been able to track the owner yet, but I think there's a good chance it's your friend's boat. They think he had an accident. That he might have gone overboard and then not been able to climb back on deck. They think his lifeline snapped."

"What about his life jacket?"

"It was down below in the cabin. Looks like he might have left it off."

"Mike wouldn't do that," Johanna said. "He grew up sailing. If there was ever a guy who didn't take chances-"

"The Sound is big water," Collier said calmly. "Tricky currents, ocean swells. A day sailor might-"

"He wasn't a day sailor, Collier," Johanna said sharply, color rising in her cheeks. "He was sailing Long Island Sound by himself when he was in junior high. He won trophies. He got caught in a nor'easter on a Sunfish and got it home in one piece. He went to Yale undergrad on a sailing scholarship, for Christ's sake. I'm telling you, Mike Constantine did not fall off any fucking boat!"

"OK," Collier said. He raised his hands defensively. "Even if that's true, the Coast Guard and the police are going to need a reason to doubt what they've got."

"What if you're right?" she asked. "What if he did tell McCarthy? He would tell el-Hamini and then maybe el-Hamini tells somebody who thinks Constantine should disappear. Look what happened to me. Isn't that enough?"

Collier rubbed at his head. "I'm not certain there's a conspiracy I'm just saying maybe there's more here than anyone thinks."

"Can't you do something about it? Don't you have any, I don't know, any jurisdiction?"

Collier shook his head. "Unless we can connect a dot, any dot, to national security, it's not my ball game and I'm not allowed to play."

Johanna picked up the decanter and poured the smoky liquid out until her glass was half-full. She took a swallow and looked at Collier. "The pacemakers he was putting in, they weren't from the U.S. The packaging was all in Arabic. I've never, ever seen that before. Is that a dot?"

Collier sipped from his own glass, a pensive look on his face. "If you can get me a sample of the packaging I might be able to make something up. It would at least be a start, maybe enough to start shaking the trees."

Johanna started to get up. "We can go now. I know where the-"

Collier gently pulled her back down. "We're not going anywhere right now," he said. "I'll call Amanda in the morning. Maybe she can be our 'Deep Throat'."

"Our what?"

"Our way in," Collier replied. "If there's a dot, I bet Amanda can find it."

Johanna suddenly felt as if all the air had been let out of her. She put the brandy down and rested her head on her drawn-up knees. She felt tears welling in her eyes and was determined she would not let him see her cry. Nobody, she told herself, was allowed to see her cry. Her breaths started coming quicker and she knew she was on the verge of decompensating. If she were in a rowing shell she would take a Power-Ten and push right through it, she thought. But right now, it seemed, her boat was too small and the water was too big. She reached out for him and Collier wrapped her in his arms. He felt so warm, she thought. She tucked her head under his chin and pulled herself tightly against him. He brushed the hair out of her face and wiped a single teardrop away with his thumb. Emotions were flooding her, clawing their way out of a place she'd kept them locked away for years. She reached up and laid her palm on his cheek.

"What's happening to me?" she whispered.

He didn't answer. He took her hand in his and touched it to his lips. She thought she could see a little shimmer in his eyes. She pushed up with her knees and cupped his face in her hands.

Then she kissed him and whatever hold she might have had on herself let go.

Chapter 25

JOHANNA'S EYES POPPED OPEN. This wasn't her apartment and this wasn't her bed, she realized immediately. His arm was around her waist and they were nestled, to borrow from her favorite T.S. Eliot poem, like two spoons. Her slowly developing wakefulness was tinged with a thread of panic. What had she done?

Johanna remained still. She couldn't feel him on her skin and in another moment she realized why: she was still wearing the sweat shirt and sweat pants he'd given her the night before. Her eyes started to focus and she could see the sunlight peeking over the window treatments. She was impressed – they were the high-end kind that you could draw from the top down or the bottom up. Currently they were flush with the sill and raised so that only about a quarter of the window was visible at the top. It amazed her that, given the current situation, this is what she chose to focus on. She began to realize just how wonderful physical affection had felt after having gone without it for so long. Deciding that she, and he for that matter, had not done anything stupid, she let her body relax and tried to luxuriate in the embrace of someone she was beginning to think might actually care for her. She wondered about him. Twice, in the space of as many days, he had been in a position to take advantage of her. And twice he had done nothing but look out for her. He was in bed with her, so she didn't think he was gay. Impotent? Not likely but possible. Why was it that the last possibility was always that he was a good and decent guy and maybe he saw more in her than just the chance for a few acrobatic tumbles?

Collier started to snore. Johanna shifted her shoulders until his head tilted a little further to the right and in a few seconds he slept quietly again. She waited a few more minutes then slipped out from under his arm.

"A Keurig," she said when he walked into the kitchen. "I'm impressed."

Collier smiled . "What good would it do for me to make a whole pot of coffee? It's a little more expensive, but if I only want one cup I only make one cup."

"And here I thought the heart-lung machine was the apotheosis of technologic achievement," Johanna said, waiting for his cup to fill. She slid it out of the brewer and handed it to him.

"Sure, it saves lives," Collier said as he took it. "But can it make piping-hot Colombian Decaf in twenty-six seconds?"

Johanna smiled and brewed herself a cup. Then she sat down at the mahogany breakfast table. "I'm going to be, um, direct here, Collier. Why didn't we- ?"

He set down his cup. "Because of what you're always telling me: it's early yet." He rubbed at an invisible spot on the table then looked up at her. "We're not old, but we're not impetuous youths, either. I know that I have more faults than California and I have made more mistakes, some well intended, than most guys I know put together. I have been a complete jerk to more women than I can count. I have faked love to get sex. I have feigned commitment to avoid loneliness." Johanna noticed that his voice had dropped to a little above a whisper. Collier took a sip of his coffee. "I don't know what you want," he said. "I'm not sure what I want. But I have never met anyone like you before. I mean, you are a very beautiful woman, but it's like there's this light inside of you. I obviously can't claim to know you very well, but I can't help feeling you try hard to keep that light covered up a lot. But when you let it out, it's just warm and brilliant and makes me want to be in it."

Johanna had to avoid his gaze, afraid she might break down.

"We all do things we wish we hadn't," she said. "I guess we have the choice of letting our mistakes teach us or letting them define us."

He smiled at her and stirred his coffee. The silence was not completely uncomfortable, she thought. Johanna was about to say something when his pager went off. Reflexively she reached for her own hip. "That's you," she said.

Johanna drank her coffee while he talked on the phone. When he hung up he rubbed at his eyes. "That's not good news," he said.

"Who was it?" Johanna asked.

"My buddy Charley at the Bureau. He said he's sending me a text message. It's always bad when he won't tell me on the phone."

"Are you going in to your office?"

"Yeah, at least for a few hours. You just stay here. I have Netflix, TiVo, Hulu, Amazon Prime, HBO and complete boxed-set Blu-Ray DVD's of Seinfeld, Get Smart, The Man from U.N.C.L.E. and The Adventures of Rocky and Bullwinkle." Johanna looked at him and he shrugged. "I'm a fan of classic TV. It's the one and only thing my father and I agree on. Anyway, we'll go get your pager, your phone and some clothes when I get back. Call The Cutter and tell them you're taking a sick day. Then hang up. Don't answer the phone unless it rings twice and then stops. If it rings again right away, pick up because that'll be me. I don't ever have anything delivered here so don't answer the door. Got it?"

"So, what – are we Boris and Natasha now?"

Collier laughed. "No, we're just being careful until whatever this is shakes out. I'll call Travis and see if he has anything new. I'll talk to Amanda. If she can get one of those pacemaker packages, I'll go to The Cutter and pick it up. We have an Arabic translator at DHS. She can take a look and see if there's anything hinky about it. There's food in the fridge and we'll pick up dinner on the way back from your apartment. Oh, and there are clean sweats in my dresser if you want to wear something different."

Johanna nodded. Collier's pager vibrated and he slipped it out of its plastic holder. She watched as he pushed the buttons. A frown came over his face.

"That's really bad news."

"What's the message?" Johanna asked.

Collier looked at the little screen again.

"The Eagle has landed."

◆ ◆ ◆

Amanda Wingfield picked up her office phone on the second ring. "Cutter Clinic International Desk. This is Amanda. May I help you?"

A smile came to her face when she recognized the voice on the other end. "Trip, darlin'," she said. "I hear you're keeping our residents out 'til all hours of the night. Even our staff is late coming in today. Who knew you were such a party boy?"

"No wonder they threw you guys out of Abu Dhabi," Collier replied. "The Cutter Clinic staff really knows how to get down."

Amanda chortled. "I'll have you know I did the invitations for that reception, Trip honey. I'd say they average age of the invitees was about sixty-three. Were you in on any of the excitement?"

"I left early," Collier replied. "Listen, I need a favor, Amanda."

"You mean crossing your path with that lovely girl Johanna wasn't enough?"

"I need a different kind of favor this time."

Amanda listened as Collier explained, nodding her head occasionally and jotting notes on a small day-glo orange Post- It pad. Her expression grew more concerned the longer she listened.

"I'd ask Dr. el-Hamini, but he hasn't arrived yet,"Amanda said.

"I would prefer you didn't mention this to Dr. el-Hamini," Collier replied. "I, I don't want to get Jo -, Dr. Roberson in trouble."

"I have to say, Trip, this is all very cloak and dagger, if you'll excuse the expression. But all right, sugar. I'll just call the Device Lab and tell them it's for one of the staff. But if any Shinola hits the fan you damn well better have my back. Do we have ourselves an understanding?"

"I promise I will have your rather magnificent b ack," Collier said.

Amanda's face brightened. "Give me at least two hours and then stroll by my desk when you see that nobody's waiting. OK?"

"Tennessee Williams would be proud, Ms. Wingfield," Collier said. "You may expect a gentleman caller."

Amanda hung up the phone and tapped her pen rapidly on the desk. She had never known el-Hamini to miss a scheduled day of work and, as far as she could remember, he had never arrived late. She was about to call his home when her phone rang again. She repeated her scripted greeting and listened.

"Why yes, in fact I just hung up with him." She listened for several more seconds. "I told him to give me two hours," she said. "All right, shug. I'll see you then."

◆ ◆ ◆

Collier dialed the apartment. After the phone ring twice he pressed the "End Call" button. Then he hit "Redial". Johanna picked up on the third ring.

"Agent Collier's secret lair," she said brightly.

"Very funny," Collier replied. "I just wanted to make sure you were OK."

"No you didn't," Johanna said. "You wanted to make sure I was still here. If I didn't answer the phone you would have called my apartment next, wouldn't you?" Collier chuckled loud enough for her to hear it. "Do you really think I would disobey a direct order from a federal agent?"

"Better not," Collier said. "Are you finding anything to keep busy?" He was drumming his fingers on the desk.

"I'm downloading 'Coma' from Netflix," Johanna said. "I've never seen it"

"It's a good movie," Collier replied. "Michael Douglas looks like a kid. Anyway, I think Amanda is going to help us out. I'll know more later. Did you call in sick?"

"I have already called The Cutter Clinic. I hung up just before you checked in on me."

"Good," he said. "Just chill for a few hours and I'll let you know what I come up with. Enjoy the movie."

"I'm sure I will," Johanna said and clicked off the wireless handset. She put down the phone and rummaged in his closet for a baseball cap, finally unearthing a crumpled Mariners' hat from beneath a pile of t-shirts. It was a fitted cap and just a little large for her, but that worked even better, she decided. She found his Wayfarers in a leather box by the door. They were tortoise-shell frames, she noticed, just like her own pair. She cleaned the lenses with the waistband of the sweatshirt and tucked them in its marsupial pouch. Then she searched the apartment for her keys, finally locating them in the little sunroom, beneath her carefully folded slacks and sweater. She was glad she'd opted for her weathered Top-Siders the night before rather than the dressier but less functional espadrilles.

Johanna looked at the clock and made some rough time calculations in her head. She picked up the remote control and hit the "Play" button. She intended to be back before Genevieve Bujold's character developed appendicitis.

◆ ◆ ◆

Collier had tried to leave the office several times but with almost eerie precision his phone had rung or his pager had gone off before he could get out the door. The last call had come from Travis Hsu.

"We finally made a breakthrough at the County Recorder's Office," the detective said. "Seems one Mister Golden B. Paul recently sold a twenty-two foot O'DAY cruiser and trailer to one Mister Michael A. Constantine for the princely sum of eighteen large plus taxes. Sorry, Trip. You want me to call your girlfriend?"

"I will and she's not," Collier replied. His sense of humor, he realized, had evaporated much earlier in the day. "Where's the boat now?"

"They matched the trailer to the one I marked down at the Don Armeni ramps," Hsu replied. "The CG wants it out of their yard ASAP. Technically it's material to an MPU investigation and it does now have a trailer so it's going to the Impound as soon as I can get a wagon with a hitch over to get it. Once the case is closed I guess we'll release it to next of kin."

Collier had a troubled look on his face. "Can you get me in to the Impound to have a look at it?"

"Why do you want to look at it?"

"I'll tell you when we get there. When can I meet you?"

"In an hour. Drive your own car. A government ride will spook them and they'll start asking questions." Hsu paused. "I'm assuming you don't want them asking questions, right?"

"Hai, shikan," Collier replied.

"That's Japanese, you asshole," Hsu chided. "You know that I'm Chinese."

"You cops all look alike to me," Collier shot back. "See you in an hour."

Johanna had the cab let her off three blocks from her apartment. The Lower Queen Anne neighborhood was quiet at midmorning and she noticed a few passing cars and fewer pedestrians. School was out but on her street there were few children. Many of the homes had been subdivided into putative apartments, often with the addition of ugly second or separate entrances. Johanna's downstairs neighbor, Flossie, was a retired obstetrical nurse who had logged forty years at Virginia Mason Hospital. It occurred to her that Flossie may have helped deliver Trip Collier into this world. She also owned the house and so she was, in addition to being neighbor and friend, Johanna's landlord. Flossie had made it a point to rent only to young doctors-in-training, a strategy which had kept the upstairs flat continuously occupied for the last ten years with trouble-free tenants who were often gone or, when home, unconscious from exhaustion. Johanna thought Flossie was showing signs of early Alzheimer's but, the way she looked at it, at least the woman was pleasantly demented.

There was a small common vestibule which enclosed their separate front doors. Johanna approached the house from its back side and walked along the narrow flagstone path, fumbling for her keys. She saw Flossie sitting in her small parlor and waved to her. As she drew her key to fit it into the lock, the other front door opened.

"Oh, you just missed him, dear," Flossie said. She was cradling a tumbler of orange juice which Johanna knew was laced with at least a shot and a half of vodka.

"Missed who?" Johanna asked.

"The man with the package," Flossie answered. Her gray hair was long and unfettered and the breeze tousled it across her forehead.

"I don't think I was expecting a package," Johanna said. "Did he leave it with you?"

Flossie shook her head. "No. I tried to get him to but he said you had to sign for it."

"Was it FedEx or UPS?" Johanna asked. Flossie looked at her quizzically. "Did he have a uniform on?" Flossie wasn't processing, she could tell. "What did it say on the delivery truck?"

Flossie smiled, finally understanding. "He didn't come in a truck. I watched him take the package and get back in his car. Must be a private courier. Would you like some juice? Oh and I have some pound cake that I just made."

Johanna gave her a frozen smile. On the back of her neck, she realized, the tiny hairs were standing at attention. "Thanks, Flossie," she said. "I just came home to get my phone and my beeper. If the man comes back with the package will you call me right away on my cell phone?"

Flossie hesitated. "Do I have it written down?" she asked.

"My number is in your cell phone, remember? Just push down on the number two button and hold it. That will speed dial my phone. OK?" Johanna put her key in the lock and turned it.

"Should I open the package if he leaves it?" Flossie asked.

"No, Flossie. Don't open the package. Just call me if he comes back. Number two on your cell phone, got it?"

"Got it," Flossie replied as Johanna opened her door and stepped inside. "Sure you don't want the pound cake?"

Chapter 26

"LOOKS LIKE YOU KNOW your way around a sailboat," Hsu said.

"It was a required class in law school," Collier replied as he examined the lifeline's truncated end. "Right after tax evasion, insider trading and country club manners. The legal stuff actually only takes a year, you know. The rest of the time is spent learning all of the rich, white guy shit."

"I can see now why you went to work for the government, Collier, and not one of the big firms," Hsu said with mock derision.

Collier held the end of the lifeline in his hand. "Look like it snapped to you?"

Hsu pushed his glasses up on his forehead and bent closer.

"Ever heard of bifocals?" Collier asked.

"Yeah, for old guys," Hsu answered. Collier held the line at different angles as he examined it.

"If it broke, wouldn't it-"

"Unravel," Collier interrupted. "This is still tightly braided. That would only happen if it was-"

"Cut," Hsu said quickly.

Collier dropped the line onto the deck. "The Coast Guard was looking for an accident, so that's what they found, Travis. Do you have any of that yellow tape you guys like so much?"

Hsu laughed. "Crime Scene tape?" he asked. Collier nodded. "There's probably some around here. You want me to-"

"Just so nobody else contaminates this scene."

"Trip, to have a Crime Scene, buddy, it usually helps to have a crime to go with it. An unfrayed lifeline is a little light on probable cause."

Collier looked fore and aft. "There's something more here, I guarantee it. Just rope it off. I don't care, make something up. If I don't have anything by four o'clock you can take it down. Deal?"

Hsu looked unconvinced but shrugged his shoulders. "The guy is still missing," he said. "Without a corpse I've still got some latitude. I can leave it isolated until tomorrow without much problem."

Collier looked at the lifeline lying on the deck. "Call me if you don't hear from me," he said. "I'm starting to get a really bad feeling about all this."

◆ ◆ ◆

Johanna sat in the rear seat of the taxi. "Where we go to?" the driver asked. She looked at his name and picture on the partition.

"Where are you from?" Johanna asked.

"Chicago," the driver replied.

"Before Chicago," she said.

"I am from Sudan. Where we go to? I have to start meter."

Johanna's first instinct had been to call Collier. But she knew he would recognize her cell or apartment phone number and know she was out and about. She thought about returning to his condominium but she decided to stick with her original plan. The packaging on the devices wasn't important, she knew. There must be something about the devices themselves. Collier would have no idea what to look for. But she would.

"The Cutter Clinic," she said.

"Main entrance?"

Johanna thought for a moment. "No, she said, "Parking garage."

He should have locked the old woman in her basement, Hajiik thought as he watched the two of them converse. He was surprised when another taxi arrived and the girl got in. He had positioned himself to take her when she went to her car. Now he was scrambling to find the cab without drawing attention to himself. Hajiik looked at his watch. He had very little time and still much to do.

◆ ◆ ◆

Collier sat in his car. He thought about calling Johanna again but decided it was too soon. He took his phone and punched in the FBI direct number. "Charley Higgins, please. Agent Collier, DHS calling."

It took almost a minute until Higgins came on the line.

"Charley, you got five minutes?"

"I'm trying to bolt early today, Trip. I got Mariner's tickets. Twinight doubleheader tonight down at Safeco."

"Who are they playing?" Collier asked.

"Orioles," Higgins replied. "I know, don't say it."

"Consider it not said," Collier replied. "I got your text. Can I come to your office? I need to run something by you."

"You got al-Zawahiri?"

"Yeah, found him in his hidey-hole," Collier quipped. "Can't believe you guys didn't look there. Seriously, we may need to do some inter-agency sharing. Maybe off the grid. Can you help me?"

"I'm always better if I'm incentivized," Higgins answered.

Collier tapped his fingers on the steering wheel, debating the price of admission. "OK," he said. "Interleague series with the Nationals, last week in July. Inside dope says Strasburg's pitching at least one of the games. Two tickets, Row One, halfway down the third-base line on the aisle. Incentivized yet?"

"When can you be here?"

"I'm parked downstairs. Give me four minutes."

Hajiik watched the taxi glide to a stop. The girl got out and, while she stood by the driver's side window to pay the fare, Hajiik pulled into a curbside parking place. He watched as she glanced around and headed into the shadows of the garage entrance marked "Physician Parking Only". He paced himself to keep her in view while trying to avoid her sightlines as she looked behind her every few steps. After a few minutes Hajiik saw the entrance door toward which she was heading. His clothing, he realized would stand out even if he were able to filch a long white coat. He would need to find paper coveralls or, preferably, a scrub suit. But that would mean letting her out of his sight. He wouldn't have to search the whole hospital to find her, he reasoned. She would be going to the cluster of offices where the cardiac doctors were. He was certain of it. Hajiik stopped, standing behind a concrete column. When he heard the entry door open and then bang shut he started moving again.

◆ ◆ ◆

"When did you say that series was?" Charley Higgins asked.

"End of July," Collier replied. "I can't remember the exact dates. Thursday through Saturday. Five games, I think."

"Consider me highly incentivized, brother agent. How can the Bureau be of service?"

Collier truly liked Higgins. It was more than the natural affinity that athletes tended to have for one another, he thought. Higgins was an impressively built African-American who had the distinction of having been not only an All-Pac 10 defensive end but also an accomplished oboist. He had been a featured soloist with the Seattle Symphony Orchestra on several occasions. Only a recent diagnosis of early rheumatoid arthritis had curtailed his musical avocation. He wore a neatly trimmed goatee which, in its graying, contrasted elegantly with his skin. Collier decided to start off with common ground.

"I got your text," Collier said and raised his eyebrows. "It makes us look a little foolish that we didn't know he was here."

Higgins gave a dismissive wave. "Nobody knew he was here," he said. "Nobody would still know he was here if he hadn't gotten ticketed for talking on a cell phone while driving on the I-5 in Oregon."

Collier laughed. "And what, he told the trooper, 'You can't ticket me, I am The Eagle'?"

"Not quite," Higgins responded with a chuckle. "But get this – he got a Washington DL as Miguel Aquila. Get it – Aquila? Greek for Eagle"

"It's Latin, actually," Collier said. "There's no 'q' or 'qu' combination in the Greek alphabet."

"OK, Latin. Geez, I hate talking to anyone from a Jesuit institution. You're all so goddamned-"

"Pedantic?"

"See? My point exactly," Higgins said. "Anyway, the trooper made a note that he didn't look like a Miguel Aquila and that bit of information pinged in the Bureau database."

"The database does Latin translations?"

"I'm sure if I put 'Collier' in the database it would come up with 'insufferable asshole' in four languages," Higgins said. "The database computer makes IBM's Watson look like your dad's first Atari."

"Where do we think he is?" Collier asked.

"He was heading north on the 5, so we assume he's in the Seattle environs. The address he gave the DOL is – surprise – a vacant lot. He's had the license for close to a year, so if there's something afoot, he's been sitting pretty tight."

"That's a mixed metaphor," Collier interjected, uncrossing and then recrossing his legs.

"I'm becoming less incentivized by the minute, here," Higgins said and pointed to his watch. "Just so you know."

Collier uncrossed his legs again and leaned forward, resting his wrists on the bullnosed front lip of Higgins cherrywood desk. "I think there's a medical scam going on at The Cutter Clinic. I think it's big enough that some people have gotten hurt over it."

Higgins dropped his shoulder. "Medicare fraud belongs to the Office of the Inspector General. You know that, Trip."

Collier leaned in further, the angle of his elbows going from obtuse to acute. "I don't think this is Medicare fraud, Charley, and the OIG only has domestic authority. This involves foreign nationals from the Arabian Peninsula and, by necessity, their money. I cleared some of these guys for entry myself. On the surface it doesn't look like much, but I'm starting to wonder."

Higgins massaged his brow, "Some guys taking flight simulator lessons didn't look like much either," he said in a weary tone. 'I can't take your tickets unless I can do something for you. And I *really* want those tickets. What is it you need?"

"All these patients had these pacemaker/defibrillator things put in by one doctor – Seljuk el-Hamini. He's been at The Cutter since it opened here, but I can't find much else on him. Bio sketch says he was born in western Afghanistan but apparently went to medical school in Baghdad during the glory days of the Ba'ath Party."

Higgins was busy writing notes on a legal pad. "Do you have the names of the patients you cleared?" he asked.

"I'll stop by the office when I leave here and e-mail them to you," Collier replied. Then he stood up. "The Cutter doctor, a resident, who sniffed this out, seems to have disappeared in a boating accident on the Sound. He told another resident, a woman doctor, about it and now she's had a near-miss encounter."

Higgins tilted his head and looked at Collier. "This woman doctor, is she, perhaps, of some personal interest to you?"

Collier tucked his chin and smiled. "It's early yet," he said. "I'd appreciate it if you could help me."

Higgins tore off the sheet he had been writing on, folded it in thirds and tucked it in the inside pocket of his sport jacket. "First pitch is scheduled for four-fifteen," he said.

Collier looked at his own watch. "I'll try to call you before that. Thanks, Charley."

Higgins waved him off. "You did say Row One, right?"

"Yeah," Collier replied. "Make sure you bring your glove."

Chapter 27

JOHANNA WAITED UNTIL TWO Women in matching blue cloth burqas wandered away from Amanda's desk before entering the warren of glass-enclosed cubicles. Amanda looked up as she approached and then laughed.

"If that's supposed to be a disguise, sugar, it is definitely not working."

Johanna doffed the baseball cap and the Ray-Bans. "I'm supposed to be sick, remember? Did you get the packages Agent Collier wanted?"

"Yessss," Amada answered testily. "I had to ask that squirrely Tipton-Kohler for them. Lord, he asked a million questions. Like I was asking to borrow the Hope Diamond you would have thought." She reached under her desk and brought out a green eco-tote bag with the name of a liquor store emblazoned on its side and set it next to her credenza. "Stand here for a few minutes and talk to me," Amanda instructed. "Then just pick it up when you walk out. What does he want them for?"

"He wants to get the packaging translated, for some reason."

"What does he think is on there?" Amanda asked. "Coded messages from the Taliban?"

Johanna laughed. "I have no idea," she lied. "When do you need them back?"

Amanda looked at her calendar display. "They do supposedly random electronic inventory checks, but I figured it out one time. It's always the number of the month of the year plus sixteen. So that's," she tapped the screen, "by Monday."

"OK, Johanna said. "I'll let Agent Collier know."

"You're awfully formal for a woman who's wearing the man's sweatshirt, dear."

Johanna looked down at her chest. "Zags Athletics XXL" was printed on the front. She decided to say nothing.

"You know there are two different devices, right?" Amanda asked.

"Different?"

"Trip wanted one of the protocol devices, with the Arabic writing, and the identical device that we use from our U.S. vendor. Didn't he tell you?"

"If he did, I forgot," Johanna lied. "Anyway, thanks. I'll probably see you tomorrow. I'm betting on a miraculous recovery from my illness."

"A little something hanging over?" Amanda asked with a wink.

"You could say that," Johanna replied. She picked up the tote bag, put the cap and sunglasses back on and walked out.

Hajiik watched her as she left the office. The lab coat he'd lifted from a hook outside the surgery department was a little tight but it would do. Its owner had been kind enough to leave his ID badge attached. Hajiik turned it around and re-clipped it to the breast pocket. This was done, he noticed, by many of the employees who apparently did not want their name or photograph easily viewed. He'd taken one of the bouffant polypropylene scrub hats and put it on. The surgical mask he left dangling below his chain. It would look odd, he knew, to have it covering his face outside of the operating theater. The Cutter Clinic's interior floor plan was expansive and he had no trouble following her from a safe distance. He was surprised when she did not take the right turn for the marble corridor that led to the main entrance. He followed, keeping his head down but his eyes up. She passed by the large double doors marking the Dugoni Family Invasive Cardiology Laboratory Suites. Whatever was in the bag was somewhat heavy, he noted, and she switched her carrying hand several times. She slowed as she approached a hallway intersection, then abruptly turned right. Hajiik looked at the sign suspended overhead; "General Radiology". He watched her hit the power button and the metal doors opened outward toward her. She walked inside. Hajiik stayed where he was until the doors closed. He surveyed the parallel hallways for an alternate entrance or exit. Finding none, he returned to a small row of four connected wooden chairs. On a table were several journals and magazines. He picked up one of the journals and sat down. Peering over the top of *The Lancet*, Hajiik waited for the girl to return.

Johanna breezed past the receptionist and worked her way past the bustling techs and into the control room where she spied a familiar face.

"Hey Connie," Johanna asked. "I need a favor. Can you help me?"

The woman wore a heavy leaded apron which made a swishing sound when she walked.

"Hi, Dr. Roberson," she said. "What do you need?"

"I have to do a presentation on arrhythmia devices and I'm way behind. I wanted to have an x-ray taken of two of the devices side by side for my PowerPoint presentation." She hoisted up the tote bag. "Can you image these and give me a digital version as a .jpg file? Then I can copy and paste it into my presentation." Johanna lifted the two packages out of the tote.

"Do you want them out of the packages?" Connie asked

"No," Johanna replied. It's just plastic and paper. Just shoot right through them."

Connie looked at the white scheduling board. "We're supposed to be getting a PA and lateral chest right now, but the floor says the lady is vomiting so we might have to do it portable. "Here," she said, motioning with her fingers. "I'll run them real quick. We can look at the pictures on the digital monitor and you can see if it's what you want. You need them separate or side by side?"

"Side by side would be perfect. Thanks, Connie."

The woman took the packages containing the devices and disappeared around a corner. Johanna nodded to some of the milling techs and waited by the image monitor.

After a few minutes Connie returned and handed the devices back to Johanna. "I never did just a device before," she said. "I had to guess on the kV settings." She glided a wireless mouse over a pad that, Johanna noticed, was imprinted like a Ouija Board. She clicked on several files in rapid succession. "There you go," Connie said.

Johanna looked up. The devices were centered perfectly in the frame. The packaging appeared like a watery outline around each one. Johanna was startled as she studied the internal circuitry the cathode rays revealed. She'd seen enough x-rays to know something was way different in the protocol devices

"OK?" Connie asked hopefully.

"Yeah," Johanna said. "Perfect." She was thinking that, if what she was looking at was what she thought it was, she needed to call Collier right away. "Thanks. Is there something I can save them to?"

"I can e-mail them to you if you're on the system," Connie answered. "Or," she opened a small drawer and rummaged around, "I can download them to a stick and you can take it with you." She held up a small, black flash drive with The Cutter Clinic logo imprinted on it.

"Put it on the flash drive," Johanna said. "Then I can take it home and work on it."

Connie put the drive in the USB hub next to the monitor. After several mouse clicks she pulled out the drive, capped it and handed it to Johanna.

"Send the bill to Dr. McCarthy," Johanna said. She dumped the devices back into the tote bag and threaded her way out toward the door.

Trip Collier sat in his office and looked at the list he had typed into the e-mail for Higgins. Something about it was bothering him. After going through it several times he finally hit upon what was odd: it was their ages. A quick tumble of numbers in his head gave them an average age of twenty-nine. The average age of the 9/11 hijackers was twenty-six, he knew. And every year of age, he'd learned in an FBI course he'd taken as part of the JTF, decreased the chances of being caught by one per-cent. But being caught at what? Why would younger men knowingly submit to a medical procedure none of them needed? The wheels were turning in his head, Collier realized, but the train was going nowhere.

Collier clicked the "Send" icon and pushed back in his chair. He was certain el-Hamini had been thoroughly vetted by The Cutter and he didn't expect Higgins to come up with much in the way of new material. If there was key, he thought, it was whatever tied together the patients who were walking around with the brand new devices in their chests. Collier looked at the clock and punched in the number for The Cutter Clinic.

"Amanda Wingfield, please. She's at the International Desk."

"One moment while I find that extension," a Jamaican accented voice replied. There was a short pause. "T'ank you for waiting," the voice continued. "I'll connect you now. And have a nice day."

Collier half-expected her to say "mon", but she didn't. He waited for Amanda to pick up. He let her finish her scripted greeting. "Hi, Amanda, it's Collier," he said. "Running a little later than I thought. What are you doing right now?"

"Well, darling, I was just reading on MSN about this poor man down in Oregon who got crushed by a grape press at one of the wineries. That would certainly spoil the vintage, I suppose."

"One would assume," Collier answered. "Were you able to get what I asked for?"There was silence on the line. "Amanda, did you get the devices."

"Well of course, I did, sugar. Didn't you talk to Johanna?"

"Johanna? Dr. Roberson?"

"I believe there is only one Johanna that we are mutually acquainted with," Amanda replied somewhat impatiently. "She was here less than an hour ago to pick them up just like you told her to. You men never listen to us when it's import-."

"Johanna is at The Cutter?" Collier asked, sitting upright in his chair now.

"Well she was forty minutes ago," Amanda replied.

"Is she still there?"

"I have no idea. Please don't tell me you didn't send her to pick them up."

"No, I didn't," Collier said. "Is Dr. el-Hamini in?"

"He didn't come in today," Amanda replied. "I haven't been able to get hold of him. Trip, honey, I took a risk getting those devices for you. I don't know what Dr. Johanna is up to, but the two of you need to get your act together."

Collier's mind was racing, trying to decide what to do next. "We will," he finally answered. "If you see Johanna again, tell her I'm on my way over to The Cutter and she should wait for me in your office."

"If is see her, I will" Amanda said. "Oh, and Trip, darlin'?"

"Yeah?"

"She looked awful cute wearing your clothes, sugar."

Tamal Hajiik could not help but marvel at the opulence The Cutter Clinic presented in every one of its public spaces. The staircases, the chandeliers and hanging art creations, the wall art – it rivaled the Baghdad palaces in every regard. He almost lost her at one turn because he was looking at a stunning crystal and stained-glass mobile suspended above the foyer of the Cardiovascular Institute. She seemed intent on getting somewhere specific, he thought as dogged her trail. He watched as she skirted the main entrance to the cardiac offices and slipped down a side hallway. He counted off the seconds after she ducked into a paneled door and disappeared. Then he went in after her.

Trip Collier smiled as pleasantly as he could to the milling patrons in The Cutter Clinic's main lobby. It looked like the General Assembly of the United Nations, he thought as he angled his shoulders to avoid a never-ending line of oncoming patients, soon-to-be-patients and entourages. As he turned off the main corridor his pager buzzed. Collier stepped into a small alcove and checked it. The message was from Charley Higgins. "CK UR PHONE" was all it said. The overhead chandeliers and the outside light bouncing off the marble made the screen on his phone difficult to see. Collier spied a sign for the men's restroom and ducked inside. He was shocked to see that, along with all the other amenities, The Cutter Clinic had thoughtfully supplied a bathroom attendant.

"Goo'day, sir," the man said. He was ancient and, if Collier had to guess, looked to be of Mongolian descent. Collier walked to the one of the urinals and made a pretense of emptying his bladder. He rinsed his hands under the copper faucet and looked for the paper towel dispenser. The old man offered him a pressed and folded towel. Collier dried his hands and exited wondering if he was supposed to tip him. A few steps down the hall he saw a small door marked "Chapel" and underneath it, "All Faiths Welcome". Collier peeked through the stained glass panel and saw no one inside. It was mercifully dark when he pushed through the wooden door and sat down. Reflexively he made the sign of the cross although there was not a crucifix in sight. He withdrew the iPhone from his jacket pocket and keyed up the recent messages. Higgins was at the top of the list. He selected the message which read simply, "Our 'aquiline' friend." Then he opened the attached picture file. Collier drew in a quick breath and looked at the picture again. Collier recognized the face who stared unsmiling into the Washington State Department of Licensing's camera. It was the man he had bumped into coming out of the men's room the previous evening at the Space Needle. He felt his pulse quicken and knew from experience that he was shifting into a state his lacrosse teammates used to call, with some admiration, "overdrive."

Time seemed to take on a different dimension as Collier rose from the padded pew and walked toward the door. Along the back wall of the chapel Christian iconography he hadn't noticed before stood out in sharp relief. He saw there was a small crucifix with a painted Christ oozing from his wounds above the door. To the left was a woodcut of St. George slaying the dragon. Collier felt for his sidearm with one hand and opened the chapel door with the other. Once back in the hallway he punched the speed dial button for his apartment.

Johanna weaved her way through the back hallways that crisscrossed the Interventional Cardiology laboratories. A few rooms were running, she noticed, but as she moved deeper into the labyrinth, they were mostly dark and empty. She felt for her ID in the sweatshirt's pouch in case she ran into anyone. Arriving at the Device Laboratories she saw that all three rooms were dark. There was a soft glow in the empty control room from the multiple power and status lights. Johanna pushed the automatic door button and went in.

Collier had abandoned calling his apartment after the fifth attempt. The he called Amanda.

"She's wearing your clothes and you don't have her phone number?"

"I need her cell phone number," Collier replied somewhat impatiently. "I think she might be in trouble."

There was a short pause and then Amanda said, "What kind of trouble? Is it because I gave her those-"

"I think she might be in danger, Mandy," Collier said as calmly as he could. "If she's still here I need to find her. Can you overhead page her or something?'

"In his infinite wisdom," she replied, "The Cutter CEO, I believe it was Dr. Poole at the time, decided that this facility would be the first completely 'wired' hospital in the country and made no provisions for the use of overhead paging."

"I don't think she has her pager," Collier said. "I really need her cell number."

"Stay on the line," Amanda said firmly. "I'll have it for you in thirty seconds.

Hajiik had lost her on the last turn. A nurse in one of the hallways had stopped him to ask if he knew where Dr. el-Hamini was today. "In Hell where he belongs," he had wanted to say but remarked only that el-Hamini was "not feeling very well at the moment." The nurse seemed to want to chat so Hajiik had feigned receiving a page by reaching for his left hip and grasping the dagger that bulged under the lab coat. If she kept talking, Hajiik decided, it would not be a pager she saw next. The nurse nodded, said something Hajiik could not hear and bustled off. He moved slowly in the partially lit corridors. The laboratory rooms, he noticed, had wire reinforced glass on the side which fronted each of the control rooms. The laboratory doors themselves had only a single, narrow wire-reinforced glass panel. He moved from room to room, pausing whenever he saw a shadow or heard voices. She could have passed through and exited on another side, he reasoned, but something told him she had not.

Johanna's cell phone chimed for the seventh time. She had booted up the control room computer without any difficulty but was having trouble finding a USB port for the flash drive. She had taken the defibrillator devices out of Amanda's tote and placed them on the counter in front of her. If nothing else, the one with the Arabic packaging was noticeably heavier than its counterpart. If she was right, Johanna thought, it would be the least important of the differences. Finally she found the port. She uncapped the little black stick and looked for the USB icon on it to tell here which way it went in. It slipped easily into the port and tiny green diode glowed once and winked out. When her cell phone chimed again she slipped it out of the sweatshirt and stared at it. It was Collier's number. She scrolled through and saw that the seven previous calls had also been from him. Johanna held the phone in her left hand and worked the optical mouse with her right. There were so many desktop icons on the monitor screen she had a hard time finding what she was looking for. Finally she located the icon for the USB drive and clicked twice. The monitor glowed, illuminating her face in the darkened room.

"Where the fuck are you?" Collier said without preamble.

"Well that's real nice," Johanna shot back.

"I know you're not at my apartment. Are you here?"

"What do you mean, 'here'?"

"At The Cutter, Johanna. We really don't have time for this shit."

"What is wrong with you, Collier? You're being a total asshole."

"Fine. You can dump me later. Right now you need to tell me exactly where you are and then you need to hide."

Johanna snorted. "Hide? Why would I need to hide?" A sound out in the hallway caught her attention. She rose up and looked around but saw nothing. She relaxed back in the chair and held the phone up to her ear again. "I'm just looking at some x-rays of those devices. As long as you're here you should really come and take a-"

"Just tell me where you are, turn off any lights and hide. Do it now, Johanna."

Something in his tone set her skin tingling. "I'm in the Control Room in Device Laboratory Number Three," she said. "But I don't understand why I-"

"OK. Find a closet. Find a crawlspace. Find a laundry hamper. I don't care, just hide and don't come out until I get to you. You need to do it now, OK?"

Johanna looked carefully at the x-ray images on her screen while he spoke. The devices were identical in size and shape, she could see that. But the internal components were completely different. Johanna didn't know what the protocol device was but, she thought, it sure as hell wasn't a defibrillator. She pushed the power button and the monitor display went dark. "OK," she said, "But this seems really stu-"

"Now!" Collier barked.

Chapter 28

SULEIMAN BAHAN WAITED PATIENTLY, a Cutter Clinic complimentary tote bag slung over one shoulder. A collective groan had gone up when he was pulled from the line after passing through the RapidScan whole body scanner at the Los Angeles Airport. He maintained a pleasant smile and nodded to the passengers in the security line behind him. Bahan held up his hands in the universal "What can I do?" gesture. Several people shrugged their shoulders in sympathetic response. A small girl with dark eyes was staring at him. He smiled at her and gave her a finger-flexing wave. She skittered behind her mother's legs and then peered out along the mother's hip, giving him a shy smile in return.

The TSA officers, he noticed, had broken from their huddle and were approaching him. "I'm sorry, sir," a sallow young man with a fierce overbite said. "We'll need to perform an enhanced pat-down. Do you have an implanted medical device, sir?"

Bahan nodded. "Yes, sir, I most certainly do."

"Would you happen to have some sort of paperwork for this device?"

Bahan feigned perplexion. "Paperwork? I'm sorry," he said, "I do not. Unless you mean this." Bahan reached into his pocket and withdrew a small blue and white card with English and Arabic writing on one side and several sets of alphanumerics on the other. He handed the card to the officer who flipped it back and forth in his hand several times.

"We're going to have you step over here if you don't mind," the young man said.

"Not at all," Bahan replied. "My safety is your priority."

Collier finally located the Interventional Cardiology suites just as his cell phone rang. He hoped it was Johanna telling him she was tucked away somewhere but was surprised to see it was Charley Higgins. Collier kept moving as he talked.

"Trip?"

"Yeah, Charley, what have you got?"

"Trip, I can hardly hear you. Where are you?"

"Inside The Cutter Clinic," Collier replied. He moved toward an open space with a huge skylight overhead. "Better?"

"Yeah, that's better," Higgins replied. "You wanted to know about el-Hamini?"

"You found something?"

"Not on him. The guy's pure as the driven sand. Funny thing about his wife and daughter though. They left for Afghanistan two years ago. Their travel application was for a two week visit and then a direct return. Apparently they never came back."

Collier pondered. "So they're still in Afghanistan? Johanna said he was leaving to meet them later this week."

"Who's Johanna?" Higgins asked.

"A friend of mine. She's a doctor at The Cutter. So they never came back, and...?"

"Well, here's the thing," Higgins continued. "They apparently never got to Afghanistan. They were supposed to change planes in Damascus but never boarded their connecting flight."

"That's not good," Collier said. His eyes darted as he talked, scanning the legions of passers-by.

"It gets worse," Higgins said. "We ran el-Hamini's phone logs. As far as we can tell there's no communication from them after they deplaned in Syria. No, 'hey we got here OK' or 'the flight's delayed', the kind of stuff you would expect. Was she leaving him?"

"Boy, I didn't get that at all," Collier said.

"The other thing," Higgins went on, "is that not long after communication from the wife and daughter stops, el-Hamini starts getting a number of unidentified calls – all from prepaid cell phones in the Seattle area. The numbers change about every three or four weeks but they don't stop. There was a flurry of them this week, especially yesterday. I'm trying to run the latest one down, but you know how that is going to turn out."

"It's in a dumpster somewhere," Collier agreed. "So what are you thinking?"

"It would fit a kidnap scenario," Higgins said. "So we checked el-Hamini's banking and credit accounts. He direct-deposited every one of his paychecks in legitimate U.S. accounts and there hasn't been an attempt to transfer even low level amounts of money out of the country. And there are no large or consistent cash withdrawals either that would make you think ransom payment."

"So what are we talking here, Charley?"

"Makes you wonder, Trip. Maybe whoever took the wife and daughter wanted something other than money."

Johanna pondered the choice for a moment then grabbed the package with the heavier device. She looked around the control room and realized there was really no place to conceal herself there. She stepped out into the small hallway and pulled open the large metal door to the laboratory suite itself. The equipment and linen cabinets were all of the small, ergonomic design favored in newer hospitals. She let the laboratory door swing closed against her hand and then guided it shut so it wouldn't clang. Without ambient light from the hallway, the large room was very dark. The ceiling mounted gantry that held the fluoroscope camera was positioned at the head end of the patient table. The control panel that governed its movements glowed with tiny amber and red LED's. Johanna heard a faint thud somewhere outside the room. She glanced through the Control Room window. A sliver of light was slowly illuminating the floor. The rear egress door, she realized, was being opened.

Hajiik pushed the door only as far as it took to slide his slender frame through. He approached the Control Desk and saw the device package in front of the bank of blank monitors and display screens. Glancing through the large rectangular window in front of him he saw only the darkened shapes of mechanical equipment. He edged closer to the desk. The package was for a defibrillator device manufactured by an American company called Guidant.

He assumed that wherever she was she might have a similar package that belonged to him. A sound from a source he couldn't immediately locate caused him to cease any movement. Hajiik cocked his head to one side and scanned his environs. When he didn't hear footsteps or the sound of a door opening, he relaxed. Then, out of the corner of his eye, he thought he saw a shadow flicker on the other side of the heavy glass.

Collier had taken a wrong turn, he knew. He backtracked and turned left down a small service corridor. For a bustling medical center in the middle of the day, this section was eerily dark and quiet. He passed doors marked "EP TESTING 1" and "EP TESTING 2." The corridor dead-ended but there was a sign indicating that the Device Laboratories were to the right. Collier turned the corner carefully, looking for movement. Seeing none, he advanced slowly, keeping his back to the wall.

Johanna waited for the intermittent hum of a cooling fan on one of the pieces of imaging equipment and then took several deep breaths. She had positioned herself at the far corner of the oversized procedure room with a peephole view of the lab's entry door. She had considered hiding in a slightly larger supply cabinet in one of the room's but realized, if she were discovered, she would have exactly zero options to defend herself or escape. Instead, she had pulled a large gray trash bin in front of her. She fluffed up the red "BioHazard" liner to further conceal her. Several boxes of intravenous fluid containers were stacked on the floor next to her. She hoped these would obscure any view of her feet from the door. Johanna had left a narrow escape route to her right, although where she could escape to, in a closed room, was a matter of some doubt she realized. As she waited in the cool, dark space she had created she briefly wondered why she hadn't just called Security on the phone in the Control Room. Then she reconsidered; she would likely have still been on the phone explaining why she needed Security when the Control Room door had opened. Johanna used her narrow sightline to survey for other options. The large red plastic "Code" button on the far wall caught her attention. It suddenly seemed awfully far away.

Hajiik quickly determined there was no one in the little Control

Room. He peered through the thick glass partition, holding the Glock-9 pistol loosely by his side. The homemade silencer caused it to be a little top-heavy but he had learned to adjust. Hajiik saw that the door just to the left of the glass partition was slightly ajar. He stepped carefully and slowly pushed it open. A vinyl apron at the bottom of the door made a schussing sound as he moved it. He ducked his head quickly around the door to make sure she wasn't behind it then stepped into the narrow hallway. He saw the metal door that, he realized, led to the large laboratory room he had seen through the glass partition. He listened for any hint of movement and then approached it. The door, he noticed, opened toward him He quietly lifted the vertically mounted handle and pulled, opening it only enough to allow him a quick survey of the room's interior.

People acted so foolishly, he thought, once they became prey.

Chapter 29

THE LITTLE GIRL FROM the security line tapped Bahan on the arm. The departure lounge at his gate was crowded but somehow she and her family had taken seats just across from him. She was wearing a white cotton sweater and a tiny faux pearl necklace. At least he thought it was fake. Who knew, he wondered, in this country of unbridled greed and consumption? The little girls in the village he'd grown up in made dolls from sticks and bits of cloth. The boys played soccer with a "ball" made of discarded packing remnants and used duct tape.

"We're going to be on the same plane," the little girl said. Her diction seemed years ahead of her age. "Are you going home?"

"Yes, you could say that," Bahan replied.

"We are, too," the girl replied. "We live in New Jersey."

Bahan blinked and decided to end the conversation. "I hope you have a nice flight," he said, tugging at the collar of his shirt. He wondered why it suddenly seemed so tight.

Trip Collier had passed Device Rooms One and Two, peeked in quickly and kept moving. The hallway was curving to his left and he hugged the wall as he moved. He'd left his shoes and socks by Room One, figuring bare feet gave him stealth and, more importantly, traction on the highly waxed linoleum floor. When he got to the Control Room he noticed that the door was open several inches. He took a breath and eased it toward him.

"Foolish woman," Hajiik said. "You think you are concealed but you are not."

Johanna held her breath and clenched her teeth. Maybe, she thought, he was bluffing.

"Whether you show yourself or not you will soon be just as dead," Hajiik said. "But if you come out I will kill you quickly and mercifully. You should have left well enough alone."

Johanna was expecting to hear a metallic click as his weapon was cocked. When she heard a footstep instead a terrifying thought formed that caused her tightly clenched jaw muscles to tremble: he was going to stab her!

Collier didn't see him at first. The glass partition limited his view of the large door that led into the laboratory. He caught sight of what he assumed was one of the pacemaker device packages sitting on the console. Collier moved slowly toward the desk and the partition window. Wire-reinforced, he noticed. As he took a third step he saw a flash. In the same instant the glass partition disintegrated.

Johanna was certain she'd been shot. The impact pushed her back against the wall. Her backside dropped to the floor, her knees now bent in front of her. She clutched the device package tightly to her chest and pushed herself up. It was then that she saw that the man – was he really another Cutter doctor? – had briefly turned his attention away from her. To her left the floor was covered with hundreds of pieces of shattered glass

Johanna dropped the package in front of her. She took two steps to her right and lunged for the green twinkling light on the fluoroscope camera's control panel. The one, she knew, that directed the movements of the big gantry tower. She pushed hard on the flat toggle-switch. The gantry's motor whirred and the tower moved quickly in its preset arc. The heavy C-arm mounted camera struck the man on the shoulder, knocking him momentarily off balance. Johanna dropped to her hands and knees and scuttled across the floor towards the red Code Button mounted on the far wall. Then she heard Collier's voice.

"Put it down, Hajiik!" Collier shouted through the broken glass and bent wire.

Hajiik turned his attention toward Collier. "It's too late," he said calmly, holding the Glock in front of him. "You kill me. I kill her. It really doesn't matter. Soon the holocaust will begin in the places you tell your people are the most safe. Your precious mirage of national security will be consumed amid the flames, the screams and the odor of burning flesh. The pictures will be seen all over the world within hours and the oppressed will rejoice."

When he had first joined DHS, Collier had taken a seminar deceptively titled "Desperate Situations and Scenarios: A Guide to Optimal Management." One of the discussions, he remembered, had centered on crazies and fanatics and how to exploit their common weaknesses, one of which was a tendency to lose focus while they were shouting jihadist or other revolutionary rhetoric. This thought raced from the hippocampus of Collier's brain, where his long term memory resided, through his dominant left cerebral hemisphere, which managed his conscious thought and impulse control, down to his cerebellum, which stored his learned and reflex movements. It then telegraphed along the motor nerves exiting from his spinal cord and out to the digital flexor muscles in his right hand in less than three-thousandths of a second.

He shot Hajiik in the neck.

Johanna punched the flat disc of theCode Button with the side of her fist and, in the same instant, saw the man crumple. She looked at the shattered window and saw Collier, his gun still trained on the body on the floor.

"You O.K.?" Collier asked without looking at her.

"Yeah," she answered. She was now taking rapid shallow breaths and knew she was on the verge of hyperventilating.

Collier disappeared momentarily and then reappeared at the laboratory door. He placed what she now saw was his bare foot on the man's wrist and then kicked the gun out of his writhing fingers.

Johanna crawled over to the gurgling figure. Blood-tinged foam was coming out of his mouth and his chest was starting to heave. "Nice shootin', Tex," she said. "Give me those white towels over there," she said, pointing to a small table.

"What are you doing?" Collier asked.

"Trying to stabilize him till the Code Team gets here. Then we'll call a Trauma Alert. Get me the towels!"

Johanna tilted Hajiik's chin up which made the gurgling better.

Collier handed her the towels.   Within a few minutes, she knew, there would be the sounds of running feet and trundling medical equipment. "Open that door all the way," Johanna directed, "So they can get their stuff in here."

Johanna pressed the towels to Hajiik's throat where a dark crimson pool was spreading. She looked for bright red arterial spurters but didn't see any. "I think you missed his carotid artery," she said while holding pressure. "Pretty sure you got the jugular, though. Why did you shoot him in the neck?"

"I was aiming for the shoulder of the gun hand," he said. "Must've kicked off the wire reinforcement and deflected up."

Johanna felt on the opposite side of Hajiik's neck for a pulse which, to her surprise, was fairly strong and steady. "He'll make it to surgery," she said. "I don't know about after that." She looked down and saw that Hajiik was trying to speak. A few gurgling syllables of another language were identifiable.

"What's he saying?" Collier asked, still keeping the gun trained on Hajiik.

"It's Arabic," a voice in the doorway said. "He says that it is too late." Johanna looked up and Collier glanced to his left, both shocked to see the source of the statement.

"I pray that he is wrong," el-Hamini said.

Hajiik's eyes widened. He twisted his head to look at el-Hamini and mumbled some wore words but the change in head position only worsened his gurgling.

El-Hamini took a step forward. Collier motioned him to stop. "He says that I am dead," el-Hamini said. "That he saw me dead. And although I stand here, he may very well be right."

Johanna could hear crash carts rumbling and the footfalls getting closer. Doors banged open within earshot. She looked up at el-Hamini. "What's in those pacemakers," she asked. "Are they bombs?"

El-Hamini shook his head. "No," he said quietly. "They are most assuredly not bombs. They are detonators."

Chapter 30

FBI Field Office
Seattle

JOHANNA FUMBLED WITH THE bright orange visitor's badge she had been issued at the front desk. She trailed the group through the last of three metal detectors and two body scanners. When she asked Collier where they were going he told her he'd never seen this section of the FBI building before. They stopped in front of a non-descript looking door which was the only visible break in a long tiled hallway. Above it was a small metal sign which said only "Maintenance Station #4". Charley Higgins turned and looked at Johanna and el-Hamini.

"At Agent Collier's request you are both being allowed to enter this room," Higgins said. "If we were under less pressing time constraints, I would deny his request. But on the off-chance that you may be able to quicken the pace of our search, I am going to allow it. What you are about to see in this room is classified and any revelations you might choose to make about its existence or location would be considered a breach of national security and a violation of not only the Patriot Act but several Executive Orders that would result in your immediate and, I should mention, indeterminate incarceration in a Federal detention facility. Do you both understand?"

The pair nodded and Higgins opened the door. They passed through a small space that reeked of industrial solvents. At the far end Higgins placed his index finger on a small screen mounted on a bare wood beam. A plywood panel with a faded green Weyerhaeuser stamp and several ugly looking knots slid soundlessly to the right. What lay beyond it, Johanna thought once she had entered, looked like something from a movie set.

Dozens of Plexiglas cubicles dotted the tiled floor. The room's perimeter was ringed with monitor screens. Some appeared to Johanna to be radar screens, other were video feeds of constantly shifting locations. Despite the number of men and women working, the room was surprisingly quiet. Higgins led them to a glass-walled conference room where, she saw, a man was already seated at the large table. As they entered Johanna could see that the table was inlaid with laptop computer keyboards. Three large monitor screens were mounted on moveable tables at one end. Johanna laughed when she saw that one of the monitors was displaying a baseball game. The man at the table caught it and gave her a smile.

"We're not total wonks, you know," he said pleasantly.

"What's the score?" Higgins asked as he escorted Collier, el-Hamini and Johanna to their chairs.

"Phillies are killing the Giants," the man replied. "Eight-nothing, top five. Arietta is working on a no-no."

Higgins smiled approvingly. "This is Agent Takashi," he said to Trip and Johanna.

Takashi nodded and, by a means Johanna could not see, clicked off the ball game. Then he addressed them. "As Agent Higgins has I'm sure already told you, we were able, with the list supplied by Agent Collier and Dr. el-Hamini's assistance, to track the twelve individuals who received these devices. My team had a man in deep cover with an unidentified sleeper we now realize" – he paused to clear his throat – "was Tamal Hajiik. That agent failed to meet his check-in deadline yesterday in Tacoma. What is most worrisome is that the individuals harboring these devices are all confirmed passengers on different airline flights leaving four West Coast airports within fifteen minutes of one another. Our current strategy is to allow the individuals to board and then to detain them once each plane is wheels-up."

"You let them on the planes?" Collier asked incredulously. Higgins shifted uneasily in his chair.

Takashi drilled Collier with a stare. "It was a command decision," he said tersely. "As in one made by a commander; a commander who has made these types of decisions before. Are we clear?"

Collier pursed his lips and nodded. "Crystal," he said quietly.

Takashi turned and looked at el-Hamini. "Doctor," he said in a tone that conveyed empathy, "You told Agent Collier you believed these devices to be detonators. Were you informed at what point detonation was to occur or what substance they are designed to detonate?"

El-Hamini shook his head. "That was not shared with me," he said, his voice barely above a whisper. "And I did not ask." Takashi leaned in toward him.

"Dr. el-Hamini," he said softly, "I know that your actions were performed under the utmost of duress: the lives of your wife and daughter. While the Bureau cannot vouch for their safe return, we will use all of the considerable reach and power of not only our government but that of our friends abroad to secure their release. As of yet, the loss of life has been minimal and our goal is to prevent large-scale destruction and the political fallout inherent if such destruction were to occur. What else do you know about the devices you implanted?"

Johanna leaned forward to hear the answer.

"They are essentially radio transmitters, all tuned to a preset frequency. They can function as medical devices but when their default settings are overridden, they will emit a continuous signal until the default settings are unblocked."

"So how does the wearer of the device override the default settings?"

"By placing a special magnet over the generator," el Hamini answered. He moved his hand to a point under his collarbone. "Here," he said.

Takashi nodded. "Under less pressing circumstances we would have the device on its way to D.C. for complete analysis. Our engineers here are working on it now, trying to find a way to disable it remotely if possible." He turned to Johanna. "You'll be pleased to learn, Dr. Roberson, that the modified device, despite its lethal intention, did manage to save your life." Johanna looked at him, not understanding. "You must have been holding it in front of you because apparently the shot that Tamal Hajiik fired at you deflected off the generator housing."

"And broke the window," Johanna said.

"It's good to be good," Takashi said, "but it is often better to be lucky." He turned back to el-Hamini. "Are you aware of any other means of disabling the devices?"

"Other than opening the metal case and disrupting the actual circuits, I am sorry but I am not," el-Hamini replied.

Finally Collier spoke up. "Do you have cargo manifests for the twelve flights?"

Takashi frowned. "Cargo, as you know, is perhaps the weakest point in the fence. It gets x-rayed and sniffed for solid explosives but, as the recent printer cartridge episode proved all too well, it is still a fairly porous line of defense. What are you thinking?"

Collier leaned in and put his elbows on the heavy glass tabletop. "At some point, you have to simplify part of the operation. The greater the variability," he said, "the less the precision. Twelve detonators, twelve individuals, twelve planes, twelve airline schedules. Somewhere, something has to be the same to minimize the risk of complete failure."

Higgins tapped on the table. "So what we need to look for is what?"

"A common source of cargo on all the planes," Collier answered. "Probably liquid."

"Can we get that?" Higgins asked Takashi.

"I can," Collier interrupted before Takashi could answer.

"I'm not sure what database you have access to that we don't," Takashi shot back in a miffed tone.

"No offense," Collier answered, "But that's where you guys lose it. If you can't hack into it you figure it's not worth knowing. Look, give me the three airports that are the furthest apart and the flight numbers. If there's one cargo source common to all three then we have to make the assumption it's on all twelve."

Takashi's fingers fluttered across his keyboard. One of the three monitors flickered to life. "Sea-Tac, San Francisco International and LAX," Takashi said. "And the airlines and flight numbers."

Collier looked around the table. "You wouldn't happen to have a piece of paper around here, would you?"

"Paper is not secure," Takashi said. "Use this." He handed Collier a small electronic tablet and a thin plastic stylus. Collier looked at it.

"And how much did this set the government back?"

Takashi half-smiled. "Twenty-nine dollars from The Sharper Image catalog," he said. "I can order you one if you'd like."

Collier took the stylus and then looked up at Takashi. "Do I have to turn it on?"

"It's pressure activated. Just write on it like a pad of paper."

Collier watched as his pen strokes turned into iridescent purple letters. "SEA, LAX, SFO," he wrote, followed by flight call numbers. Then he looked at Higgins. "Phone?"

"Not in here," Higgins replied, rising from his chair. "I'll take you to a soundproof room with a secure line."

Collier got up to follow him. "Geez, Chief," he said in mock exasperation. "Where's the Cone of Silence?"

When the door closed Takashi turned to Johanna. "Dr. Roberson," he said gently, "did Mr. Hajiik say anything before Agent Collier subdued him?"

"Subdued him?" Johanna replied. "You mean when he shot him in the frickin' neck."

Takashi paused a beat. "We prefer the term subdued in these situations," he replied evenly. "Now can you remember if he said anything?"

Johanna shook her head. "He called me a foolish woman. Said I should have left well enough alone. Then the fucker said if I came out he would kill me quickly, like he was doing me some kind of favor."

"In his cultural frame of reference, he was," Takashi said.

"Well in my frame of reference he wasn't," Johanna replied. "Anyway, he said some more stuff to Trip but I was trying to get to the Code button and I didn't really hear it."

"Dr. el-Hamini?" Takashi asked. "Collier told us Hajiik thought you were dead?"

El-Hamini interlaced his fingers in front of him on the table. "I knew he would come for me," he said. "And I knew if he were successful that you would never be able to stop his madness. I waited until I knew he was in my house. I arranged my bedroom to look like I had committed suicide by taking tranquilizers and injecting myself with potassium. Then, as I heard him coming up the stairs, I did inject myself. Not with potassium but with something called Adenosine." He looked at Johanna. "As this young doctor will tell you, Adenosine stops the heart very effectively but only for a short period of time. We often use it in my laboratory when we are placing devices and need the heart still for just a bit. I was briefly unconscious after the injection, but he must have felt for a pulse and, finding none, believed that I had done his work for him. Once I had recovered I tried to contact Dr. Roberson so she could put me in touch with Agent Collier but I could not reach her."

"I didn't have my phone or my pager until this morning," Johanna interjected. Takashi cocked an eyebrow but said nothing.

"Finally," el-Hamini continued, "I contacted my secretary Amanda who, concerned for my safety, told me about Agent Collier's request for the devices and Johanna's, I mean Dr. Roberson's, visit to pick them up. That's why I was at the hospital when this occurred."

Johanna noticed that Takashi took no notes. It then dawned on her that every word she had uttered in the room was probably being recorded and transcribed. She thought about el-Hamini's gambit. Adenosine, she mused. How brilliant was that!

"You took quite a risk," Takashi said to el-Hamini.

"Not really," he replied. "If the adenosine did not kill me then Hajiik surely would have and certainly much more painfully." El-Hamini dabbed at the corner of his eye. "I love my wife and my daughter more than you can know," he said with a catch in his voice. "But some ransoms, I realized perhaps too late, simply cannot be paid." He turned his head and Johanna could see him struggle to regain his composure.

She was about to reach an arm out to comfort him when Collier and Higgins pushed through the door.

"Wine," Collier said emphatically. "All three flights were loaded with wine shipments from a vineyard in the Willamette Valley. Get this – Eagle Ridge Winery. Fuckin' A, what a narcissist. Anyway, I've got my guys in Portland running down their Bills of Lading. The sonofabitch was smart – he used six different ground shippers - but I guarantee you there's an Eagle Ridge Wine shipment in every cargo hold on those twelve flights."

"Eagle Ridge," Higgins interjected. "Wasn't that where a worker was just crushed to death in the grape press? Cordoba, Cardoza – some Mexican name."

Collier sat down. "Yeah, and I'll bet when you run that down you'll find out the guy was about as Mexican as Omar Sharif. That's why Hajiik was on the I-5 yesterday when he got pulled over. He was on his way back from the Willamette."

There was silence at the table for a moment. Then Takashi spoke up. "Agent Collier," he said. "What was it that Hajiik said to you just before you," - he glanced at Johanna – "as Dr. Roberson so eloquently put it: shot him in the frickin' neck?"

Collier looked at Johanna who just shrugged. "I don't know. Some shit about it being too late. That our national security would go up in flames, screams and burning flesh. Then he said something about the pictures being-" Collier stopped himself and Johanna saw a look a surprise and then fear come over his face. He turned immediately to Higgins. "Charley," he said. "You can't let them board. You have to move now to stop them!"

"The Director said the order from the Pr-'" Higgins stopped himself. "The order was explicit that they were to be taken only after they were in the air."

Collier looked at Takashi whose face told him he also now understood completely.

"They're never gonna take off, Charley," Collier said as he stood. "That's been the plan all along."

"Exactly!" Takashi said, rising simultaneously.

Johanna looked at Collier. "What?" she asked.

"They're going to blow them up while they're still on the ground."

Chapter 31

BAHAN REACHED FOR THE handkerchief in his pocket and dabbed at his brow. Then he twisted the air blower above him until it was open all the way. He fingered the circular magnet in his pocket, hoping to extract it without the man seated next to him on the aisle noticing it. Bahan ran through the timetable in his head. He pushed up the plastic shade and looked out the window. A large tanker truck was parked just off the tip of the wing. "Jet A" was emblazoned in red on its side. He scanned as far as the little window would let him. Several other planes, fully laden with fuel he knew, were within a few dozen meters in each direction. And, he reasoned, there were certain to be fuel trucks in the vicinity. His perspiration was increasing and he dabbed more frequently at his forehead. "Consumed by the purifying flames," The Eagle had told them. "Crossing the threshold into Paradise."

Overhead bins were being snapped shut above his head as the flight attendants hustled up and down the crowded aisle, urging late boarding passengers to take their seats. His mouth felt like cotton. A baby was crying somewhere behind him. Across the aisle, in the row ahead, two teenage girls giggled and tossed their hair as they donned headphones for the noisy ascent that, he knew, would never come.

Bahan's head was buzzing. He was having a hard time understanding the cabin attendant's patter over the intercom. Near the open First Class curtain he saw one of the crew holding the seat belt buckle assembly aloft and demonstrating its operation. He gripped the magnet tightly. A flight attendant stopped at his row and he froze. In the same instant he hoped and feared that he had been discovered; prayed that she would demand he accompany her to the front of the plane and through the door. He would be jailed, beaten and tortured, of course. But he would live. He was about to blurt out his surrender when he realized the stewardess was talking to the large man next to him. When the man had loaded his roll-aboard into the compartment above Bahan had noticed his large silver belt buckle with the name "Lyle" engraved on it.

"You can put it back down once we're in the air," the stewardess said. The man's beefy arm jostled Bahan as he pushed up the tray-table and locked it into the recess in the seat ahead of him. Bahan gripped the magnet tightly but the sweat from his hands was making it slippery. He pressed it against his trouser leg and stared straight ahead.

"Y'OK, partner?" Lyle asked. He tipped back the brim of his white cowboy hat. "Ya' look a bit peak'ed."

Bahan didn't understand the phrase. He smiled weakly and closed his fingers even tighter.

El-Hamini looked stricken. He sat in a chair with his head cradled in his hands. Johanna sat with him. They could see Collier, Higgins and Takashi through the walls of the conference room. They were huddled over a desk in the center of the larger room. On the big monitor screens, numbers flashed and live video shots, now almost exclusively of planes parked at airport Jetways, rotated in sequence. Johanna sensed the urgency in their exchanges as she studied the expressions on their faces. She saw Collier walk over towards the door to the conference room. He motioned through the glass for her to come over.

"Is el-Hamini alright?" Collier asked.

"As alright as he can be, I guess," Johanna answered.

"I mean, can he come out here and give us some input?"

Johanna looked at the defeated form seated at the table. "I'll talk to him." When she turned around she was surprised to see el-Hamini already standing, one hand braced to the rolled metal edge of the conference table. His eyes were red and puffy but they were dry, she noted. She was about to ask him when he spoke.

"I will help in any way I can," he said. "Will you go out there with me?"

Johanna nodded and reached for his arm. She pushed open the conference room door and held it for him. He seemed, she thought, to be getting a little stronger with each step.

Collier pulled up a rolling chair and pointed to it. Johanna led el-Hamini over and helped him sit down. Two men who Johanna had not noticed before were now standing at the table. In front of them, on what looked like a cafeteria tray, the device that had stopped Hajiik's bullet lay in pieces. She stared at the divot in the generator cover trying to imagine the hole it would have left in her chest. The two new men were speaking rapidly to el-Hamini.

"Yes," she heard him say. "Any strong unipolar magnet should suffice. The ones we use are usually circular to provide a uniform field."

One of the men, Johanna judged him to be barely old enough to be out of college, placed a square metal piece over the dissected device. "We figured it must be an extremely high or extremely low frequency signal. Otherwise normal radio waves would set off the explosives." The other man, who appeared a bit older, produced an instrument the likes of which Johanna had never seen.

"It will hopefully pick up the transmitting frequency," Collier said.

The younger man moved the magnet several times over the device. "Nothing," the older man said.

"The bullet impact may have damaged it," Higgins interjected.

"We're running out of time," Takashi said. "We've put a hold on all the planes; told them to stay at the gate. But it's a crapshoot now. Who knows what the detonation time is supposed to be?"

"They won't do it until they feel the plane pull away from the gate," Johanna said.

The men at the table stared at her in surprise.

"What?" she said. "It just makes the most sense. They'd still be close enough to do catastrophic damage but they'd know no one could get to them."

"Are there air marshals on the planes?" Collier asked.

"Only on four of them," Takashi answered, "but their instructions were to wait until take-off. We could change that but if all it takes is a wave of the magnet, we don't want to spook these guys now." He looked at Johanna. "If you're right – and you just may be – you might have bought us enough time to figure a way to stop this."

"Flip it over," Collier said.

"The device?" the younger man asked.

"No, the magnet. Just flip it over."

The younger man carefully turned the magnet and passed it over the device.

"Well fuck me," the older man said with a laugh. "Three hundred and fifteen Megahertz. Tremendous signal strength. Regular as a clock." He looked at Collier. "Just tell me you majored in Electrical Engineering in undergrad," he said.

"Nope," Collier replied. "Eighth grade science fair project, St. Peter's Parochial. Made the same mistake." As he finished his statement the engineers looked at each other.

"Oh, shit," the younger one exclaimed and looked at Takashi. "Are there military posts or installations at any of these airports?"

"At four of them," Takashi replied. Why?"

"Get hold of them right away and tell them to shut down any and all LMRS radio communication immediately. You have to be clear – no radio traffic whatsoever."

"Is it that sophisticated?" Higgins asked.

"Worse," the older engineer replied. "It's that simple. It's a fucking garage door opener."

"Ladies and gentlemen, this is Captain Gary Levinson. Ah, Tower Flight Control has just informed me we're in a very short hold situation here at the gate to allow a plane that's low on fuel to use our runway. They anticipate no more than a ten minute delay and then we'll have you on your way to Newark. At this time we do ask you to turn off – and I mean turn off, not silence – all electronic devices. We appreciate your patience and I'll be back to announce our departure very soon."

Bahan now had a full sweat going and his palms were running water. He released his grip on the magnet for what felt like only a second when it fell from his lap and onto the floor.

"Let me get that for ya," Lyle said. He twisted his bulk in the tiny seat and reached down for the circular magnet that had come to rest between his feet. In doing so he pinned Bahan's wrist against the armrest. Lyle grabbed the magnet and straightened his back. "Here ya go," he said. But instead of placing it in Bahan's lap Lyle simply pulled his forearm straight up and pushed the magnet toward Bahan. He tried to say no but Lyle's meaty paw was within inches of his shoulder. His right shoulder, Bahan realized in a panic. He struggled to pull his hand free from under the armrest. As if in slow-motion, he saw Lyle lean toward him, the object in his hand moving even closer. For a moment Bahan thought that he could feel the first rumblings of the explosion beneath his feet. There was a high pitched screeching sound and the passengers around him instinctively put their hands over their ears. Bahan closed his eyes tightly and uttered the Takbir in little more than a whisper.

Chapter 32

"DR. EL-HAMINI," TAKASHI SAID. "I'll need you to accompany these two gentlemen if you don't mind." Johanna saw the heavy vests and the side arms under the green FBI windbreakers and knew that it didn't really matter whether he minded or not.

"Of course," el-Hamini said. "I understand completely. May I say just a word to Dr. Roberson before we go?"

The men in the vests looked at Higgins who nodded. El-Hamini approached Johanna and reached out to take her hands in his. "It may be a bit before I am back in the lab," he said. "I am sorry about your friend Michael. I am sorry that I was not man enough to stop it." Johanna tried to interrupt but he stopped her. "I don't know when or if I will see my lovely daughter again. If I do, I hope that I can help her become a woman like you. That is my wish for her. My wish for you is that you find someone as fine and brave as yourself to share a happy life with. Don't wait too long, my dear. Sometimes the finest gifts are those set right in front of us." He squeezed her hands and then let go. "*Allah alim*," was the last thing he said to her before he was led away.

Johanna bit on her lip to hold her composure.

"You OK?" Collier asked.

"Yeah," she answered. "Where are they taking him?"

Collier shrugged. "He did the right thing," he said, "but he's got some splainin' to do, as you can imagine."

"Any word on that guy? What did you call him -The Eagle?" Johanna asked.

"I don't want to violate any patient privacy laws," Collier

replied, "but apparently your cowboy trauma surgeon cleaned up the mess I made in his neck. Guess I just missed his windpipe. Let's just hope he can still talk when he wakes up."

Johanna straightened her shoulders. Higgins, Takashi and the two engineers were drinking Diet Cokes and looking severely relieved as they sat at the table. "Can I have that piece that the bullet hit?" she asked Collier.

"I'm sure once it's not needed for evidence Charley can get it for you," he answered.

"So what was the whole garage opener thing?" Johanna asked.

"You remember Occam's Razor?"

"The simplest solution is usually the best?"

"That's it," Collier replied. "They way the engineers explained it, it's a coded signal with one specific receiver programmed to accept it. And every time it generates a signal it also generates a new security code. Fortunately, I guess it's a pretty easy signal to jam."

"Why did they shut down the military radios?" Johanna asked.

"It seems the military operates on a nearby frequency and there was at least a theoretical chance that one of their radio transmissions would accidentally send a detonation signal to one of the receivers."

Johanna still looked puzzled. "So what was that stuff about the deafening screech in the cabins? Was that the jamming signal?

Collier shook his head. "No. They just used that like a flash-bang to distract the bad guys long enough to grab them. Not very pleasant for the people on the planes, apparently, but it beat the alternative."

"Will the passengers ever know how close it was?"

Collier shook his head. "Not unless you tell them. I guess the airlines are already getting calls from attorneys who were on board claiming pain and suffering, not to mention permanent hearing impairment and demanding some form of settlement."

"It's a great country," Johanna said.

Collier smiled. "And we aim to keep it that way," he said.

"What will happen to the patients, I mean the terrorists, with the defibrillators?"

"Right now they're being classified as enemy combatants. Apparently they're none too happy to be alive, either. Except one guy at LAX who broke down crying and tried to kiss the air marshal when he cuffed him. He was sweating like a pig they said. Looks like the fourteen virgins will have to wait."

"That's OK," Johanna said. "That's what virgins do best. They wait. Oh, and for the record, pigs don't actually sweat."

Collier laughed. "Ok, then. Good to know." He waved at Higgins. "Charley, I take it this doctor is free to leave?"

Higgins smiled back. "With the thanks of the Bureau and several hundred irate and surely litigious airline passengers. And remember what I said about what you saw here."

Johanna shook her head in assent.

"Sorry there's no reward, doc," Higgins went on, "But maybe your friend Trip here can get you lifetime TSA Pre-Check."

"I'll ask him, Johanna said, casting a sideways glance at Trip Collier. "I'm pretty sure he works at the airport."

Chapter 33

"JESUS, COLLIER. YOU LOOK like a monkey humping a football."

Johanna was sitting in her Vespoli racing single, holding water. The oar handles were tucked against her midsection and the blades lay flat on the water at right angles to the shell, concave side up. There was no current in the shallow eddy where they were practicing and very little wind, so Johanna's rowing shell was almost motionless.

"This is a lot harder than it looks, you know," Trip Collier called back. The setting August sun sparkled off the flat water of Lake Union. Further out from them a women's eight glided by followed by a few scattered scullers in boats like Johanna's. "What's this thing called again, an Arrow?"

Johanna laughed and flipped her ponytail. "That's Aero, Collier, as in aerodynamic. You couldn't fall out that boat even if you tried!" She noticed she was drifting away from him a little so she took two lazy strokes on the oars then rested them in her lap again. "Relax your grip!" she yelled to him. "Bend your knees! Let the boat get set, then try rowing it!"

Collier raised a hand to wave and let the port oar handle slip from his grip. The boat rocked precariously from side to side until he grabbed hold of it again and steadied himself. Johanna turned her head so he wouldn't see her laughing.

"It really helps to know you're enjoying this so much!" Collier yelled back plaintively.

Johanna pivoted her shell and rowed over until she was just abeam of him.

"Did I ever tell you I tried this once before, when I was in college?" he asked.

Johanna shook her head. "Did you do better or worse that time?"

"Oh, way worse," he said. "I stayed dry for about a minute, but it was on one of those little yardstick boats like yours."

"You'll get it," Johanna replied. "I started out in an Aero and I still think it's the best boat for everyday scullers. Like I said, relax. That boat is so stable it won't let you fall out. Once you quit worrying about dumping you can concentrate on rowing. Come on, I'll row with you."

Collier took a few tentative strokes, his seat sliding only a few inches forward with each one.

"Good!" Johanna yelled, gliding along effortlessly beside him. "Now lengthen your stroke and go a little faster."

"I bet you say that to all the new scullers," Collier called back without turning his head. Johanna flipped her oar and soaked him with a blade-full of lake water. Collier laughed and kept on rowing. She kept pace with him and was impressed at how quickly he was acquiring something that actually looked like a rowing stroke. After they covered about two hundred yards she pulled up next to him.

"I'll meet you back at the rowing club dock. Getting in can be a little tricky so I'll rack my boat and be there to help you."

"What if I beat you there?" Collier said between strokes.

"Yeah, as if," Johanna replied. She pushed her oars forward and held her blades just above the water. With an almost imperceptible grunt she slid forward on her seat, brought her chest up to her bent knees and, having achieved full compression, dropped the blades in and extended her legs using the large muscles to pry the boat forward. The narrow, teak-veneered hull almost lifted out of the water with each stroke as she powered ahead. Within ten strokes Collier was a slowly receding figure just off her stern. Every third stroke she would whip her head around to look for traffic ahead of her. Since it was an evening during the week, there were only a smattering of boats in the rowing lanes. Johanna found her rhythm and was almost in a trance for the next fifteen minutes. It occurred to her during this reverie that she really didn't care if she ever rowed competitively again. She was beginning, she thought, to find a balance in her life that had eluded her; a balance that, for so long, she could only find sitting atop a narrow hull on flat water, racing to someone else's idea of a finish line. Her breaths were coming quicker and she was moving fast enough to generate a soothing breeze. Some dockside loungers gave her approving whoops as she flashed by. It felt so good, she thought, she really didn't want to stop – so she didn't. She looked between her feet at her NK StrokeMaster and saw that her rating was forty-two strokes per minute. She didn't even feel like she was working that hard. Her sense of well-being, she realized, was being naturally enhanced by the rush of endorphins her brain was mainlining into her bloodstream, but she didn't care. The last ten years of her life played in her head like a little movie. The psychological letdown after the Olympics; the search for direction and the decision to try and find a purpose for her life in medicine. She was finally happy, she thought. She was an accomplished woman in a respected profession. She didn't need a medal to make her feel good about herself anymore. She had someone she cared about and someone she was sure cared about her. As she pushed her physical limits she had the nearly orgasmic emotional release that came with knowing she was finally ready to love somebody. She was finally, she knew, going to be able to love herself. She needed to find Collier, she thought, and let him share in her bliss.

As she started to power down Johanna realized that the sounds of the world around her, which had all but disappeared for a while, were slowly returning. Glancing to her right she saw that she had overshot the Seattle Rowing Club by at least fifty yards. She lifted her blades and let them bounce on the wind-riffled surface of the water. There were people on the club's floating docks and they appeared to be waving at her. Johanna tucked her oar handles and waved back. Then she realized something – they were motioning for her to row in.

Johanna flipped her port blade and moved the oars in opposite directions, spinning the boat on its center like a compass needle until she had the bow pointed at the large SRC sign behind her. She took a few half-slides then rowed quickly, angling herself parallel to the gently bumping dock as it came up on her left. She lifted her starboard oar by pushing down on the neoprene-covered handle.

The blade's convex surface bounced lightly over the boards. Someone grabbed the shaft of the oar and Johanna's momentum stopped.

"What's all the fuss," she asked, nodding toward the group huddled by the club's small outboard coaching launch.

"I guess one of the Novices dumped about a half-mile up," a lean woman of about fifty in a neon unisuit told her. Johanna's gut became hollow.

"Guy or girl?" Johanna asked, her voice a whisper from both exertion and dread.

"Not sure," the woman said. "They're going to take the launch. You want to go?"

Johanna shook her head. "Push me back out," she said. "I can get there before they get that rust-bucket started."

The woman crouched down and grabbed the shaft of Johanna's oar just above the blade, lifting it slightly. Then she pushed straight out until Johanna got purchase with the other oar. The woman gave a little wave. Johanna dug in, took two half-slides, and then, despite her recent exertions, launched into a full Power-Ten.

For the first thousand yards she berated herself for leaving Collier by himself. She had assumed he could swim but realized she had never actually asked him. She slowed her rate to a steady thirty-six, turning to look ahead of her with nearly every other stroke. She saw a small knot of boats and the women's eight in the distance, about thirty yards from the shore. Taking a little pressure off her port oar, she angled towards them. If Collier had been rescued, Johanna hoped for his sake it had not been by a boat full of college girls. The empty feeling in her gut grew as she passed the spot where, even if he were rowing slowly, she should have passed him. She just couldn't believe he had managed to fall out of that boat. And what if he were hurt or drowned? She'd been the one pushing him to try the sport that she loved. Johanna started biting off her breaths, as much with anger as with effort.

When she was within a hundred yards she slowed her stroke and glided towards the little group of boats. The eight and a little motorboat were tight to each other's bow, she noticed. She dipped her starboard blade in every few seconds to adjust her angle as she got closer. There were raised voices and someone was trying to yell instructions. The eight drifted broadside and blocked her view. She could see the crew of girls was leaning to one side. Just beyond them she saw the empty Aero, floating upright, its oars askew in the swivels. Johanna took a quick series of half-slides and made her way around the little grouping. Then she saw him, near the empty number two seat in the eight's bow. His head was just above the water and he wasn't moving. One of his arms was draped across an outrigger. Johanna held her breath. Then she saw other arms reaching and suddenly she understood.

Back at the dock a small crowd had gathered. The Seattle Fire and Rescue wagon was on the scene, its red and orange strobes flashing in sequence. A Harbor Patrol cruiser from SPD idled just off the dock, the Aero and its shipped oars perched awkwardly on the aft deck. Johanna peeked over the shoulders of the paramedics, a worried look on her face.

"Are you sure I can't help?" she said. "I mean, I realize I'm just a board-eligible cardiothoracic surgeon, but I am certified in Advanced Cardiac Life Support, Advanced Trauma Life Support, Advanced Pediatric Life Support and Conscious Sedation." There was no response. "Did I mention," she said in somewhat louder tone, "that I also passed Senior Life Saving when I was a junior in high school?" The little group ignored her. "And rowed in the Olympics?"

A boy who Johanna figured for no older than twenty, with EMT in eight-inch blue sewn-on letters across the back of his shirt, looked up. "I think we're OK here, doc," he said. "Just a little shook up is all. Probably be OK to go home."

"Fine," Johanna said testily.

"Hey, don't take it personally," a voice from the inside the little group said. "It's all about liability."

"Leave it to a lawyer," Johanna said and resumed pacing the bobbing dock. Finally a head popped up from the crouching group.

"What time is it?" Trip Collier asked, his t-shirt still not quite dry.

"It's almost eight." Johanna replied. "Why?"

A young girl was being lifted to her feet.

"We have a table at The Wild Ginger," Collier said. "But I'm sure they'll hold it 'til nine."

"We don't need to go out to dinner."

"Yeah, we do," Collier said. "We really do."

Johanna recognized the waitress. She had served them over a year ago, the first time she'd met Trip Collier for dinner. Apparently, they'd made an impression.

"Hey, I remember you guys," the woman said. "Armagnac. Right?"

"That was *his* idea," Johanna said and pointed across the table.

"Well, it must have worked," the waitress said. "Here ya' are."

"Here we are," Collier said with a grin.

"Can I start you off with a cocktail?" the girl asked, "or would you like to see a wine list?"

Collier shook his head. "We would like a bottle of Mumm DVX, preferably the nineteen ninety-nine. Can you do that?"

"I'll check with the sommelier and be right back," she said.

'What's DVX?" Johanna asked.

"America's best champagne," Collier answered. "If you ever go to Napa, you should visit the Mumm estate. It's spectacular."

It did not escape Johanna's notice that Collier had said "if you" and not "if we." She tried to smile between pursed lips. Perhaps, she thought, she was reading this all wrong.

"So you really thought I was the one who fell in the water?" Collier asked with exaggerated incredulity.

"Well, yeah," Johanna said sheepishly. "But just until I got down there."

"Oh," Collier retorted, "And saw that I had jumped out of my shell to rescue that girl in the water? And held her head up until her boat came back to get her? And then hiked her up on my shoulders so she could climb back in? That's when you realized I wasn't a complete spastic?"

Johanna started to laugh. "Yeah," she said. "Right about then."

"How did she ever manage to fall out of a boat that big?" Collier asked, shaking his head. "With eight other people in it, no less?"

"She didn't fall out," Johanna replied and picked up her dessert spoon. "She caught a crab. That's what it's called when you bury the blade too deep in the water. The blade got stuck" – she held the belly of the spoon below the edge of the linen tablecloth – "but the boat kept moving at full power" Johanna moved the salt shaker and rested it against the end of the handle. "It's a lever. If one end moves" – she quickly flicked the belly of the spoon –"so does the other." The salt shaker launched across the table and landed in Collier's lap. "That's what I mean she didn't actually fall out,

Collier. She got flung out. And it was very nice of you to save her."

Collier reached down and picked up the salt shaker. "I got something in the mail today," he said. Then he reached under the table and produced a large brown envelope. "Actually, it came through Charley Higgins. He wanted me to make sure you got a look at it before he had to have it back." He passed it across to her. She was about to open it when the waitress returned.

"Claude will be bringing your sparkling wine up from the cellar shortly," she said. "Would you like to order anything to start?"

"I think we'll just sip the champagne while we look at the menu," Collier told her. "Thanks."

When she had slipped out of earshot Collier looked over at Johanna.

"Claude," he said and made a stupid face. "I'm sure there's an extra charge for Claude."

Johanna laughed and opened the unsealed flap on the envelope. She reached inside and pulled out a piece of blank cardboard. She pushed the envelope open with her fingers and peeked inside. Then she reached in and withdrew the photograph.

Johanna held the glossy picture in front of her for several minutes. She took her napkin and blotted her eyes.

"She's beautiful," Johanna said. "She's just beautiful." She put the picture down in front of her. The smiling face of Seljuk el-Hamini beamed up at her, his arm around a girl of about sixteen with dark hair and large eyes whose irises were the color of a child's cats-eye marble. "She has eyes like the girl on the cover of – oh, what was it?"

"National Geographic," Collier answered.

"But his wife is…?"

"She's OK," Collier said gently. "She took the picture."

Johanna smiled and wasn't sure if she could keep from crying. "How did they find them?"

"I don't know all the details," Collier said. "Even Charley Higgins doesn't know all the details. But apparently through some amazing cooperation between a CIA station chief in Syria and some black ops guys under the command of God-knows-who, and maybe - but maybe not - Seal Team Six, they got them out. I guess when the Glorious Mission failed and it was let be known that The Eagle was grounded, the guys that were supposed to behead them got cold feet and disappeared." Collier took a sip of his ice water.

Johanna decided to do the same. "Anyway," he continued, "they left them locked in a cellar in Damascus for three days. No food, no water. His wife was doing poorly so the daughter, she-"

"Saaleha," Johanna interjected. "Her name is Saaleha."

"OK, so Saaleha digs out a hole under the door with nothing but a pottery shard and manages to find her way to the American consulate. They were able to find his wife before she died of dehydration and somehow they get them both out of the country."

"Where are they now?" Johanna asked.

Collier shrugged. "Charley has no idea and neither do I. Not in the continental U.S., I'm certain of that. Charley said the State Department took over and everything after that became classified. Eyes Only, Need to Know type of classified."

"Well I'm happy they're all safe." Johanna drained her ice water. "I suppose The Eagle…"

"Well, you know he lived, obviously," Collier replied.

"Yeah," Johanna said with a laugh, "there were guys with machine guns outside his hospital room. Only Dr. Tuggle was allowed to see him. They brought in military nurses and M.P.'s to empty the bedpans and change the dressings. What about after that?"

Collier looked to see if their waitress was approaching. "Well I'm sure the el-Hamini's have better government accommodations than Mr. Hajiik," he said. "Let's just say he's probably still in a black hole somewhere, literally and figuratively."

"Good," Johanna replied as Claude glided up to the table. She was surprised to see that he was a middle-aged black man with remarkably straight long hair and an uncanny resemblance to Rick James.

"DVX, nineteen-ninety-nine," he said in a butter-smooth voice. Collier smiled at Johanna as Claude cut and removed the foil. Then he loosened the wire cage with the requisite six half-turns and slipped it into his pocket. He glanced at Collier then draped his linen towel over the cork and held it tightly with his left hand. With his right hand he grasped the barrel of the bottle and separated it from the cork with three quick twists of his wrist. The "pop" was muted but audible and, Johanna noticed, not a drop was spilled. Claude set the mushroomed cork down in front of Collier who examined it briefly and nodded his approval.

"A special occasion for you two?" Claude asked as he poured.

"Anniversary perhaps?"

"Yes to the first, no to the second," Collier answered.

"Enjoy," Claude said and padded silently away in what Johanna thought looked like black ballet slippers.

"When do you have to be in San Francisco?" Collier asked.

"My contract starts September first," Johanna said and shifted in her seat. "But I got a call today from PCH – the Philadelphia Children's Hospital. They have an immediate opening for a congenital heart surgery fellow and McCarthy gave them my name."

Collier frowned. "Is he trying to make sure you're as far away as possible?"

Johanna squinted. "I don't think so," she said. "I did a really good job when I was on Dani Rivers' service. I'm betting this came from her."

"So what are you going to do?"

Johanna reached out and grasped the stem of her champagne glass but did not pick it up. "I don't know," she said. "It's two more years of training. And it's pretty far away."

Collier smiled. "Far away from what?"

"Don't do this to me," Johanna said in a soft voice but with a sharper tone. "Don't mess with me. If you're OK with me leaving, whether it's down the coast or across the country, then I can deal with that. I know how to take care of myself, you know."

"I do know," Collier replied. "You're a real-life Lara Croft."

"Must be the guys I hang out with," she said, releasing her grip on the glass. She let her shoulders sag and suddenly decided he had brought her here just to say good-bye.

"Let's toast before Claude's perfectly poured DVX warms up," Collier said cheerily.

Johanna knew she was pouting but did her best to find a brave smile.

"And what exactly is it that we're toasting to, Agent Collier?"

"To everything that comes next," he said and touched her glass. She smiled wanly and took a long sip. It was marvelous champagne, she thought. She set her glass down.

"And what, exactly, comes next?"

Collier was about to answer when their waitress returned.

"Have you had a chance to look at the menu or do you still need a few more minutes?" she asked somewhat impatiently.

Collier took a deep breath and turned to the girl. "We'll be sharing orders of the Singing Fish Satay, the Dungeness Crab Cakes, the Tuna Manada and the Pad Thai. And we'd like all of it Thai hot, please. We're in no hurry, so if we could just have a few minutes before the first course, that would be great."

The girl finished scribbling on her pad, picked up the unread menus from the table, smiled tightly and headed toward the kitchen.

Collier exhaled slowly and turned back to Johanna who was looking at him with raised eyebrows.

"Sorry," he said. "Hope you don't mind that I ordered for us. She wasn't going to leave us alone until I did and there are some things we really need to talk about."

OK, here it comes, Johanna thought.

"Sounded like good choices," she said.

Collier took another drink of his champagne. Johanna thought he suddenly looked nervous and uncomfortable. "I got something for you," he said quietly. Johanna wondered if it was a lovely parting gift.

"You didn't have to do that," she said. "I mean, I understand. I really do."

He surprised her by laughing. "Oh, I'm pretty sure you don't," he said and reached carefully into his jacket. He gingerly handed her a small, tri-folded brochure. It was four-color, she noticed, and printed on heavy stock.

She reached out and took it from him with both hands, holding it by the edges. "Are you selling me a time-share?"

"Just look at it," he said. "Do you know what it is?"

Johanna looked at the first page and then opened it, scanning the copy and the pictures with an increasingly puzzled expression.

"Do you recognize it?"

She held the brochure in her hands and looked across at him "Yeah. I know what it is. It's a Maas Double rowing shell. Why do you have –"

"I ordered one," Collier said. "They hand-make them one at a time in Richmond, California. I actually called and talked to Chris, the boatmaker. It won't be built for another week and we wouldn't get it until–"

"OK. Stop. Why did you order this?" Johanna interrupted.

"So we can row together," Collier said. "At least this way if I fall out you'll be the first to know about it."

"How are we going to row-"

"Oh, yeah," Collier said. "I forgot. Before we can row together you have to agree to accept the terms on the back."

Johanna rested her elbows on the table and dropped her shoulders in supplication. "Collier," she said, "I am really lost here. Terms on the back? The back of what?" He had a weird little smile on his face that she did not think she had ever seen before. He pointed to the brochure that she held.

Johanna turned it in her hands. Mounted on the back panel, on a piece of transparent double-stick tape, was the most beautiful diamond ring she had ever seen. Unable to speak she looked at Collier and then back at the ring. The flickering table candle made it look like the stone was on fire.

"Oh my God, Trip," was all she could get out. Collier reached over and pulled the ring off the tape. Her eyes welled up and she could feel her nose starting to run. Collier was still smiling. She wasn't sure if she'd taken a breath.

"So?" he asked.

"Well," she said hoarsely, wiping at her nose. " I mean I - I do really like the boat," "So, yes, I accept the terms."

Collier reached across and took her left hand in his. "I have never met anyone like you, Johanna Roberson. I am positive that I will never meet anyone like you again. But what's more important is that I know that I love you and I don't ever want to live without you. If we can row together I bet we can do anything together. Maybe even wallpaper. I'd really like to try."

Johanna brought her hand to her mouth. She could feel the tears staining her cheeks. Trip reached across and wiped them away with his thumb. Then he put the ring on her finger. "Can we row in San Francisco?" he asked. All Johanna could do was nod. "Can we row in Philadelphia?" She sniffled loudly and nodded again. "OK, then the rest is just logistics," he said and squeezed her hand. She couldn't tell if it was her own watery vision or the flickering of the candle but she thought she saw a tear in his eye as well. The he leaned across the table and kissed her.

"Let's toast again," Collier said. "Now that you know what we're toasting to."

Johanna raised her glass and tapped it against his, rim to rim.

"To everything that comes next," she said. They both drained their glasses.

The waitress returned with their first course and looked at Johanna's hand. "Oh shit, I lose," she said as she set down the steaming plates.

"You lose? Lose what?" Johanna asked.

"My bet with Claude," she answered. "He said it was 'marry me' champagne. I said it was 'thanks for everything' champagne.

Johanna let out a huff. "'Thanks for everything' champagne? Are you serious?"

"I've waited a lot of tables, honey," she said. "It happens more than you think. I'm just glad I was wrong. Either way, that first bottle is on us. Congratulations and enjoy. You guys are going to make beautiful babies."

Collier shook loose the ice clinging to the chilling bottle and refilled their glasses.

"What kind of champagne did *you* think it was?" Collier asked with a twinkle.

Johanna sipped from her glass, swallowed and smacked her lips. She looked down at the ring.

"I would never question the intentions of a federal agent," she said and reached out her hand for his. "It's just a good thing you bought the right boat."

◆ ◆ ◆

Perimeter of Mihail Kolgalniceanu Airport
Southeast Romania

The rumble of a landing transport plane awoke him after hardly more than an hour of fitful sleep. The cover was still in place over his half-meter-square outside "window." In what he could only guess was the more than a year that he had been "temporarily detained" in this filthy box, he was permitted only hour-long periods of natural light. Once he talked, they promised, he would be allowed to see the sun for himself. It had been several hours since he had been taken to the fungus-encrusted showers for his weekly hosing – no soap or disinfectant was ever used – and his regularly scheduled tonsorial humiliation. With his wrists chained to the corroded pipes and a bite-block in his mouth, his upper lip was dry-shaved with a dull disposable razor. As was customary, he was forced to take a quick look in a hand mirror at the stubbled and nicked empty space under his nose and then returned to the cage.

He had known about the "black sites" since the invasion of Afghanistan and had at first thought he was on Arab soil. Now, somewhere in the Balkans was his best guess. He still had trouble turning his head to the right, a sequela of the surgical reconstruction performed on his blasted neck. The resultant scarring had pulled his head into a permanent tilt, as if he were always cocking an ear to listen for something important. His fingers traced lightly over the hard ridges and the deep pits, mapping them.

Conversation was never permitted and rarely did he even hear the voice of another person, save for his captors and the occasional American interrogator. Once, on a still night, he thought he heard the call to prayer. His once-dormant religious fervor had been re-ignited during the long months of constant debasement. The Russians were pimps and he resolved never to deal with them again unless it was in vengeance. He now believed that even if there was only one true *jihadi* within a thousand miles, for that one he would not give up hope.

The slat at the bottom of the rusted door creaked as it dragged in its bolt. He leaned forward and waited for the day-old toast and the sediment-laden cup of water to appear. When it arrived, he picked dried mouse turds off the stiff bread and waited for the opening to be sealed once again. To his surprise, the slat remained unobstructed. In the dim light he could see the toe of what looked like an antique mosque slipper. The foot it covered lingered for a moment. Then Hajiik heard words being whispered. Whispered, it took him a moment to realize, in the language of his homeland.

"Stay strong, brother," the voice said. "Soon, very soon, you shall fly again."

ACKNOWLEDGEMENTS

The author wishes to thank those whose help and support brought this story to the page: Joe Marquart, Bob Rocca and Ann Donahue Croce, my HS writing teachers and first real mentors; Fr. Joe Feeney, S.J. who brought literature to life in college; and my Professors and gifted fellow students in the M.A. Writing program at Lenoir-Rhyne University, especially Prof. Laura Hope-Gill.

Also thanks to Terry Persun for his formatting expertise and Graphic Artist Jim Zach who designed the cover art and layout.

A special thanks to friend, reader and teacher, Seattle author Bob Dugoni, who helped me rediscover and develop my writing voice.

PRAISE FOR "SURF CITY CONFIDENTIAL"

"A gripping debut. Waters creates a cauldron of colorful characters simmering in an intricate plot. The revelations come in a wild, tense finish. One of the best books I'll read this year."
—Robert Dugoni, #1 NY Times, Wall Street Journal & Amazon Besteslling Author

AMAZON READERS AGREE: 100% FIVE STARS

"Set in a small coastal town in the late sixties, this is a fast paced story that kept me turning pages into the night. This book is a very impressive first novel, comparable in pacing and character development to the work of Ken Follett or John Sandford."

"A real page-turner set in a milieu that will be familiar to many readers - the Jersey Shore. The book delivers on its promise and then more! Perfect summer (or any other season) reading."

"Enjoyed this so much! Having grown up in that era I was amazed at the detail. Remembered things I hadn't thought about in years. Love the dialogue and surprise ending...."

"Difficult book to put down! Many twists and turns to keep your interest to the end! One really great read."

"SURF CITY CONFIDENTIAL" is available in Paperback and e-Book formats on Amazon.com and at select local booksellers and libraries

ABOUT THE AUTHOR

DANIEL J. WATERS is a native of Southern New Jersey. He graduated from Bishop Eustace Preparatory School, St. Joseph's College in Philadelphia and the University of Medicine and Dentistry of New Jersey and has been publishing stories and essays since 1981; his work has appeared in the *Journal of The American Medical Association, The New Physician, The Examined Life* (University of Iowa) and *Intima: A Journal of Narrative Medicine* (Columbia University) and *Typishly: An Online Literary Journal*. He has practiced open-heart surgery for thirty years and is the author of " A Heart Surgeon's Little Instruction Book" and " A Surgeon's Little Instruction Book", pocket collections of surgical advice and aphorisms as well as the novel *Surf City Confidential*. He holds a Graduate Certificate in Narrative Healthcare and a Master of Arts in Writing from The Center for Graduate Studies/The Thomas Wolfe Center for Narrative at Lenoir-Rhyne University in Asheville, NC. He and his wife Pamela have three grown children and live in Iowa.

Visit our website at www.Bandagemanpress.com

Contact the author: drdan@bandagemanpress.com